GREAT
HEXPECTATIONS

Also by HP Mallory:

THE JOLIE WILKINS SERIES:

Fire Burn and Cauldron Bubble
Toil and Trouble
Be Witched (Novella)
Witchful Thinking
The Witch Is Back
Something Witchy This Way Comes

THE DULCIE O'NEIL SERIES:

To Kill A Warlock
A Tale Of Two Goblins
Great Hexpectations
Wuthering Frights

GREAT HEXPECTATIONS

Book 3 of the Dulcie O'Neil series

HP MALLORY

GREAT HEXPECTATIONS
by
H.P. Mallory

To Kill A Warlock

This book is dedicated to the memory of my cousin,
Shelby Elizabeth Barnes
1990–2011

Acknowledgements:

To my mother: thank you and I love you

To the most important men in my life: my husband and son,
I love you both

To Caressa Brandenburg and Alexandra Fields-Gerrity:
thank you so much for entering my "Become a character in
my next book" contest and I really hope you enjoy seeing
yourselves in print!

To Caitlin Boberg: thank you for entering my contest to
name this book and coming up with the title Great
Hexpectations! I absolutely love it!

To my beta readers: Sofia Oberg, Evie Amaro, and Mary
Genther, thank you so much for your help!

To all my readers: I cannot thank you enough for your
continued support—you all mean the world to me!

ONE

So Knight was right—I hadn't exactly surrendered myself to the idea of going on a date with him. In fact, I'd been doing a damned good job of trying to talk myself out of it because the sensible part of me thought it wasn't a good idea to mix business with pleasure. Granted, Knight and I didn't work together anymore (not in the technical sense of him being my boss), but I still managed to find myself on cases with him, so for all intents and purposes, we were working together. And as any smart person will tell you, business should be just that, business.

Okay, so that was the practical side of me. The less practical side of me couldn't stop thinking about the last kiss Knight and I shared in my kitchen—when I'd been straddling the incredibly hot man, er Loki (Knight is a creature called a Loki—forged from the fires of the Netherworld god, Hades), and played the game of "let's see how far my tongue can go down your throat." I would've actually had sex with him right then and there if it hadn't been for my best friend who coincidentally was staying with me. And, really, looking back on it, I'm glad Sam was my roommate that evening because I wasn't quite ready to surrender to my more carnal feelings for Knight. Not yet anyway.

So you're probably wondering what in the hell is wrong with me, right? Why would I not want to get involved with an incredibly hot and mostly nice guy? (Well, Knight can be a bit of a cocky bastard but I guess that comes with being the head of the Association of Netherworld Creatures here in Splendor, California—think police detective). So, yes, he's the best looking guy I've basically ever seen in my life and yes, he seems to be into me; but I guess I have hang-ups, namely my ex-boyfriend, Jack, who cheated on me and really screwed me up.

My first issue with Jack is that he's human. Now, before you start thinking I'm some sort of weird alien life form, I'm not, (although I once spent about five hours transformed into a mass of green goo). I'm a fairy and I'm attractive, if I do say so myself. I'm also a law enforcement agent working as a consultant at the moment for ANC Splendor, and, yes, for Knightley Vander.

But, back to the subject of a date with Knight. Yes, I'd gone back and forth, basically having a full-blown argument between my rational side and the side of me that hadn't gotten any in a while. The side that hadn't gotten any in a while won, but, not for the reasons you might be thinking.

I'd decided to go on a date with Knight for two reasons: first, because he mentioned that he didn't think I would go on a date with him—that I'd talk myself out of it (I guess he's beginning to know me better)—and I wanted to prove him wrong. Second, as I mentioned earlier, Knight is a Loki which is a creature I'd never come across before, since they seem to only exist in the Netherworld. But, that's not why I wanted to go out with him … Knight has this weird condition, for lack of a better description, where his eyes start randomly glowing. So, naturally, I was curious as to why the hell his eyes glow and he said he'd tell me the hows and whys of it but only if I agreed to go on a date with him.

Sigh.

So, here I was, dressed in my evening best and waiting for the Loki to show up. I was wearing a short red dress with long sleeves and a plunging neckline. The material had to have Spandex in it because it seemed to hug my curves.

And, no, I hadn't magicked this one, although, as a fairy, I could have, had I wanted to. Sometimes, though, it just takes too much creative juice to make your own clothes; after a while, my wardrobe starts to all look the same. This outfit was purchased from the Juniors' section of Macy's in preparation for my date with Knight.

Looking at my reflection in the mirror, I stepped into my black stiletto heels and said a silent prayer that I wouldn't stumble and kiss the pavement. Truth be told, I really wasn't used to high heels—I preferred my tennies because they were the best shoes to fight in. When you're in law enforcement, you never know when you might need to pull out a can of whoop-ass. And pulling out a can of whoop-ass is definitely easier when you aren't wearing stilettos. But, tonight, I planned to leave the whoop-ass cans to Knight, that is, if we even needed them.

I ran my fingers through my elbow-length honey gold hair, covering the tips of my ears. As a fairy, my ears come to points at the top and I'm not exactly thrilled with them. I always wear my hair down to cover the points. I once actually considered getting ear surgery but decided I wouldn't allow myself to be so vain.

My eyes are green, as in the color of emeralds, and I've got an oval-shaped face with decently plump lips. People seem to think I'm pretty but I don't really see myself that way. It's not like I'm self-conscious or anything—I'm just less concerned with my looks than with making sure my body is fit and healthy. That's because, really, as a fairy, my body is my best weapon. Beauty won't save you in a fight.

As I glanced at my small frame (I'm five foot one), I was pleased to see that, if anything, I looked leaner. Yes, my breasts still filled out my C cup bras and my hips remained on the curvy side, but the rest of me was solid, sculpted. My muscles were well defined which was good news—it meant I'd be that much faster and better when it came to combat.

At the sound of the doorbell, I grabbed my black leather jacket and my purse and, after nearly tripping over my ridiculous heels, I started for the living room.

I glanced through the peephole and after ensuring it was Knight, I pulled the door open.

"Hi," I said.

Knight didn't answer. Instead, he made it very obvious that he was taking me in from head to toe, his gaze pausing a little too long on my bust. Well, it did serve me right, I guess—the dress had a pretty deep neckline and I was wearing my Wonderbra.

"Um, hello Knight," I grumbled again and pointed to my face as his eyes continued to ogle my bust line. "If you're waiting for my boobs to talk, don't hold your breath."

A huge smile appeared as his gaze moved back up to my face. "Nicely done, Dulce."

Knight, as I mentioned before, is basically the definition of gorgeous. He's insanely tall, (I'm not exactly sure how tall but over six-three for sure). He's like looking up a flag pole. His hair is pitch black and his eyes are blue, that is, when they aren't glowing. Tonight he had the beginnings of stubble decorating his chin and cheeks and looked every inch the rogue that he is.

"Thanks, are you ready?" I asked, never exactly comfortable with compliments, especially compliments from a Loki.

"Aren't you going to say I look nice?" he asked, holding his hands out as I examined his figure. He was wearing dark grey slacks and a black, v-necked, short-sleeved dress shirt. The sinewy muscle of his forearms hinted to the fact that this guy was built like an ox—strong, almost intimidatingly so.

"You look very handsome," I said reluctantly and managed a half smile. "Handsome" didn't even begin to express the way he looked. "Handsome" paled in comparison. "Killer sexy" might have been more apropos.

"Wow, handsome, huh?"

"Stop trying to get more compliments out of me," I retorted and started for the door, grasping the doorknob. "So where are you taking me?"

"It's a surprise," Knight answered and offered his arm. I closed the door behind me and then took his arm, silently appreciative of the fact that he'd offered it. It definitely would make walking down my driveway in stilettos that much easier.

"You look beautiful, by the way," Knight said and snuck another glance at me, this one at my backside. "Not that you don't always look beautiful."

"Thanks," I answered and felt something warm boil up inside me—something decidedly girly and decidedly unlike me.

"I was pretty surprised you didn't talk yourself out of our date," Knight commented as he opened the passenger door of his silver BMW M3 for me.

I smiled up at him. "I came close, believe me."

He chuckled. "I DO believe you."

He walked around to the driver's side and opening the door, seated himself before he glanced over at me again. "So what made you decide to see it through?"

I shrugged and figured I'd go for honesty. "I wanted to find out about that eye glowing bit."

He nodded and looking over at me, offered me a boyish smile. "I had a feeling that would do it."

"So seeing as how we're on a date and that was the agreement, spill the beans."

He chuckled again as he started the engine and the Beemer purred beneath him. I couldn't help but think everything would purr beneath him.

"Our date isn't over yet," he said with an evil smile. "I'll tell you at the end of it."

"I thought you'd probably milk it," I said and shook my head, sighing over the injustice of the whole thing.

5

"Gotta pull out all my tricks with you, Dulce."

For the next ten minutes, we made small talk as Knight managed to break more than one traffic law as we drove through downtown Splendor. There weren't many people out and about for a Friday night, not that Splendor was a happening spot. In fact, it wasn't happening really at all. It was more of a bedroom community, although we did have a decent population of Netherworld creatures.

Those with superhuman abilities had come out of the proverbial closet fifty years ago. Even though things had definitely simmered down since the dawning of the truth regarding the fact that vampires, werewolves and witches not only existed but had also been living among humans undetected for hundreds of years, we were still subject to ignorance and misunderstanding.

Knight pulled into the parking lot of Bliss, a nightclub that had just opened and played rival to the only other night club in Splendor, No Regrets, which was run by the vampire Bram, whom I guess I could call my friend.

"I thought we were doing dinner and drinks tonight?" I asked, turning to face Knight.

He shrugged and coaxed the Beemer into a spot by the back door. Then he glanced over at me with a wide smile as he turned the engine off and opened his door. "Will you just trust me?"

I undid my seatbelt and was about to let myself out when Knight appeared beside my door and opened it for me. Yes, he was lightning fast but I wasn't really surprised. As a Loki, Knight has a plethora of powers but he'll never tell me everything he's capable of. That relegates me to picking up on his abilities here and there, basically whenever he feels like showing off.

I took his proffered hand and stood up, quickly finding my balance. "You know, Bram won't like the fact that we're here and supporting his competition," I remarked, feeling a little guilty over the fact.

6

"What the hell do I care?" Knight asked with a bit too much acid in his tone. Yep, Knight didn't like Bram and vice versa. I think it was because they were both jealous of one another.

"Well, I care because I need Bram's support," I answered, throwing his nasty tone back at him as we started for the door of Bliss. Bram seemed to walk the line between good citizen and outlaw. I usually kept a blind eye to his less than noble pursuits because he was good about giving me leads when it came to catching the bigger bad guys.

"What Bram doesn't know won't hurt him," Knight answered dismissively and, nodding his head at the bouncer, the smaller man approached the double entry doors and held one of them open for us. Knight offered him a smile and allowed me to enter before he came up behind me, putting his hands on either side of my hips as he steered me through the crowd.

I glanced back and him with a frown to which he merely responded with an innocent grin. Facing the club again, I took in my surroundings, immediately making note of the exit routes. Hey, you never know when you're going to need one. As to the club itself, the place was pretty packed. A strobe light highlighted the patrons as they danced in the center of the room, making the crowd appear like some sort of pulsating, throbbing creature. Timbaland's "Scream" belted out through the speakers and I felt myself hungering for a Captain Morgan and Coke. The dance floor was square and large, and a bar occupied the far corner, while lounges fringed the sides.

Knight tightened his grip on either side of my waist and piloted me through the mass of undulating people, pulling me into him when some drunken guy stumbled out in front of me. The guy looked embarrassed and quickly allowed the crowd to swallow him up again as Knight directed me to an empty table which boasted a few purses and … Trey's manbag?

7

"Surprise!"

Before I had the chance to think another thought, Sam, Dia and Trey all jumped out from wherever the hell they'd been hiding and greeted me with large smiles and jazz hands. I felt myself go into fight or flight mode and had to calm myself down, talking my heart out of having an attack while I took a deep breath.

"What's going on?" I asked, turning to face Knight with total confusion written on my face. It's not like it was my birthday or anything.

Knight smiled smugly and nodded at the booth, motioning for me to take a seat. "I thought you needed a night out on the town with your friends because you've been through a lot lately."

And that was the truth. I'd been through a crap load lately. Hmm, within the last six months, I'd nearly been killed by a Kragengen shape-shifter—a voracious predator that had been feasting on some of Splendor's citizens. And if that weren't enough to cause my stress levels to spike, more recently, I had to defeat a Dreamstalker, who attacked me under the guise of my dreams. But, wait, it gets better ... I also suffered through the tragedy of learning that my old boss, the prior Head of the ANC, not to mention my very close friend, Quillan, had been double dealing all along and turned out to be one of the bad guys. Yes, I had had one hell of a year.

I glanced at Knight and smiled. Sometimes he did things that surprised me, things that were not in line with his tough guy persona. Sometimes he made me wonder.

"Girl, you need a drink!" Dia said with a huge smile as she enveloped me in her arms.

Dia Robinson was one of my newest friends but that didn't diminish our friendship, which was bonded strong. Dia was the Head of the ANC for one of our bordering communities, Moon. She and I worked very closely on the last case which involved the Dreamstalker.

8

"It's so good to see you," I said as I held her tightly, taking in her bright red halter top and matching pants. Red must have been her favorite color because it seemed she was always wearing it. I had to admit, it did compliment her beautiful chocolate skin and the perpetual glow that seemed to surround her. Dia was one of those people you couldn't help wanting to hang out with.

She pulled away and smiled down at me with her full, beautiful lips just as my best friend, (a witch working for the ANC), Sam, appeared and gave me a big hug. Then it was Trey's turn. Trey is a hobgoblin, also employed by Knight and the ANC, and, although I'd never cared for him much in the beginning of our acquaintance, I definitely considered him a friend now.

"'Sup, Dulce?" he said, lifting his chin like he thought he was Eminem or something.

I couldn't help my laugh. Trey is anything but cool although he tries so hard to play the part. He's short, overweight, always sweaty and perpetually lusting after anything with boobs. But he's got a heart of gold.

"Thanks for coming out tonight, Trey," I said.

"Okay, what's everyone drinking?" Knight asked and offered us all a cheery grin. He took everyone's orders while I sat down at the table and the other three followed suit.

"Wow, this is a surprise," I started. "And you drove all the way from Moon, Dia?" Moon was a good two-hour drive from Splendor.

"Honey, there's no way I was going to miss it. 'Specially when your Mr. Sex on a Stick said I'd better make it out or suffer the wrath of the Loki." She paused for a second or two, running her perfectly manicured nails against her lips. "Course, that's a punishment I just might want to sign up for!"

"Oh, God," I muttered. Dia was like a cat in heat whenever she was around Knight. However, all women were like that really. "I'm happy to see you, Dia."

9

"And I'm happy to be here, girl. Got to know your BFF a little better," she said, glancing at Sam who just smiled.

"Yeah, I guess I was sort of passed out during our introduction," Sam said with a smile. The truth of the matter was that Sam had been in a coma. She'd been one of the Dreamstalker's victims and Dia, Knight and I had worked tirelessly to save her. But, I didn't need any more reminders of the hell my life had been lately. Instead, I fully intended to drink away the memories and lose myself in the moment—surrounded by the people closest to me.

Two hours later and I was inebriated. I'd downed four Captain Morgan and Cokes and now found myself dancing in front of Knight, who was sitting at our table with his legs stretched out before him, watching me with a glimmer in his eye as he sipped his whiskey.

"So I thought you wanted some alone time with me?" I started, swaying my hips to "All The Right Moves" by One Republic. "What happened to that?"

Knight smiled and I felt something blossom in my stomach—something repressed, something carnal. I wanted him.

"Of course I want some alone time with you."

"So why didn't you take the opportunity tonight?"

He shrugged. "Because tonight is about you. It's not about what I want. It's about what you need and I thought you needed a night out to release some steam."

I nodded and suppressed the incredible desire to throw my arms around him and kiss him. Sometimes he was just so … nice. "Thank you."

"You're welcome, Dulce." He sipped his whiskey again, his eyes never leaving mine. "I'm trying to prove I'm not a bad guy."

I was taken aback and stopped dancing, instead swaying with inebriation. "I don't think you're a bad guy."

He shrugged. "Maybe not, but you're still holding back." Then he laughed. "You're a tough nut to crack. The toughest I've come across yet."

"Maybe that's why you keep coming back?"

He sipped his whiskey and his eyes began to lighten, an eerie glow usurping their otherwise bright blue. His damned eyes were glowing again, the same way they had the first time I'd seen them do it—when we were at Bram's restaurant. I bit my tongue, wanting to ask him what the deal was but I knew he wouldn't enlighten me. Not yet—our date still wasn't over.

"Nope, that's not why I keep coming back," he said simply and the glow in his eyes died away. Before I had the chance to respond, Sam came up behind me.

"I have to pee, Dulce, wanna come?"

I didn't want to come but it was unspoken girl law that if your friend had to pee, you had to accompany her. I nodded and smiled at Knight in apology as he smirked. I wasn't sure why, but I was convinced his gaze didn't stray from us as we made our way through the crowd, eventually disappearing into the bathroom.

"So are you going to have sex with Knight later or what?" Sam asked, her words slurring until it sounded like she was talking underwater.

"Sam!"

She waved away my faux shock. "Come on, Dulce, when are you gonna give the poor guy a break?"

"Ah, so you're on his side now?" I asked in mock annoyance, propping my hands on my hips.

Sam started for the stall but didn't stop talking, she just raised her voice. "I think we both mislabeled him. Knight's not a player. He really likes you."

I sighed deeply, not really sure what to think or what to say. All I was sure of was that I really didn't want to wait in the bathroom for her, listening to her pee. "I'll wait outside for you."

I started for the door and exhaled all my tension. Did Knight really like me or was he actually just a player? Would he treat me as badly as Jack had? Would I even be dumb enough to put myself in that situation again to begin with? I mean, I liked my life as it was. Granted I really didn't have much of a romantic life, but did that really matter? I had friends …

"Dulcie."

It was like I was in slow motion, my brain trying to place the voice but finding it difficult with my alcohol-induced stupor. But, when I focused on the man standing before me, complete with his sickening sweet smile, I wanted to throw up.

"Jack."

I didn't even recognize my own voice. Instead, my heart was hammering and my blood seemed to be increasing in temperature, boiling me from the inside out. My breath was coming faster and shallower and it was all I could do to stay standing.

"Wow, didn't think I'd see you here."

"Yeah," I managed to reply as I tried to get control of myself. *Dulcie, you can handle this. Just calm the hell down. Just act cool.*

Jack looked the same as he had all those years ago. Still tall and dashingly handsome; still the same warm brown eyes I'd lost myself in; still that charming, boyish smile. His eyes raked me from head to toe.

"You look great, like you haven't changed since the last time I saw you."

The last time he saw me … the time I'd caught him in bed with another woman. And then all the emotions, all the feelings of anger and hurt started churning in my gut again, feeling as fresh as if I'd just walked in on him again.

I didn't realize my hands had fisted at my sides until I glanced down at them. My body absolutely and totally wanted to knock him out. And that was when I realized I needed to just walk away. Before I had the chance, I was blocked by what looked like an Amazon. She approached Jack and took his hand and it was like déjà vu. She wasn't the same woman I'd walked in on all those years ago, but that didn't even matter. Standing beside him, she was his height—a full six feet. And she was gorgeous with long black hair and boobs that were so big, she could probably get away with driving in the carpool lane.

"Who's this, Jack?" she asked in a sweet voice laced with alcohol.

As far as my buzz was concerned, it had packed and moved out at the exact moment I found myself standing in front of my ex.

"This is Dulcie," he said with that same smirk, his eyes never leaving mine. They were hungry, predatorily so. "My ex."

The woman's eyes widened. "The fairy?"

Jack was a human and, apparently, so was this chick. Her humanity was something that should have struck me immediately since I have the ability to detect Netherworld creatures from humans as soon as I get close to one. I can tell a werewolf from a vamp from a goblin from a ditzy brunette in less than three seconds. But, where the hell that ability was right now was anyone's guess.

"Yeah, the fairy," I managed to answer.

The woman smiled, revealing a set of perfect white teeth set behind sumptuous, full lips. I could never accuse Jack of dating anyone less than beautiful. "Well, isn't she just the cutest, lil' thing? I could just pinch her, she's so cute, like a lil' lightnin' bug."

That was when I realized she had a southern accent. Scarlett O'Hara had just lost all her charm and, as God was my witness, I'd be damned if I ever drank another sweet tea.

"Yeah, I'd say Dulcie has some lightning in her," Jack said with a laugh and another carnivorous gaze, this time at my bust.

Even though I wanted to either blast their righteous smiles off their righteous faces or, at the very least, run away and hide, I did neither. My feet were cemented in place like my ankles had just gone on strike.

"You okay, Dulce?"

I heard Knight's baritone voice come up behind me at the same instant that his arm weaved through mine and his hand found my waist, grasping it and pulling me into him. I couldn't even speak, and from the looks of it, neither could the skyscraper. Instead, she just stared at Knight like she'd never seen a god before.

"Hi," she said and paused for a few seconds. "Who are you?"

"Knight." He glanced down and offered me a little smile, squeezing my side as if to say he knew exactly what I was going through and that he was there for me, that he would see me through this. Then he faced the woman again and extended his hand. "I'm Dulcie's fiancé, it's nice to meet you."

At that moment, I wanted nothing more than for the room and everyone in it to melt away around us, leaving only Knight and me. He'd saved me. Just when I thought I was going to shrivel up and die, he'd ridden in on his white steed and slayed my dragon.

"Hi, Knight," the woman said in as flirty a voice as she could muster. "I'm Sunshine."

Knight chuckled and shook his head. "I'll bet you are."

"And I'm Jack," the jerk in question said as he thrust his hand out and the smile he'd been wearing only seconds before was now nowhere to be found. Instead, he wore a deeply etched frown and it was obvious he was put out either because I had a fiancé or because his date was still staring at Knight in total and complete appreciation.

14

"Good to meet you," Knight responded, without offering his hand in return. Instead, he glanced down at me and smiled. "Was wondering where you'd gone to, Dulce." Then he started to walk away, pulling me with him and when he smacked my ass and smiled at them, he added, "I just can't get enough of her, she's so damned beautiful," I didn't even mind.

When we were out of their line of sight, he looked at me with concern in his eyes. "Are you okay?"

I just nodded, still feeling shell-shocked. Then I glanced up at him and felt something that I hadn't felt in a long time, something I couldn't even characterize but it was real and pounding its way through me. "Thank you."

He just nodded. "Sorry about the ass smack but wanted to play it up."

"No," I was quick to respond. "I mean it … thank you."

Knight didn't say anything for a few seconds but bit his lip like he was trying to find just the right words. Then he turned to face me and there was something deliberate about his expression. "Dulcie, he's an asshole, you know that, right?"

At first I was confused because it wasn't as though Knight had ever met Jack, so how could he know the situation between us? But then it suddenly occurred to me that Knight knew exactly who Jack was. He knew because he'd inserted himself in a dream that I'd had about Jack a long time ago. That was one of Knight's abilities—he could basically highjack my dreams whenever he wanted to.

"Trust me, I know he's a jerk. I was just surprised to see him, that's all."

"Okay," Knight answered although he didn't sound convinced. "Did it weird you out at all? I mean, what I said?"

"Weird me out?" I shot back at him with a little laugh. "No, you were like my knight in shining armor."

He chuckled. "No pun intended?"

Warmth suffused me as I glanced back up at him. "No pun intended."

TWO

By the end of the evening, I was drunker than I'd been in a long time. After the little incident with Jack and Dixie's tallest woman, I found myself wanting nothing more than to lose myself in alcohol. Granted, it probably wasn't a great idea, but I wasn't concerned with great ideas at the moment … no, all I was concerned with was inebriation and the quickest route there.

"Dulce, I gotta get to bed," Sam said and collapsed into the booth next to me. "I feel sick."

"You're a witch, charm away your hangover," I argued, not wanting the night to end. If the night ended, I'd go home, which would leave me with nothing to do but think. And given the events of the evening, thinking wasn't such a great idea.

Sam shook her head. "I'm too drunk to focus on a charm. I think it's a few Advil for me and the sack."

"Girl, I'm right there with you," Dia said with a laugh. Although she'd had just as much to drink as we did, she didn't seem drunk in the least. Nope … instead, Dia looked like she'd just been sipping on water all night. The same couldn't be said for Trey, who sat beside Knight, and had already fallen asleep, drooling into his man-bag.

"What are we going to do with him?" Sam asked as she pointed to the sleeping hobgoblin.

Knight laughed and shook his head. "Leave him to me." Then he seemed to think better of it and scrutinized each of us. "I'll give all of you a ride home."

"You've been drinking too," I pointed out, still not okay with the fact that our evening was coming to an end.

Knight faced me and smiled. "As a Loki, my metabolism is faster than yours. I process alcohol within a couple of hours."

"Of course!" I said and shook my head. "How could I have thought otherwise?"

Knight didn't respond but offered me a knowing grin before reaching for Trey and hoisting him over his shoulder as if he weighed nothing which just hinted to Knight's strength because Trey weighs … a lot. I draped my purse over one shoulder and Trey's man-bag over the other. Then Dia, Sam and I followed Knight out of the club.

Knight reached inside his pants pocket and produced the key to his Beemer, beeping it unlocked as I opened the rear door and watched him deposit Trey, rather unceremoniously, into the backseat. Trey grunted once he hit the seat and then rolled over onto his side, leaving a line of drool across the black leather. I glanced at Knight, who offered me a frown. Then I remembered Dia and the fact that we were a long way from Moon.

"Dia, you can crash at my house if you don't want to make the drive home," I suggested.

Dia looked at me and raised one eyebrow before facing Knight and giving him a flirtatious smile. "Girl, the only house I'm crashing at tonight is the sexy Loki's; otherwise, I'm driving my bootylicious self back home."

"Is that an invitation?" Knight asked with a grin.

"Honey, I've lost track of how many invitations I've sent your way. Just goes to show that you've got too much fairy on your mind."

Knight glanced at me and nodded. "You could say that."

"Oh, God, let's go," I said, feeling entirely uncomfortable with all the sexual innuendo.

Knight chuckled as he walked around to the driver's seat. Sam opened the rear door, pushing Trey out of the way so she could fit beside him. Before I could take a seat, Dia grabbed my arm and pulled me closer to her, leaning in to whisper: "Girl, you make your damned move on that fine man or you are seriously gonna upset my inner diva."

"I wouldn't want to do that."

"No, you sure as hell wouldn't. I know you're a smart girl, Dulcie O'Neil, so you make a play on that man before he comes to his senses and realizes I'm waiting in the wings." Then she winked.

I laughed and said nothing more, but gave her a knowing smile when she cocked her eyebrow at me again. After hugging me and saying good-bye, she started for her red Ford Mustang. She got into the driver's seat, gunned the engine and, with the radio blaring, disappeared into the darkness of Splendor's city center.

I faced Knight's BMW again and seated myself, glancing over at him as I did so. He was watching me with a curious look on his face.

"Don't tell me you have stellar hearing ability too?" I grumbled.

He smiled and turned on the engine. "Okay, I won't tell you." Then he motioned to my door, which was still wide open. "Ready?"

I didn't respond but closed the door and looked back at Sam who was already draped over Trey's shoulder and sound asleep despite his snoring—something that sounded like a cross between a vacuum struggling with pennies and a chainsaw biting steel. If Trey ever managed to land a girlfriend, I'd be amazed.

"Did you have fun tonight?" Knight asked with a boyish expression.

I smiled, thinking about the evening. I had had fun at times and then there had been that whole Jack situation which hadn't been fun. But, all in all, I actually felt good about it—it was almost like I now had closure; like somehow I'd had the last word. And that had all been due to Knight.

"I did, thank you again."

"So seeing your ex didn't ruin the evening, I hope?" Knight continued. "If I'd known that was going to happen, I'd have just stuck with dinner and drinks."

"Ah, so your Loki powers don't include seeing the future?"

Knight chuckled. "Can't say that they do." He stopped at a red light and faced me, losing his smile. "Answer my question, Dulce, is everything okay?"

I sighed as I considered it. Was I okay? Somehow, I felt numb to the whole thing—indifferent even. "Yeah," I said and nodded, almost in surprise at my own admission. "Seeing Jack really wasn't that terrible. I mean, sure, I would have preferred not to have seen him, but I'm … okay."

"Good, I was worried."

"Don't be worried. I'm good."

Knight chuckled. "Maybe that's because you find yourself attracted to a particular Loki?"

I remembered Dia's parting words about pursuing Knight. The truth of the matter was that I was attracted to Knight, and always had been. Maybe I just needed to run with it, abandon myself. Dulcie O'Neil never abandoned herself to anything and maybe tonight was the night to change that. "That could be why."

Knight didn't say anything but continued beaming as if that was really all he wanted to hear—the fact that I was into him. Well, I *was* into him. On overload.

Before I knew it, we pulled up to Trey's house and Knight threw me a disarming grin as he put the car in park and undid his seatbelt. "I'll just be a minute."

He stepped out and opened Trey's door, pulling the smaller and fatter man into his arms. Then he lugged Trey over his shoulder and started for the front door. I glanced back at Sam and noticed she was awake and I suddenly wondered how much of Knight's and my conversation she'd overheard.

"Are we home yet?" she asked groggily.

"Nope, not yet," I started and not wanting her to get any ideas, added, "and you're staying at your house tonight."

Apparently she wasn't too drunk to get my gist. "Wow, Dulce, you planning on scoring?"

I nodded as I thought about it. "Maybe."

Sam giggled but quieted once Knight resumed his place behind the wheel. "One down, two to go."

Five minutes later, we reached Sam's house and with a quick hug and wink, Sam was safely inside and it was just Knight and me. We drove the ten minutes to my place in silence, just listening to the mindless chatter of the DJ. When Knight pulled in front of my apartment, I suddenly felt nervous, my heartbeat pounding in my chest as my palms went clammy.

"Here we are, Dulce," he said as he put the car in park.

I nodded and it seemed it took me an eternity to undo my seatbelt and grasp the handles of my purse. I opened the door and was about to step out when I thought better of it.

"Do you, uh, do you want to come in?" Holy Hades, I hadn't meant to sound so schoolgirl embarrassed.

Knight's smile was wide as he shook his head. "Not when you're drunk."

I felt something crumble inside me. I'm not good at putting myself out there and even less good when it comes to dealing with rejection. "Drunk? I'm really not that drunk," I said even though I could hear the doubt in my own voice.

"When something happens between you and me, it will be because you want it to happen. Not because you're under the influence of alcohol or something else."

I could read into the "something else" he was referring to—Mandrake, an illegal narcotic I'd had the displeasure of becoming addicted to during our last case with the Dreamstalker. And, yes, I'd come onto Knight at the time and, yes, he'd denied me … so this was now denial number two.

"I don't know what to think when you play the part of a gentleman," I said with a quick smile, not exactly sure how I felt about the turn of events. He didn't want to come in and have sex with me but his reasons were admirable … somehow I was okay with that. More than okay with it, actually. I respected him because of it.

"I'm a good guy, Dulcie. One of these days you're going to realize that and when you do, things are going to be very good between us."

There really wasn't anything more to say so I stood up, thinking about retiring to my bed. Then it suddenly dawned on me that I'd forgotten the whole reason I'd agreed to go on this date in the first place.

"So our date is over, what's with the glowing eyes bit?"

Knight chuckled and shook his head. "The date's not over."

I threw my hands on my hips. If there's something I hate more than anything else, it's playing games. "Knight, the date is over. You're dropping me off and going home. You said at the end of our date you would tell me."

He nodded. "Right, and it's not the end of our date."

I sighed deeply. "So when will the end of our date be?"

He shrugged. "I'm picking you up tomorrow morning at nine a.m. sharp so don't oversleep. Oh, and dress in your riding gear."

"What?" I demanded. "What riding gear?"

22

"We're going to take a little joy ride," he answered as I realized he meant my motorcycle riding gear. Yep, I must have been pretty drunk because it wasn't like I was a horse enthusiast ...

"You don't have a bike?" I asked, feeling the cloud of alcohol starting to descend on my mind. I was tired and I'd have a mean hangover in the morning. Good thing for me that I could heal it with a little fairy dust.

Knight shook his head, still beaming up at me. "Don't worry about it. Now, before you let all the warm air out of my car, let's go."

"Let's," I started. "I thought you weren't coming in?"

He opened his car door and closed it behind him at the same time I did. "It's impolite not to walk a beautiful woman to her door, Dulcie. And, furthermore, it's even more impolite not to ensure that beautiful woman's apartment is safe."

"You're really taking this gentleman stuff to extremes," I said with the beginnings of a small smile that revealed the fact that I liked it when he played this part.

He glanced at me and winked. "Maybe that's because I am a gentleman?"

I scoffed. "Hardly."

We reached my front door and I pulled my key out. Once I'd opened the door, Knight sidestepped me and pushed the door wide. As he walked into the living room, the lights came on and it wasn't like he'd clapped to activate my nonexistent clapper. Nope, this was just another of his Loki abilities ...

I followed him into the apartment and closed the door behind me, watching him disappear down the hallway and, I imagine, into my bedroom where he could play the part of protector to ensure no one was hiding out. My yellow Labrador, Blue, pawed at the sliding glass door, wanting to be let in.

"Just a second, boy," I called out, my attention momentarily arrested by the sight of Knight in the hallway.

"All good?" I asked.

"All good, Dulce."

I nodded and suddenly felt the incredible desire to kiss him. But I didn't act on my impulse because I wasn't sure how he'd take it and I really wasn't in the mood for denial number three.

He started for the door and paused with his hand on the doorknob, turning to face me. "Good night, Dulcie. Remember tomorrow morning at nine a.m. sharp."

I didn't say anything but merely nodded and watched him as he smiled again and ducked out of the door, jogging down my front walkway to his Beemer. I waved to him and watched his sports car disappear down the street before I remembered to let Blue back in.

Knight, as usual, was true to his word. The next morning he appeared on my doorstep right at nine a.m. At the sound of the doorbell, I pulled open the door and found him dressed in head to toe riding gear—black with grey etching. The leather clutched his thighs like a second skin and the riding jacket just accentuated his already incredibly broad shoulders. He smiled down at me, gripping his helmet in his hand.

"Love a woman in leather," he said, shaking his head.

I glanced down at myself and took in my black leather pants and long-sleeved black cotton T-shirt. My riding jacket was still hanging behind the door.

"So where's your ride?"

Knight stepped aside with a knowing grin and I immediately noticed the sparkling black motorcycle sitting in front of my house.

I sighed—it was all I could think to do. Whatever Knight did, it was always to the utmost. He just didn't seem happy with mediocrity. "Since when do you like motorcycles?"

Knight smiled boyishly. "Since you started riding one. Figured I needed to keep up with you."

The only reason I'd purchased a bike was due to the fact that my Jeep Wrangler had been totaled in the situation with the Dreamstalker and I couldn't afford anything other than a motorcycle. My owning one was due to an economical need, not a need for speed. Apparently, the same couldn't be said for the Loki.

"Okay, so what is it?" I asked and offered him an encouraging smile. I mean … it WAS a beautiful bike.

He glanced behind him and grinned like a new parent. "Ducati Superbike 1198."

"Okay, you realize there is no way in hell I'm going to be able to keep up with you on that?" My bike, a Suzuki DL 650, paled in comparison. To begin with, my Suzuki was about half the size of Knight's Ducati.

Knight didn't say anything but smiled again—one of those "I know something you don't know" smirks and fished inside his jacket pocket. Then he handed me a key.

"What's this?" I demanded.

"The key to your new bike."

"What?" I started, in shock, first glancing at the key and then Knight's smug face. "You bought me a motorcycle?"

He shook his head. "The ANC did. You can't hope to work on Netherworld cases on a bike that may or may not get you where you need to go." His smile deepened. "Think of this like a company car … only it's a company bike."

"It's true what they say," I started.

"And what do they say?"

"That the people highest up in a company take the most advantage," I finished with a self-impressed smile.

Knight frowned and with the slope of his shoulders, looked disappointed. "You can accept the mode of transportation provided by the Netherworld or you can choose to ride your own bike, it's up to you." He paused a moment or two. "But, you might at least want to see it."

I shrugged and he must have taken it as a sign of interest because he turned around and started down my entryway, pausing just beyond the edge of my building. I followed him and that was when I saw it. Sitting a few feet in front of his bike was a smaller one, just as sporty and dangerous but instead of a shiny black, this was deep crimson. And, yes, it was gorgeous.

"What is it?" I asked, in awe.

Knight chuckled, the tone of his laugh victorious. "Ducati Diavel."

I swallowed hard before facing him again and couldn't deny the fact that I was always impressed with Knight's antics. He definitely wasn't predictable. "How did you manage to get them both here?"

Knight laughed. "Leave it to you to ask the logistics questions. The dealer dropped yours off this morning." He extended his hand. "Do you want to see it?"

I just nodded and took his hand as he led me outside and, instantly, I was in love. Um, with the bike. It was sleek, with lines that were so sharp, it looked like it could cut you just by sitting on it.

"Wow," I muttered as Knight chuckled.

"You approve?"

I gulped down my excitement. "Um, it's beautiful, thank you." Suddenly remembering myself, I glanced up at him. "I'm not giving up my bike," I added with a determined expression. "I'll use this for work-related business only." He frowned and I continued. "If it's a company bike, it should be used for company business."

Knight shrugged. "I guess that's fair enough." He paused and then a huge smile lit up his face. "Well, this visit is work-related."

"Work-related?" I repeated dubiously, crossing my arms against my chest.

He nodded. "We have lots to discuss. Once we get to where we're going, that is."

"And where would that be?"

Knight didn't answer but put his helmet on and started for his bike. I was left with no choice but to follow him. I grabbed my helmet from the chair by my door and locked the door behind me, feeling a little hesitant and unsure about the new motorcycle. Maybe it was too much bike for me?

"That's for me to know and you to find out," he said with a wicked grin as he mounted his bike.

And damn it if he didn't look like a wet dream come to life. "It's going to take me a little while to get used to it," I started, still feeling overwhelmed.

He nodded. "I'll go slow." And the wicked smile on his lips told me that was a double entendre if ever I'd heard one.

I didn't respond but mounted the bike and, putting the key in the ignition, turned it on. The power of the engine was obvious in the way it purred beneath me. This was going to be one hell of a ride. Hopefully I'd arrive in one piece.

"Ready?" Knight called as he peeled into the street and circled, coming up beside me. I could smell the rubber of his tires.

"Show off," I muttered.

"Come on, Dulce, show me what you've got."

And he was already down the road. I glanced at the bike beneath me and shook my head. What other choice did I have? I revved the engine, said a silent prayer that I wouldn't kill myself and gunned it.

I met Knight at the end of the street. He smiled at me and took a right so I followed him, speeding to keep up with him. I caught him at the next stop sign.

"Didn't you say something about going slow?" I yelled.

He shook his head. "I wasn't talking about driving."

He gunned the engine, disappearing around a bend in the road as I fought to catch up with him. I wasn't sure if my bike was as powerful as his—it definitely wasn't as big so maybe the power wasn't quite there either. Or maybe I was just making excuses.

Knight paused at the base of Highway Seven, which led up to Giant's Gorge, a canyon with lots of twists and turns—the perfect course for a bike ride. He glanced back at me and smiled, taking off before I had the chance to discuss our route. This time I wasn't as reserved. I peeled into the street and easily caught up with him.

For the next ten miles, we rode alongside one another, taking the twists and turns of the road as they came. And I had to admit that the Ducati was an amazing ride—it was incredibly fast and powerful.

We reached the top of the canyon and the paved road became dirt. Knight pulled into the large, flat open space and killed his engine, standing up as he removed his helmet. I followed suit and took my jacket off. I draped the jacket over the bike and left my helmet on the seat as I approached Knight and lost myself in the beauty of the view from Giant's Gorge. We were so high, I could see the town of Splendor below us, the cars and people appearing as tiny as ants, busily being busy.

"How do you like the bike?" he asked.

I glanced at him and inhaled deeply. I couldn't help it. Knight is a gorgeous guy but something about him clad in leather, standing next to an incredible street bike was almost too much for me to handle.

"It was really something," I said, forgetting what I was talking about.

And at that moment, I realized what I intended to do. My needs and wants were clearer to me than they had ever been. I approached Knight, never taking my eyes from his.

"You kept up okay," he said in a throaty voice, which got huskier the closer I came.

I didn't respond but stepped up to him and looped my arms around his neck. The surprise in his face was priceless.

"Knight, I'm not drunk or on Mandrake."

He chuckled deeply. "No, you aren't."

"I want you to kiss me."

Before the last word was out of my mouth, Knight's mouth was on mine. And his kiss was demanding, hungry, needy. I ran my hands through his hair as his tongue entered my mouth, eagerly meeting my own. I'm not sure how long we kissed, how long my hands caressed his silky hair or how long our tongues mated, but when he pulled away from me, we were both panting.

"That was unexpected," he said.

There was something inside me that wasn't satiated, something that was raring to go, and something that wouldn't be denied. "That isn't all I want."

More surprise in Knight's eyes. "What do you want, Dulcie?" he asked and his voice sounded raspy, gravelly.

I inhaled, asking myself the same question even though I didn't need to. I knew what I wanted, what I'd wanted since the moment I met Knight. I knew what my body was demanding, what I needed. Him.

"Tell me what you want," he repeated with urgency in his tone.

"I want you," I said in a small voice, glancing up at him. The lust swimming in his eyes made me feel weak and wobbly in my knees, like I was going to keel over right there.

29

"Where?" he insisted, grabbing hold of my wrists as he pinned me against his chest. "Where do you want me?"

I swallowed hard, never breaking eye contact. "Inside me."

And those must have been the magic words because Knight said nothing more but lifted me up and took a few steps before pushing me up against a large boulder. Then his lips were on mine again and his kiss was even deeper, more passionate.

He ground his hips against me and I could feel the obvious stirring of his excitement from between his legs.

"Are you okay with this, Dulce?" he whispered as he trailed a line of kisses down my neck. "Because if you aren't okay with it, we need to stop now." He kissed me again and then pulled away, glancing down at me.

"No, don't stop," I whispered and arched my back when I felt his hands plying my breasts above my shirt.

"Tell me you're okay with this."

He stared at me with the look of ravenous hunger in his eyes and his face was flushed. "I want this, Knight, I want you. I'm more than okay with it."

He smiled and then his lips were on mine again while his hands explored my breasts, my hair, my face, before pulling me into him.

"You don't know how many times I've thought about this, about you saying those words to me," he said, losing his voice as he buried his face in my cleavage.

I didn't say anything but allowed him to loop his hands underneath my shirt and pull it up and over my shoulders, revealing my breasts as they strained against my bra which suddenly felt entirely too confining. Knight dropped my shirt on the ground and focused on my breasts, his cheeks flushed. His gaze found mine as he reached around and undid my bra, pulling the straps slowly down my arms as if he wanted to torture me. I felt the sting of the air on my nipples and didn't have to glance down to know they were standing at attention.

"Beautiful," Knight said as his gaze settled on my breasts. He plied them with his hands before bending down and taking one nipple captive in his mouth, his tongue teasing. I ran my hands through his hair and dropped my head back, closing my eyes as I enjoyed the flush of excitement and anticipation building up within me.

A moan escaped my mouth and I felt Knight break away from me. I opened my eyes and faced him in confusion.

He was breathing hard, his chest rising and falling with the exertion. "Dulcie," he started and then his voice seemed to trail into the distance.

"What?"

"This isn't just sex for me."

"It isn't just sex for ..."

"No," he interrupted me. "You don't understand. I, hmm ..." He glanced down at the ground as if he was trying to find the right words.

"Knight, just tell me."

He looked up at me again and his eyes were glowing.

"Your eyes," I started.

"This may not seem like the best time to get into this but before anything more happens, we should ... we need to."

I swallowed, not really sure where this was going but very curious all the same. "Go on."

Knight looked down at my breasts again and outlined my still alert nipples with the pad of his index finger. Then, before I could take another breath, he hoisted me into his arms and carried me to his bike, where he settled me on the seat.

"To understand everything, I need to explain about my species," he said and his voice was deep, heavy. He continued to run his fingers in large circles around each of my breasts, toying with my nipples as he did so.

"Okay."

"The Loki, as you know, is a creature forged from the fire of Hades. Hades is the King of the Dark World."

"The Dark World?" I repeated, suddenly at a loss.

Knight nodded. "During the creation of the Netherworld, there were various rulers—Hades was the God of the Dark World which lies deep in the center of the Netherworld and is responsible for all creatures that possess incredible strength, power and speed."

I was glad Knight was explaining everything to me because I'd never been to the Netherworld and all of this was completely foreign to me.

"So, have you seen the Dark World?"

He nodded and a chuckle escaped his lips. "Yes, you could say that. I spent my entire youth and early adulthood there, training."

"Training for what?"

"The Loki is a soldier, created in Hades's own image—large, powerful, fast and strong."

"Sounds like you in a nutshell."

He nodded. "We are the warriors of the Netherworld, Dulcie. Our mission is to protect and enforce Netherworld law."

I nodded. "Hence your position with the ANC?"

"Yes," he started and looked as if he wanted to say more but didn't. "Technically, all Loki were to remain in the Netherworld and that's why you never came across one of my species before."

"But you aren't in the Netherworld," I started.

He shook his head. "That's a story for another time," he said quickly.

"Okay."

"So going back to the creation of the Loki warriors," he started and seemed to lose his train of thought while he watched his fingers circle my breasts. "You are so beautiful," he said, glancing down at me.

I smiled. "The creation of the Loki warriors?" I prodded.

He chuckled and nodded, picking up where he left off. "As the warrior class, reproduction is a vital and complicated subject for us." His voice trailed off and he dropped his attention to his feet and took a deep breath. "Sex with me won't be what you're used to."

"Why?"

"Because I will want to claim you."

"What?" I started. "I don't even know what that means."

"It means that ..." he dropped his attention to my breasts again and stopped touching them. His eyes found mine and he continued. "My eyes glow, Dulcie, because my body has identified you as my mate."

"What?" It was all I could think to say.

"I was surprised when it happened as well." He took a deep breath. "I always knew I was attracted to you, well, really, that you drove me to complete insanity." He chuckled and I just raised an unimpressed brow as he continued. "But it goes much deeper than that. It's not a conscious decision. I'm wired to reproduce with a woman who can tolerate my seed, Dulcie. She must be physically strong enough."

"Um, no offense but I'm not interested in having kids anytime soon." Truth be told, I wasn't convinced I ever wanted kids. It seemed like I'd missed the line where God was handing out maternal instinct.

He chuckled again and shook his head. "Neither am I."

"So why are you telling me this?"

"So you'll understand my biology, my genetic makeup, why I am the way I am."

Loki Biology 101 aside, this whole sex conversation was sort of tripping me up. "Okay, going back to this sex thing, you can't tell me you haven't had sex with other women before?"

He shook his head. "Of course I've had sex with other women, but not at the same level that you and I would."

"Why? How does that work?"

He exhaled deeply. "With other women, I'm basically infertile. I can only procreate with the … right woman."

I shook my head, trying to come to terms with what he was saying. "So if you and I have sex …"

"We could protect against you getting pregnant."

"We could?" I demanded. "Because, like I said, I'm not ready for Loki juniors anytime soon."

He laughed. "And I said the same, Dulcie. Yes, human contraception works on me too."

This was the strangest conversation I'd had in a long time but luckily for me, I was still on the pill. Why, you might ask considering my sex life had been non-existent for the past couple of years? Because I liked having short periods. And maybe I was hopeful that my sex life would someday pick up …

But back to the fact that Knight wasn't farming for a wife and children … "Amen to that," I said with a smile.

THREE

Granted, I was interested in knowing Knight's history—why he was the way he was and why his eyes glowed but his timing sort of sucked, for lack of a better word. I mean, I guess he had to tell me about the whole sexual bit before we got too hot and heavy and he "claimed" me without me being aware of it. And, depending on what that claiming thing meant, maybe it would have seriously freaked me out? Especially if I hadn't been prepared for it. As it was now, I was still sort of freaked out but more in an anxious and excited sort of way. I had the feeling that sex with Knight would be like nothing I'd ever experienced before.

"So going back to the part about you wanting to 'claim' me, as you called it, what the hell does that mean?" I asked, trying not to lose myself in the fact that his fingers were caressing each of my breasts. "I mean, the last thing I need to deal with is you turning all caveman on me."

He nodded and cocked his head to the side as if to say he was contemplating my words. It wasn't exactly the response I'd been hoping for. I'd hoped for something more along the lines of: no jealousy, no possessiveness and definitely no loincloths or clubs.

"I might be a bit possessive and possibly jealous," he admitted.

"Might be?"

He shrugged. "It's never happened to me before. This would be a first. Who knows, maybe I'll be just as awesome as I always am." Then he laughed.

I shook my head before my thoughts returned to this newest bombshell he'd dropped into my lap. Why could nothing in my life be simple? "So how do you know all this if you've never experienced it?"

"I've talked to Loki men who have."

He trailed his index finger over my nipple and down the side of my breast, continuing his descent to my stomach until he reached the waist of my leather pants. Staring at me, and never taking his eyes from mine, he undid my button and unzipped my fly. I stilled his hand before he could undress me any further.

"So we're in unchartered territory here?" I asked in a small voice—a voice that was currently choking on the frog lodged in my throat.

"Looks that way, yes," he answered and moved his eyes down the line of my body to where my red lace panties peeked out from underneath my pants. "Damn," he said, shaking his head, outlining the lace as he did so. "Could you be any sexier?"

I didn't know how to answer that question so said nothing; although I must admit I definitely enjoyed the fact that Knight appeared to be so into me. I mean, come on, how could I not? But, really, my focus needed to be on this subject of "claiming" me, as he termed it. I needed to understand what that meant in order to make a decision as to whether or not I was okay with it. "So if we do this, what are you going to want from me?"

"A relationship." Knight's answer was immediate. He didn't even have to think about it.

At his words, something inside me cracked and I felt warmth spreading through me. It was like Knight had just slammed a sledgehammer into the bulwark of my emotional defenses, attempting to break down the wall I'd been working so hard to erect over the past few years. But while I could definitely feel the beginnings of panic welling up from within me, there was also a feeling of pleasure, of gratitude to Knight. I didn't want to continue living the way I had been. I wanted to experience love again. But, aside from those rosy feelings, I also didn't want to go into anything blindly and I needed to understand what I could be getting myself into.

"I don't want a jealous, overbearing and possessive man on my hands."

He nodded. "Fair enough."

"If that happens, can you control it?"

"I'd like to think so." Then he paused for a few seconds, studying me. "Sounds like you're okay with the relationship part?"

I shrugged. I guess I was okay with the relationship part. I mean, it hadn't freaked me out ... that much. And I did still have that warm and fuzzy feeling ... I nodded even though I was surprised by my own admission. "Yeah, I, uh, I think I could handle that."

Knight smiled broadly. "Wow, listen to you ... willing to get back up on that steed again?"

I started to nod but then something occurred to me. Something that probably wasn't going to be the greatest subject to broach, but one I wanted to, no needed to, all the same. "Knight, if your body considers me to be your ... mate ... what if things don't work out between us?" Just call me the cynic, I guess.

He frowned. "Why wouldn't things work out between us?"

I shrugged. "I'm playing the part of devil's advocate. What if we dated and just decided we weren't well matched?" I paused for a few seconds. "I guess what I'm asking is ... is there a way out of this mate business should we need one?"

He studied my face for a few seconds, his expression not giving away his thoughts. "Yes, there is."

I smiled and felt a little uncomfortable, like maybe I shouldn't have mentioned the negative. But then I chided myself—I was not the type of person who went into anything blindly. I needed to know where my escape routes were should I ever need them. And, apparently, in matters of the heart, I was no different.

"It's okay, Dulce," Knight said with a smile.

"Okay?"

"It's just who you are." I realized he was talking about the fact that I was considering this subject from all possible angles. "And because you weigh the pros with the cons, you're great at your job as a Regulator." His smiled broadened. "And it's also one of the reasons I like you so much."

Maybe it was the way he said it, maybe it was the words themselves, but his comment flipped a switch in me—it flipped me into the position of extremely turned on. I didn't respond but clutched the back of his neck and forced my mouth on his, wanting nothing more than to feel his tongue lapping at mine.

A few minutes later, he pulled away and merely gazed down at me as he ran his fingers through my hair, pushing an errant tendril back behind my ear. "Does this mean you've made a decision?" he asked.

I thought about it. The pros: I liked Knight ... a lot. I wanted him and I always had. And somewhere inside me I knew we'd be good together. I trusted him. The cons: maybe he'd be jealous and possessive but, then again, maybe he wouldn't.

The pros definitely outweighed the cons.

I nodded as I glanced up at him. "Yes, I've made my decision."

Knight's hands continued palpating my breasts as he spread my legs, pushing himself into the V of my thighs. "And?"

"I want to be with you, Knight," I said in a wispy, breathless voice.

He didn't say anything but his smile spoke volumes. He glanced down at his body which was still wedged between my legs and began grinding against me, teasing me mercilessly.

"Is that all you've got?" I asked, feeling bliss as it spread from my core through my entire body. Holy Hades, did I want him.

He chuckled and shook his head and, before I could take another breath, he lifted me from the Ducati and carried me a few paces before gently placing me on the ground. He took off his jacket and laid it out like it was a picnic blanket right beside me, making me laugh. I mean, why settle for an impromptu leather jacket-blanket since I was a fairy and had a little something called magic? I balled my left hand into a fist and shook it a few times until the tell-tale signs of fairy dust began slipping out from the cracks. Then I closed my eyes, imagined a large, thick blanket and released my magic, which spilled like glitter against the dirt, only to immediately create the exact blanket I'd just visualized.

"Impressive," Knight said with a smile.

I didn't respond but allowed him to lift me and place me on top of the blanket, as he pulled my pants down the swells of my thighs and let them fall around my ankles. He pushed on my shoulders as if to say he wanted me in a reclining position so I acquiesced, sitting down and stretching my legs out before me. He never took his eyes from mine as he leaned over me, his fingers finding my panties again. He started rubbing me up and down above the lace. I arched back and closed my eyes, wanting nothing more than to focus on the strength of his fingers as they massaged me. He slipped my panties to the side and then his finger was on me, rubbing me back and forth as I bucked beneath him.

"There now," he said with a raspy voice.

"Give me more," I whispered.

He chuckled. "What was that, Dulce, I couldn't quite hear you?"

I opened my eyes but said nothing, and simply grabbed his finger, forcing it inside me. The shock and hunger in his eyes was reward enough. I released my grasp and allowed him to penetrate me with two fingers, letting him build his own rhythm as I leaned back and enjoyed it. He pulled his fingers out and I felt him toying with my pants, releasing them from around my ankles. I stabilized myself on my elbows and watched him as he stood up and pulled his shirt over his head, revealing a chest to which I've never seen the equal. Muscles landscaped his chest and his tan skin contrasted against the light dusting of dark hair, which adorned his lower stomach, vanishing beneath his belt line.

"You are stunning," I whispered.

He shook his head. "I'm nothing compared to you."

I could argue that point but wasn't going to waste my time. Instead, I wanted to see what was under his pants. "Take it all off."

He offered me a cock-eyed expression and a smirk but shrugged and undid his pants, pulling both his boxers and leathers down his sculpted thighs. But it wasn't his thighs that captivated me. Nope, that honor was reserved for his penis, which was, in a word … beautiful. It was long and thick, longer and thicker than any I'd ever seen before and there was a part of me that cringed in trepidation at the mere thought of playing host to such a … Titan.

"Wow," I said in disbelief, never pulling my eyes from him.

He chuckled. "Another Loki trait."

He laid back down next to me and pinned one of my legs between his as he started running his hands down my body again.

"Where were we?" he asked as he bent down to kiss me and his fingers found the junction of my thighs. "Ah, I was going to taste you," he answered his own question.

I didn't even get the chance to consider his statement before his head was between my thighs and his tongue was lapping at me with long, forceful strokes. I strained against him, lost in the bliss of his mouth and felt an orgasm seize me from the very core of my body. I shook against him and he grasped my thighs, steadying me. But he didn't break the seal of his tongue; if anything he was more forceful, more demanding.

"Knight, I need you now," I groaned.

He pulled his head up and smiled at me. "How bad?"

"Bad."

He cleared his throat and faced me again with a wicked smile as I watched him shift himself until he was directly above me, supported by his hands. I leaned back against the blanket, preparing myself for his entry. He lowered himself down and that was when I felt the head of him pushing against me, just enough to allow an explosion of butterflies in my stomach. He pushed forward and I felt myself stretching to accommodate him.

"Are you alright?" he whispered.

I just nodded as I continued to thrive on the sensations of him as he entered me—something between incredible pleasure with just a trace of pain. It had been a long ass time since I'd had sex and my body was making that clearly evident.

He still wasn't all the way inside me and was going so slowly, it seemed like it might take him all day to finally arrive. "Just do it," I said, bracing myself.

And so he did. He pushed and filled me. As soon as the entirety of him was ensconced inside me, I felt the beginnings of an orgasm rain down within me. I gripped his shoulders and moaned out as the orgasm overtook me, all the while amazed by the fact that I'd just had one so quickly. Usually, it took at least fifteen minutes … Usually, just at the time I was about to climax, Jack had already finished and was on his way to dreamland.

But the last person I wanted to think about now was Jack. Not while I was with the most beautiful, arresting and sexy man I'd ever met. No, I didn't want to spare another thought for my ex-boyfriend. It almost seemed sacrilegious.

"Did you," Knight started as he glanced down at me with a smile.

"Um, yes," I said somewhat sheepishly.

He chuckled. "That was fast." He continued to push inside me, his eyes never straying from mine and that smile still firmly in place. "Are you ready for another one?"

I swallowed hard. No point in lying. "Yes."

As I watched him, the intense blue of his eyes began to give way to a subtle glow, a white light that seemed to eclipse the entirety of his eyes.

"Your eyes," I said in awe.

Knight smiled but said nothing because there really wasn't anything to say. We both knew what was happening. He was claiming me, making me his. And the thought made me giddy inside.

He started pushing harder, faster and I wrapped my legs around his middle, thinking sex had never been this arousing before. I could feel myself teetering on the brink of another orgasm as my body suddenly began to spasm, my legs shaking.

"Knight," I started, suddenly feeling frightened.

"It's okay," he crooned in my ear. "Don't fight it. It's your body reacting to mine."

I exhaled my pent-up breath and closed my eyes, allowing my body its response. I tightened my thighs around his waist as he grasped me by the hips and held me at an angle, plunging into me as deeply as he could.

That was all it took. I could hear my screams as another orgasm took control of my body. With a chuckle, he allowed my hips to touch the blanket again and I opened my eyes to find him studying me. Our gazes locked as his body pulsated within mine, erotic and sensual.

He pushed into me as deeply as he could and then began grinding his pelvis against me, his penis as far inside me as it could be. I grasped his shoulders and dug my nails into his back even as I realized I could have been hurting him.

"Sorry," I started.

"No," he interrupted as he gazed down at me. "I like it."

Smiling, I increased the pressure of my grip and allowed myself to get lost in the feel of him up to my hilt as he continued to grind against me, rubbing that soft nub that sent me into another round of orgasms. I closed my eyes and thrust my hips upward, screaming out his name as I erupted into my own state of bliss.

"I love listening to you," he whispered and started kissing my neck as he began pulling out and pushing back into me again. The grinding bit had merely been for my own benefit—Knight was a generous lover.

"That was amazing," I said, still breathless. "No one's ever done that to me before."

He smiled and I could see the pride in his eyes. "There's plenty more where that came from."

But suddenly I wanted nothing more than to witness his own surrender, to watch him as he used my body to reach his own blissful euphoria. I wanted to watch him orgasm, wanted to watch his face, feel him. "It's your turn," I said.

He nodded but said nothing more. Course, he didn't really need to—his body was doing all the communicating. He pushed inside me and then started a quick rhythm, going

43

faster and harder and deeper. All the while, his eyes were shut tight and small moans escaped his lips. At the point at which I thought I could no longer handle him, he pushed one last time, his eyes glowing all the while, and then collapsed against my chest, panting with exertion.

I wrapped my arms around him and played with the hair at the nape of his neck, running my hands through the thick, silky locks. "Wow," I said with a smile.

He pulled up until he was on his elbows and smiled at me in return. "Wow, huh?"

"That wasn't quite as I imagined it would be."

His smile faltered. "Oh?"

I patted his back. "In a good way, Knight. I, uh, I've never come so many times before."

"Really?" There was that look of accomplishment, of pride on his face again. "Then you don't regret it?"

"Regret it?" I asked in shock. "How and why would I regret it?"

He chuckled. "I'll ask you tomorrow."

Even though he was laughing, I realized he was partly serious. And you know what they say about jokes—that they always contain an underlying element of truth. But jokes and truth aside, what it came down to was that I didn't want Knight to think I regretted being with him. "Why would you think that?"

"Because I know you too well and I know that once you're alone, you'll start thinking and, invariably, you'll put up those walls of yours that I've just fought so hard to tear down."

While it sounded like he had my general behavioral patterns down pat, it was merely a generalization. Yes, I was like that with most subjects, but I wasn't about to let him think the same thing would happen in this case. "Knight," I started. "That isn't going to happen."

"Well, if it does, just talk yourself down. Or better yet, call me and I'll remind you why we're good together."

44

"Okay," I said with a laugh as I allowed him to kiss me.

Five hours later, I sat at my desk in my humble apartment, staring at the blinking cursor of my word document. So far, I'd managed to type:

The Vampire Raven, Book Two of A Vampire and a Gentleman series by Dulcie O'Neil

Yes, I had aspirations to be a writer—not just a hobbyist writer, but a full-fledged, career author who penned novels. I'd finished my first book, A Vampire and a Gentleman, which had been based on the exploits of my "friend" and vampire, Bram. That book had actually garnered the attention of the leading agent in paranormal romance, Barbara Mandley, from Great Fiction Agency and, even more amazingly, she loved the book and offered me representation a few days later.

Owing to my last case, when I nearly succumbed to a Dreamstalker (a goblin who hunted and killed his victims during sleep), I never had a chance to respond to Barbara. But, now I did have the time. And, based on the fact that it appeared my creative skills hadn't yet announced themselves, maybe an e-mail to Barbara was exactly what I needed to focus on.

Pulling up Firefox, I logged into my Yahoo e-mail account and, finding Barbara's e-mail address, quickly replied, typing:

Dear Barbara,

Thank you very much for offering to represent my book and me. I'm very excited to accept your offer of representation. Please advise what next steps will entail.

Sincerely,

Dulcie O'Neil

I sat back in my seat and rocked forward, thinking about the fact that I was about to embark on a career path very different from law enforcement. And it wasn't a feeling that was entirely joyful. The truth of the matter was that I loved my position as Regulator and, even now, I enjoyed my job of consultant Regulator to the ANC and to Knight. I'd been in law enforcement for the majority of my adult life and my identity really was wrapped up in my work—being a Regulator had shaped me; it had taught me how to be tough, how to survive and what was important in life. It defined me—in my blood, in my veins. It was me.

But would the life of a writer allow me to continue in my role of consultant Regulator? I mean, with book deadlines, marketing and signings, would I have the time to continue in law enforcement?

It was interesting, but this was the first time I'd actually considered any of this. I mean, it's not as though I'd ever come close to seeing the fruition of my dream of becoming a writer in the past. But, now, with Barbara endorsing me, I couldn't help but imagine all the publishing houses going into a tailspin to try and acquire the rights to my book. I mean, Barbara had to know what was hot and what would sell, right?

Yes, I was firmly convinced that if my writing career took off, I would have to step down from the ANC … and from Knight. And while I was concerned about how Knight would take the news, I was more concerned about how I would take it. Would it change me as a person? Would I get bored? Would my creative juices dry up? How would I handle deadlines? How would I deal with the loneliness of being an author?

I exhaled and realized my heart was pounding.

"You don't have to think about this now, Dulce," I announced out loud and to no one, suddenly thinking it was very strange that I was talking to myself.

The phone rang and I welcomed the interruption, since this latest realization completely depressed me. I reached for the receiver and brought it to my face.

"Hello?"

"Sooooo?" Sam asked expectantly.

"So what?" I repeated, pleased to hear her voice on the other end. Whenever I had a problem, Sam could always talk me through it.

She sighed. "So, did Knight hit the homerun?"

I laughed. "Um … yeah, I guess you could say he did."

Sam squealed and, at the thought of Knight hitting his homerun, I could feel my cheeks beginning to color.

"So, spill the details, girl!"

So I did. I told her about my multiple orgasms, about how incredibly hot and passionate Knight was as a lover and how his eyes had glowed.

"Wow, so you guys are like in a relationship then?" Sam asked.

I was quiet as I considered her question. "Yeah, I guess we are."

"And are you okay with it or have you freaked out yet?"

I shook my head. Why did everyone think I was going to freak out? I was a grown woman, for Hades sake! And it wasn't like I'd never been in a relationship before … As soon as that thought left my head, I realized I was trying to deceive myself. It made complete and total sense that everyone thought I was going to freak out because, when it came to relationships in general, that was what I did—freak out.

"I'm fine with it, Sam. I mean, it wasn't like he blindsided me and forced me into something. It was my decision, remember? I'm the one who said I was good with it. I'm the one who said I wanted it."

"Okay, good, I just wanted to make sure you weren't having an episode. Because if you were freaking out or if you're about to freak out, I'd remind you of all the good things about Knight … like, um, how insanely hot he is, how smart he is, um, how much he likes you, um, that he's super funny and that he puts up with Trey at work all day." She giggled. "He's actually a really nice guy, Dulcie."

I got her gist. She still thought I was in the process of freaking out or getting close to it. "I'm fine, Sam."

As I said the words, I thought about them. Somehow, I was fine with everything. I didn't have the feelings of panic that usually accompanied thoughts of entering into a relationship. I didn't have heart palpitations or the feeling that I couldn't breathe. Somehow, and I had no idea how, I was okay with everything. And, yes, I was slightly surprised by myself. Okay, the truth was it amazed me.

"Wow," Sam said.

"I know, pretty crazy, huh?"

She laughed. "Just goes to show that when you find the right one, you just know it."

The right one. Wow, maybe I had found the right one. Maybe Knight was truly the guy for me? The thought caused a flurry of butterflies in my stomach and my body suddenly ached for him. I wanted nothing more than to see his boyish smile, feel his big arms around me, smell that spicy scent that characterized him.

I missed him.

"Dulce?" Sam asked and I realized I'd completely lost track of our conversation. "You still there?"

"Sorry, I guess I'm just sort of floored by this whole thing."

She giggled. "Just go with it. I've been waiting for this to happen to you for a long ass time." She was silent for a few seconds. "I'm really happy for you, Dulce."

I sighed. "Thanks, Sam. I, uh, I'm really happy for me too."

And it was the truth.

FOUR

It was the day after Knight and I had sex and I couldn't wait to see him again. In fact, I tried to keep myself preoccupied all day with mindless things like taking my dog out for a very long run, going to the grocery store, washing the Ducati and tidying up the apartment. Anything to stop thinking about Knight and how incredible our sex had been. None of those diversions worked, however … Knight was on my mind and then some.

Now it might sound strange that I didn't pick up the phone to call him considering he was all I could think about. But really, I hadn't been in a relationship in such a long time, I couldn't remember what the rules were, or if there were any rules at all. I definitely didn't want Knight to think I was needy or possessive. And I didn't want to think I was needy or possessive. But would a phone call have been considered needy or possessive? No, probably not. Of course, it had only been one night and one day since we'd last seen one another. And wasn't there some rule about waiting two days to call or was that to return a call? Or maybe that was if you weren't yet in a relationship? Holy Hades, this stuff was going to be the death of me.

What it came down to was that I didn't want to change who I was. *Being in a relationship should in no way, shape or form change me*, I repeated to myself. I'd just continue living my life in the same manner I always had. Just because I was now having intense sex with Knight and it would be an ongoing thing (Woo Hoo!) didn't mean that I had to act or be any different. No, I was still the same headstrong, stubborn and emotionally calm Dulcie I always had been, right?

Then why in the hell did I feel like this? Why could I not stop thinking about the sexy-as-hell Loki? Why did I keep replaying the events from the day before? Why could I not concentrate on anything other than remembering his eyes as he pushed inside me for the first time?

My cell phone rang and I lurched for it, not even realizing why I felt so frantic. This just wasn't like me. Reading Knight's name on the Caller ID caused a flurry of excitement in my stomach and I wasn't sure whether I wanted to kick myself or do a happy dance.

Thankfully, I managed to restrain myself from doing either.

"Hi," I said, the tone of my voice belying the fact that I was happy to hear from him.

"Hi, sexy."

I giggled and felt like shooting myself. "What's up?" I asked after clearing my throat to ensure the giggle was dead.

"How are you ... feeling about things?"

"Feeling about things? What do you mean?" I asked, although I couldn't really say my focus was on the conversation. Instead, I tried to beat down the decidedly girly feelings that had suddenly welled up within me like a bad chick flick.

"I just wanted to make sure everything was good, that you didn't regret what we did yesterday?"

Ah, how was I feeling about *those* things ... Now we were on the same wavelength. "I don't regret anything, Knight."

I could hear him exhale his relief. "Thank Hades for that," he said with a chuckle and then paused for three seconds. Not that I was counting ... "I, uh, I was thinking about you, Dulce. Missing you, really."

I smiled. I couldn't help it. "Is that so?"

"Yep, and I was wondering what you're up to tonight?"

I felt heat color my cheeks and those girly feelings were now in complete control of my body. The strong and reliable side of me wanted to vomit. "I don't have any plans."

"Do you want some?"

"Sure."

"Good because I wasn't sure how I was going to go to sleep tonight without at least kissing those beautiful lips of yours."

I giggled again. Dammit.

"Pick you up at seven for dinner?" he asked, his chuckle revealing his extreme amusement at my giggle. Double dammit.

"Sure," I answered. Then, not wanting to leave him out in the cold, I quickly added, "I, um, I missed you too, Knight."

He took a few moments to respond. "I like hearing that."

And, truthfully, I liked saying it.

###

When I heard a knock on my front door at twenty minutes to seven, I was surprised to find Knight was early. And, I'll admit it, I was also happy. I mean, I'd finished getting ready long before and was just sitting around my living room, trying to kill time.

I stood up, completely not okay with the fact that my nerves were on full steam ahead. This was the part about being in a relationship that I didn't like—the fact that I felt anxious all the time and jittery, like I'd just downed a full pot of coffee. I glanced down at myself, running my hands across my short black skirt. It was so short, in fact, that I couldn't bend over. My legs were bare and I opted for black four-inch wedge heels. On top, I was wearing a plunging red halter top with my Wonderbra so my C cup boobs looked like DDs. I mean, it was silly really because Knight already knew what he was getting and DDs weren't on the list.

My hair was down as usual since I'm not exactly thrilled with my pointy ears but I put some extra time into my makeup. I chose to go with a smoky eye, rosy cheeks and a high gloss red lipstick. I'm not a vain person but I looked pretty damn great, if I do say so myself.

I took the few steps to the front door and inhaled a deep breath as I pulled open the door, excited for Knight's reaction. But, what I got wasn't exactly what I'd been expecting ...

"Jack?" my voice barely made it out of my throat. "What the fu ..."

"Dulcie," he interrupted, his eyes widening as his gaze settled on my bust for a good three seconds and then moved down to my legs. I'm not sure how long it took him to work his way back up to my face. Asshole.

"What do you want and why are you here?" I demanded in a less than friendly voice.

He brought his eyes back up to mine and they were heavy with lust. He flaunted that know-it-all smile of his and ran his hand through his hair. He was very handsome. I couldn't deny it—it was a fact. And there was something inside me that wanted to remember how things had been between us, something that wanted to focus on the happy times but I wouldn't allow it to take control of me. I was over Jack. Jack was history and Knight was my future.

"I came to talk," he offered.

"I'm busy and I don't have time to talk to you." I started to close the door, as if charading that he wasn't welcome anywhere near me but he merely stepped forward and blocked my attempt. Guess he wasn't good at taking hints.

"Please, I'll just take a few minutes of your time." He looked me up and down again. "It's pretty obvious you have plans."

"Yeah, I do," I quickly added, not wanting to encourage him at all. It was good that he was aware I had plans—even better that he realized he hadn't scarred me for life—that I'd moved on. He nodded and dropped his gaze, as if my plans were causing him some sort of inner turmoil.

"What do you want, Jack?"

He sighed and, looking up at me, immediately glanced away for what appeared to be dramatic effect. "I … I need your help."

"My help?" I asked dubiously, crossing my arms against my chest and exhaling my frustration. "What the hell could you possibly need my help for?"

"Can I come in?" He actually took a step forward without waiting for my permission.

"No."

"Please, Dulce, just for a few minutes?"

"Don't call me Dulce. It's Dulcie."

"Please?" he asked and frowned.

I'm not sure why I did it but I stepped aside and allowed him to enter. Seeing him in my apartment again flipped something in me, some latent memory that I'd locked away. All of a sudden, it was as if time had rewound and we were back to the old days, when we were in love, or at least, I was in love with him. Whether he had genuinely cared for me was anyone's guess. I started to close the front door behind me but, thinking better of it, decided to leave it open. Why, I wasn't sure but I felt more comfortable knowing the door was open and that I could tell him to leave any second.

Truth be told, I still wasn't sure why I'd even allowed him inside. I had nothing to say to him. Maybe it was the fact that he'd asked for my help. I guess I had a hard time denying people who needed me? Or maybe I was just reaching …

"Okay, what the hell do you need my help with?" I demanded, my hands on my hips. I was angry, yes, but whether I was angrier with him or with myself for allowing him to even talk to me, I didn't know.

He walked into my living room and glanced around, as if wanting to make sure everything still looked the same as it had two years ago. It did.

He faced me again and smiled. "You really look amazing, beautiful."

"Cut the crap."

"I was thinking the same thing when I saw you at Bliss," he continued, as if he hadn't heard me or just didn't care. "You're gorgeous."

"Why are you here, Jack?"

He glanced away and then, as if noticing the couch for the first time, walked up to it and didn't wait for permission but sat down, making himself at home. I'd give him two minutes to tell me why he needed my help and then he was out of here. And hopefully whatever help he needed could be referred to the ANC because I wasn't about to take on any cases where Jack was concerned.

"I need your help because I made a huge mistake."

"A mistake?"

He nodded and stretched his arms out against the couch back, leaning back as if he belonged there. "Yes."

"And when do you plan to inform me what that mistake was?" I cleared my throat. "I can't help you if I don't know what your problem is."

He leaned forward and sighed before glancing up at me again. "My mistake was that I let you go."

"Oh, for fuck sake," I started as I neared the door, feeling anger welling up inside me. I was a total moron to think that Jack had legitimately come to me with some sort of problem. I was a total dumbass for ever believing he could be civilized about anything. "You can leave now."

He stood up but didn't look concerned. "Please, Dulcie ..."

"No, don't 'please' me, you asshole. It's ridiculous that you came down here and gave me some stupid sob story about making a mistake and needing my help when you're just here for your own selfish needs." I took a deep breath but I wasn't quite finished laying into him. Not yet. "And that stupid apology of yours? Yeah, it's about two years too late."

"I thought you might take it that way ..."

"Then you should have listened to yourself and talked yourself out of coming here because you're wasting your time." Then I remembered Knight and the fact that he was due to arrive any minute. And that wasn't a situation that sounded in any way good. "I'm with someone else now, Jack."

"I know," he said as he dropped his gaze, rubbing the back of his neck. "That's why I'm here. I didn't want you to end up with some asshole when it's me you should be with." He paused again. If I had fifty cents for every time he paused, I'd probably have five dollars by now. "I had to let you know how I felt," he finished.

I couldn't even believe I was still standing here listening to this bullshit. "Well, you've had your say so you can leave now and live the rest of your life in peace, knowing you finally said whatever it was you wanted to say."

"I'm being serious, Dulcie."

"So am I."

He took a few steps closer to me but made no motion to leave. He reached out, as if he were going to touch my cheek, but I pulled away. "We were good together."

My jaw was tight. "You cheated on me."

"It's something I've regretted all this time."

55

I snickered and it was an ugly sound. "You really expect me to believe that?"

"Yes, because it's the truth."

I shook my head and laughed acidly. Did he really think I was buying this total crap? That I was so stupid to succumb to this trite bullshit? Did this work on other women? It must have. And speaking of other women, an image of the southern belle he'd been with at Bliss dropped into my head like a bomb. "I'm sure your southern Amazon would like to hear you say that."

He wore his confusion. "My southern Amazon?"

"That woman you were with the other night at Bliss," I said hurriedly, waving my hand in front of me dismissively.

"We're through," he said and sighed dramatically. "I couldn't stop thinking about you, Dulcie. I couldn't be serious about her. I don't love her."

As if he'd ever loved me. As if he'd ever loved anyone …

"You don't love anyone but yourself," I said snidely and glanced at the clock on my wall, realizing the seconds were ticking by and Knight would be arriving soon. Jack needed to vacate the premises immediately because I didn't want Knight to see him here—it would take too much explaining and it would look bad. "You need to leave, Jack."

"I just want you to hear me out."

"I have."

"But you aren't listening."

He was really starting to upset me because he wouldn't take no for an answer. "I *am* listening. You're just pissed off because I'm not falling for your bullshit."

I wasn't prepared when he moved toward me and pushed me against the wall of my living room. I tripped over my heels and had to stabilize myself against his chest which only fueled his fire because before I knew it, his mouth was on mine. His kiss was sloppy, urgent and he was desperately trying to pry my lips open with his tongue. I pushed against him furiously, but he kept me pinned to the wall, his hands now on my breasts. I turned my head and broke away from him and tried to free my hands but he held them at my sides as he stared down at me.

"Get the fuck out of my house, you son of a bitch," I seethed.

"I know you want me, Dulcie. And I want you. It can be good like it was before."

"It was never good and I never want to go back." I glanced down at my left hand, wondering if I could get enough movement to shake my fist for some fairy dust. But then I remembered the ANC mantra that I wouldn't use magic against a human. Dammit. I glanced up at him again and narrowed my eyes. "I can't stand you."

"Tell me you can't stand me again, Dulcie," he said, confusing me, but once I felt his fingers underneath my skirt, inching up my thigh, I got his gist.

"Get away from me!" I screamed and bucked against him, suddenly feeling afraid. Jack had never been the violent sort and had never forced himself on me in the past but I had to wonder if the rules had changed. He just seemed so determined. I tried to calm myself down; then I thought about reasoning with him. When I spoke, my voice was sharp but low. "You could go to jail for this, Jack. I'm an officer of the law."

"Are you really going to report me, Dulcie?" he asked, the look on his face saying he didn't believe I would—not by a long shot.

"You just made a big fucking mistake." It was Knight's voice and I felt my stomach drop. That bad situation I'd been worried about earlier was about to make itself known and judging by the fury on Knight's face, it was about to make itself known in a big way.

In less time than it takes to blink, Knight had Jack by the back of the neck and with one pull, yanked him away from me. Jack's eyes went wide and before he or I could guess what was going to happen next, Knight impelled his fist into Jack's face. The smaller man flew backward with the force of Knight's blow and landed on the floor.

"Didn't you hear her say no, you son of a bitch?" Knight fumed, his chest rising and falling with his elevated breathing.

Jack wasn't a small man. Compared to Knight he was small but he wasn't used to losing a fight and I could see the anger erupting inside him. He wasn't going to back down—I could read as much in his narrowed eyes and tight jaw.

"This is between Dulcie and me," he spat out as he got to his feet and glared at Knight.

"I want you to leave, Jack," I yelled at him, fear spiraling within me as I considered how bad this situation could get. Knight couldn't afford to get into a fight—not while he was the head of the ANC. And a fight with a human would be even more problematic. Not to mention the fact that he could do major damage to Jack and, although I believed Jack deserved it, I don't like fights.

"The only person who needs to leave is you," Jack yelled at Knight at the same time that he cocked his arm backwards and allowed his fist to unfurl against Knight's face. Knight's head bobbed slightly but it didn't appear that the impact had done much to him. Instead, his eyes began to glow but not in the way they had when I witnessed them earlier. This time the glow somehow hinted at Knight's anger or maybe I was just getting that from the fact that he looked like he was irate, his face red and his eyes narrowed.

Jack looked at him in shock. "What the hell are you?"

But I didn't give Knight the chance to respond. Instead, I was too worried about what he was going to do to Jack. "Knight," I warned. "He isn't worth it."

Jack faced Knight and smiled in an ugly way. "You backing down? Think your tough shit but maybe you aren't so tough?"

"Knight," I said again, watching him as he battled with himself over whether or not to teach Jack the ultimate lesson. But he had to realize it wasn't worth it. Not when it could mean his entire career? Knight dropped his fists and stood up tall, exhaling as he did so. I could feel relief coursing through me, easing the stiffness of my composure.

"Fucking coward," Jack said and snickered as he shook his head.

"He could kill you, you moron," I shouted at him, watching Knight to ensure he wasn't going to lunge at Jack. He appeared to have his temper under control. Point for him.

Jack faced me and smiled but it was laced with venom. "Let him try."

"Get the fuck out of here," Knight said, his voice strained. "I'm giving you one last chance."

Jack laughed this time, like the whole thing was just a big joke. "Dulcie and I go way back, asshole. This is about us, not you."

"I'm warning you," Knight was shaking with anger.

"Knight, let me handle this," I said, suddenly afraid for what a Loki temper entailed. Especially given the fact that he and I were now romantically involved—somehow it seemed like that fact alone had escalated this whole situation into something that resembled a time bomb. I took a few steps until I was standing directly between them. Then I faced Jack. "Jack, you aren't welcome here. I don't know what more I can say to get through your thick skull. I don't want anything to do with you. So just save yourself from further embarrassment and leave."

It was like Jack didn't even see me. Instead, he looked right past me to Knight. "You need some pointers on her favorite positions? Maybe how she loves having her …"

But Jack was unable to finish his statement. Instead, I didn't so much see Knight as I heard him lunge for Jack. He moved lightning fast, sidestepping me, and before I could even argue, he pushed Jack down and brought his fist down onto Jack's face.

"Knight!" I screamed and felt like I was running through quicksand as I threw myself on him. "Stop it!"

But Knight wouldn't stop. He continued throwing punches into Jack until I was worried he'd do serious damage. I jumped on top of Knight and grabbed his arms, feeling like I was a gnat trying to stop a tornado.

"Stop it!" I screamed again. "Knight, get off him!"

Realizing I wasn't making any difference, I dove down on top of Jack and watched Knight pull back, just as he was about to bring his fist down on me.

"Dulcie, what the fuck are you doing?" he screamed.

"I'm stopping you from killing him!" I yelled back, pushing my hair out of my face as I looked up at him. "What the hell is wrong with you?"

Knight backed away and turned to face the wall, running his hands through his hair as he took a deep breath, probably asking himself the exact same question.

I glanced down at Jack and found he was still coherent though covered in blood. He rolled over onto his hands and knees, trying to catch his breath. Apparently Knight had knocked the wind out of him.

"Are you okay?" I asked him.

He glanced up at me and it looked like Knight had broken his nose. It was already bruising and blood was gushing out both nostrils uncontrollably. He pushed away from me and stood up, suddenly hunching over as if he couldn't catch his breath. Then he took a few steps forward until he was at the entry of the door. He leaned against the doorjamb and glanced back at me.

"She isn't worth shit," he said and spat on my floor. Then he turned around and hobbled down my front walkway, finally getting into his car. Once he sped away, I felt like I could breathe a little easier. That is, until I wondered if Jack would alert the police about what had just gone down. Course, he probably had no idea that Knight was tied to the ANC. I could only hope so anyway. And, furthermore, Jack wasn't the type of man to willingly admit he'd been bested in a fight so maybe he'd keep it to himself.

I stood up and glanced around my living room, at the blood stains all over my floor. I started for the kitchen so I could get a dishtowel, but Knight grabbed my hand and stopped me.

"Don't ever put yourself in the middle of a fight again," he hissed.

I glanced up at him and felt my face flush with anger. I pulled my arm out of his grasp and continued into the kitchen, reaching for a wet dishtowel on the sink while trying to get control of my temper. But it appeared that wasn't going to happen. "You aren't the one who should be pointing out what I should or shouldn't have done."

"What do you mean?"

I brought the dishtowel to the living room and began soaking up the blood, hoping it hadn't already stained my wood floors, cheap though they were. "You lost control of yourself. What the hell were you thinking?"

"I knew where my limit was."

"Bullshit!" I railed, pausing to glance at him before returning my attention to the blood stains. "What the hell are you going to do if this gets back to the ANC?"

"I'll handle it." He shook his head and stretched his fingers out as if they were hurting him.

"If your hand hurts, it serves you right," I said tartly as I stood up and returned to the kitchen, turning on the faucet to wash out Jack's blood from the dishtowel.

He glanced over at me and frowned. "Thanks, Dulcie."

But I wasn't about to let him make me feel guilty for his bad behavior. "What the hell was that back there? You completely lost control of yourself."

"No, I didn't."

61

"Don't try to pretend like you didn't, Knight. I was there and I saw what happened. If I hadn't gotten in the way, who knows what you would have done to him." I paused as I considered it. "He's human, you know?"

"Of course, I fucking know that!"

Then something dawned on me, something I hadn't previously considered. "Is all of this because of what happened between us?" I didn't wait for him to respond because I was already convinced the answer was a resounding yes. "I said I didn't want you going caveman on me, remember? That I didn't want a jealous and possessive man on my hands."

"This has nothing to do with us, Dulcie. He was forcing himself on you and I intervened." He paused for a second or two. "I would have done the same thing whether you and I were in a relationship or not."

I couldn't argue that because I imagined it was true. But it wasn't the fact that he'd gotten involved that upset me; it was the degree to which he'd gotten involved.

"I'll admit that the sight of him with his hands all over you upset me," Knight added.

"I could have handled the situation myself."

He frowned. "Sort of like you were handling it when I got here? With him holding you down while his other hand was under your skirt?"

I swallowed hard, trying to keep control of my temper. "I am a law enforcement officer and I know how to defend myself."

"Then why weren't you?"

I glared at him. "This isn't about me, Knight, so stop turning the tables. You need to face the fact that you royally screwed up back there."

"Should I have just watched him have his way with you then?"

"I would have gotten control of the situation!" I insisted again, feeling myself flush with anger. "The point

I'm trying to make is that now I don't know where we stand!"

Knight narrowed his eyes as he considered my statement. "What do you mean?"

"I mean that I don't want you to act like this. I don't want to deal with your jealousy and your arrogance."

"Jealousy? This has nothing to do with jealousy, dammit. Will you listen to yourself?" He slammed his fist into the wall and the entire room shook. "I heard you tell him no and he didn't back away, Dulcie. Should I have waited until it was a rape before I intervened?"

"Stop blowing it out of proportion," I yelled and before I realized what I was saying, the words were already out. "I knew this would end up being a mistake."

"What?" Knight's expression was hard to read but there was definitely a wounded look in his eyes.

"I told you what I didn't want and it looks like this situation has turned into exactly that." I could feel something bubbling up within me that felt like fear mixed with anger and I had to wonder if I wasn't making a mountain out of a mole hill. Maybe I was overreacting? Maybe I was taking this too far? Maybe I truly was scared about the fact that I was in a relationship again and wanted to subconsciously sabotage it?

"Dulcie, tell yourself whatever you need to in order to keep that wall of yours up but this whole situation has nothing to do with it and I'm not going to stand here and take the blame for this." He started for the door but turned to face me. "Just realize that this failed because of you, not me."

I didn't know what to say so I didn't say anything at all. I just watched him as he took a few steps, then he turned back to face me again.

"Oh, and you're welcome for saving your ass."

Before I could respond, he threw my door shut behind him.

FIVE

It was Friday night when Jack and Knight got into their confrontation. After Knight and I had argued and Knight walked out, I hadn't talked to him all day Saturday and now it was Saturday night. And I wasn't sure what to make of the fact that neither of us had called each other. The more I thought about it, though, I realized the answer was pretty, glaringly obvious. We were done. Over. Kaput. No longer.

I'd managed to last in a relationship for all of one night and one day. I wasn't sure why, but I felt like I deserved some sort of raspberry award—"Dulcie O'Neil, so dysfunctional she can't keep a man for longer than twenty-four hours."

It's just as well, half of me said, *because it was pretty obvious that Knight had become that jealous and possessive guy you expected. Maybe he's always been that way? He's cocky—you've always known that. And just because Jack wasn't right for you, doesn't mean that Knight was. And, really, maybe Knight was just a rebound anyway? I mean, you hadn't dated anyone else after Jack, right? It's better this way—better to keep your guard up and not fall for men and their bullshit.*

The other half of me didn't exactly agree. *Knight wasn't acting jealous or possessive. Yes, he was pretty hard on Jack but maybe that was just to teach him a lesson. From*

Knight's point of view, it looked like you couldn't defend yourself and that Jack was taking advantage of the situation. And you know Knight, yes, he's cocky but you also know he's so much more than that. You need to admit to yourself, Dulcie, that you screwed up. You freaked out just like Sam and Knight both knew you would and you looked for the nearest emergency exit. This isn't Knight's fault; it's yours.

Anyway you looked at it, I was at an impasse. It seemed like one minute I was resolute in the fact that Knight was a jerk and someone I wanted nothing to do with; and, the next second, I couldn't help but think I was completely wrong. And when you, yourself, can't figure out what the hell to do with your love life, you call your best friend.

I picked up the phone and dialed Sam's number. She answered after the second ring.

"Hello?"

"Hi, it's me."

"Hey, Dulce, what's up?"

I sighed. "I'm having man problems. What's up with you?"

I could hear the clanking of a metal pan hitting the oven. Sam's middle name should have been Betty Crocker. "Oh, I just made Trey some chocolate chip cookies with an itch charm to relieve that rash that's all over his face. Have you seen it?"

If I forgot to mention earlier, Trey was a hobgoblin who worked for the ANC and helped us out a lot with the Dreamstalker case. Invariably, there was always something wrong with him. "No, I haven't been privileged enough to see Trey's rash, Sam."

She sighed as if Trey's rash was occupying her mind, front, right and center. "It's really bad and he keeps making it worse by scratching it."

As much as I liked Trey and was concerned for his well-being, I didn't really want to spend the next Hades-only-knew-how-long discussing his skin ailments. "Oh well, tell him I hope he feels better soon."

I could hear her turning a dial, probably setting the timer on the oven and then the sound of her heels as she walked across her tiled kitchen, no doubt about to throw herself into her favorite, over-stuffed, Pottery Barn living room chair.

"So what's the problem with Knight?"

I didn't even know where to start but I managed. I told her about Jack showing up, the fact that he wouldn't leave and Knight arriving just at the moment that Jack had his hand up my dress. Then I continued with the part about Knight attacking Jack, ending my happy little story with the argument that ensued between Knight and myself.

"So what's the problem outside of the fact that Knight might be in a load of shit if this ever reaches the ANC?" Sam asked.

"Well, yeah aside from the ANC issue which could be a total cluster fuck in and of itself, I, uh, sort of blamed the whole confrontation on Knight and I guess ..." I took a deep breath. "I, uh, freaked out like you were worried I would."

Sam sighed, which tacitly said she definitely thought I shouldn't have blamed Knight. Dammit. I hate it when I'm the bad guy. "So call him and say you're sorry."

I glanced at my fingernails and started picking at my cuticles, trying to accept the fact that this mess was something wholly owned by me. "You think I should?" It was a rhetorical question.

"Are you sorry?"

Was I sorry? That was the million dollar question. Half of me was sorry, yes, and the other half was still fighting with the first half. But I must admit it was a losing battle because the more I thought about it, the guiltier I felt. And that had to mean one thing. "Yeah, I guess I am." I stopped talking and zoned out on my wall for a few seconds as the truth of the situation sunk into me. "This whole thing is my fault."

"Yeah, sounds about right," Sam was quick to respond. "But that's not a big surprise, is it?" Then she giggled.

And the truth of the matter was that it wasn't a big surprise—not really a surprise at all. Deep down, I'd known the truth of the situation before I called Sam. I guess I just needed a second opinion. "Well, that's the answer I was expecting."

Sam took a deep breath and exhaled until it sounded like I was having a conversation with the wind. "Dulce, I'm not going to tell you what to do and I know how difficult relationships are for you, but I think you need to look at the situation and ask yourself whether or not you acted fairly. I'm sure there is some truth to the fact that Knight was jealous and a little too hard on Jack. I mean, it sort of goes with the territory, you know? You *are* his girlfriend and any man walking into that situation with you and Jack would probably have reacted the same way." She paused for a few seconds. "But didn't it feel good to watch Jack get his ass handed to him?"

I laughed as I thought about it. I hadn't realized it at the time but, looking back, it did feel pretty good that Jack finally got what he should've gotten two years ago. "Um, yeah, I guess I can admit taking some adverse pleasure in that."

Sam just laughed and I felt suddenly incredibly grateful for her friendship. It's not like I'm normally an ingrate where Sam is concerned or that I have ever taken her for granted; but sometimes you just have a moment when you realize how important your friends are and how much they mean to you. And Sam just has a way about her—she's always right. "If you're ever looking for a career change, I think you'd make a really great therapist."

She laughed. "Well thanks, but I'm not so sure about that."

67

Then it occurred to me that Sam hadn't really talked much about her own dating life lately. In fact, the last date (of which I was aware) she'd had was with the vampire, Bram. That situation was completely over and done with (not to mention ancient history). "So how's your love life?" I asked.

"Um, well," she started and then giggled which meant there was definitely a story in the makings. "I do sort of have a crush on a guy."

I was surprised. This was the first I'd heard of it and suddenly I felt like a bad friend. Granted, the last few weeks had been pretty hectic for all of us—Sam especially. During the Dreamstalker case, Sam had fallen into a coma and nearly lost her life. Given those events, I guess it wasn't so weird that I had no clue she was actually interested in someone.

"Spill the details," I said with a smile.

"I met him the other day when I was at training."

By training, she meant that she had attended a required ANC class, whereby she was probably learning the latest in potions and spells as well as new moves in self-defense/offense. Given the fact that she'd met her mystery man in training, though, I could only imagine it must have been some sort of weapons training. Either way, it was pretty clear he was ANC, which was good in my books.

"What training?"

I could hear her tapping her permanently manicured fingernails against her table. "Oh, defense moves training. I, uh, volunteered to let him take me down."

I laughed. "And has he taken you down in more ways than one?"

It was her turn to giggle. "No, not yet but I think he's getting pretty close."

"What's his name?" I asked, wondering if I might know him. The ANC branch in Splendor was pretty small and I knew all the employees.

"Alex," she said with a smile. "He's from Estuary and he's new to the force." Estuary was one town over from Splendor. And, no, I didn't know any Alexes.

"What is he?"

"A were."

I nodded. In general, weres could be trouble because they had an incredible amount of energy and without the right discipline, they usually resorted to breaking the law. But, as with most generalizations, not all weres were trouble. This being a case in point.

"I'm really happy for you, Sam. I just hope he deserves you."

"Well, we'll find out." She paused and I could hear her heels against her floor again. "So is everything copacetic?"

I thought about it. I'd gotten the answer I expected and now I knew exactly what I'd have to do. "Yep."

"And you're going to call Knight and apologize to him and beg him to take you back?"

"Um, I don't know about 'the begging him to take me back' part but, yeah, I'll call him."

Sam laughed. "I'm sure it will be fine, Dulce. Knight is a good guy and he happens to be completely in love with you."

"In love with me?" I repeated, my tone dubious as I considered it. Knight in love with me? I couldn't see that exactly, not that I knew what love was; but he did seem to like me and I really liked him. So, basically, what it came down to was the fact that I screwed everything up and now it was time to play the part of repentant woman. "Thanks, Sam."

"Welcome. Call me later."

We said our good-byes and I hung up the phone. I didn't put it back on its cradle, though. Instead, I just stared at it in my lap as I tried to summon up any courage I possessed. I mean, it's never fun eating humble pie; and I was about to have multiple helpings. I took a deep breath and picked up the phone, dialing Knight's number as my hand shook. I really wasn't good with this apology stuff.

It rang and I felt the breath catch in my throat. He didn't pick up. It rang again and my heartbeat started escalating until I could feel the drumming in my ears. He didn't pick up. Third ring … nothing. After the fourth ring, his answering machine kicked on and I felt myself panic. *Should I leave a message or hang up?*

I hung up.

Then I sat there for another few minutes while I weighed the reality of what had just happened. *Was Knight at his house, screening his calls? Did he know it was me and just didn't want to pick up? Was he really that angry with me? Or maybe he had a woman over? Maybe he was numbing himself in the arms of someone else? Angela from Bram's nightclub, maybe? Or someone I didn't know?*

I felt anger brewing up within me and stood up, trying to calm myself. My mind was racing, taking me into territory that was completely ridiculous and, more so, painful.

At the sound of my dog, Blue, scratching at the sliding glass door, wanting some company, I walked through my kitchen and pulled it open, giving him a big smile and a pat on the head.

"What am I going to do about my life, boy?" I asked, leaning down to accept his doggie kisses. "Ah, thanks." Then I sighed and scratched him behind the ear. "Life would be so much easier if it were just you and me."

Blue batted his tail against my legs and nudged me with his gigantic head.

Thank Hades for dogs.

It was Monday morning. I slept in too late and awoke to the shrill ring of the phone interrupting my slumber. I sat

70

up, rubbing my eyes. The sliver of sun infiltrating my drawn shades acted like a knife to my eyes and I shaded them, feeling for the phone which sat beside my bed.

"Hello?" I said in a voice that implied whoever was calling better have a damned good reason to be waking me before … what time was it? I glanced at the clock. Before ten a.m.

"Dulce." It was Sam and she sounded worried.

"What's up?" I asked, sitting up straighter. Worry in someone else's voice is never a good thing.

"Have you talked to or seen Knight?"

I felt something in my gut begin to stir—something like butterflies, only more malevolent. This felt more like the beginnings of angst mixed with dread. "No."

Sam took a deep breath. "He never showed up for work this morning. I don't know how many times we've tried calling him at home and we've tried his cell phone, but he doesn't answer."

It wasn't like Knight to be late to work. His life was his work. I felt the angst mixed with dread turn into worry, verging on panic. "I tried him the other night and didn't get an answer either."

"I'm worried, Dulce. Can you go check on him? Make sure he's okay?"

I sighed, long and hard. It wasn't that I didn't want to go check on him, but I was suddenly worried that maybe it was just an innocent situation. Maybe he'd simply overslept (um, he'd never done so in the time I'd known him, but anyway) and my arriving on his doorstep, when he hadn't bothered to return my call, might become an embarrassing state of affairs. Especially if he had company.

Damn, Dulcie, what is wrong with you? Why do you keep thinking he has a woman over? I reprimanded myself. And I was right—I was being a total idiot. If there was the slightest chance that Knight was in trouble, I needed to put my personal feelings aside and make sure he was alright.

71

That's all there was to it. "Yeah, of course I will. I'm headed there now."

"Okay, I'll keep thinking good thoughts."

I stood up and cradled the phone between my head and shoulder as I grabbed my stretch pants, which were draped over my chair and pulled them on.

"I'll let you know as soon as I find him," I said before hanging up. Grabbing a long-sleeved shirt from my closet, I yanked it over my head and reached for the Op 6 which was underneath my bed. Even though the Op 6 was a small gun, similar to a Smith & Wesson five-shot revolver, the length just spanning the width of my palm and fingers, the dragon blood bullets were lethal to all Netherworld creatures.

I snatched my shoulder holster from my night table and, securing it around myself, fitted the gun inside it while reaching for my leather bike jacket. Glancing at the keys to the Suzuki, which were just beside the keys to the Ducati, I delayed for only a second. The Ducati *was* faster and if I needed nothing else at the moment, it was speed. I grabbed the Ducati keys and started for my bedroom door, running hell-bent through my living room. I paused long enough to grab my helmet and then started for the front door, exiting as I locked it behind me.

The sun met me full bore and I pulled on my sunglasses, my mind racing with thoughts about Knight. *Was he in trouble? Was he hurt? Had Jack somehow gotten revenge?* I pushed the thoughts from my mind, focusing on my first hurdle which was to go to Knight's house. *What if he isn't at his condo? Where should I go next?*

"Just focus on one thing at a time," I said to myself as I hurried down my front steps, reaching the Ducati in mere seconds. I threw my leg over the seat, secured my helmet on my head and turned the bike on. It purred beneath me and, pulling onto the street, I gunned it.

It usually took me about ten minutes to reach Knight's upscale neighborhood from my less-than-desirable area but

72

when I turned down his street only moments later, I wasn't even sure where the time had gone. I parked the bike and turned off the engine, removing my helmet before placing it on the seat. Then I jumped down and inhaled deeply as I started for Knight's door.

Hopefully, this whole thing would just be a matter of over-sleeping. Hopefully, Knight just wanted a weekend to himself where he could ignore his phone and somehow, he'd forgotten it was Monday morning. Hopefully, there wasn't anything questionable going on; and I was doubly hopeful that I wouldn't find a woman in his house … Guess I was about to find out.

I strode up to the front door and pounded my fist, knocking twice before I remembered his doorbell. I buzzed. After waiting a few seconds and realizing no one was coming to answer it, I rang the bell again. And waited. Nothing. I rang it again. And waited.

I had to face it, Knight wasn't home. I tried turning the doorknob and found it was unlocked. Hmmm, something was very definitely rotten in the state of Denmark because Knight never left his doors unlocked. When you work with criminals every day, you very quickly learn how important locks can be.

I pulled my cell phone from my pocket and called for backup. It wasn't smart for me to do this alone. After hanging up, I put the phone back in my pocket and started searching the perimeter of Knight's condo, just to see if anything seemed out of the ordinary—broken windows, open doors, ripped screens, etc. After securing the perimeter, I came to the conclusion that nothing seemed unusual or looked as if it had been disrupted. If someone was responsible for Knight's … disappearance (for lack of a better word), he probably knew who that someone was. In any case, it didn't appear like anyone had broken in.

I walked back around to the front of the building, pretty sure that anyone that might have been here was long gone

73

but, still, I wasn't about to take any chances. Not until I had backup as my aid. So I waited.

I don't know how long I waited—maybe five minutes. But while five minutes might not sound like much, to me, it felt like forever. And I'm sure it had everything to do with my replaying visions of Knight in all sorts of distressing situations. At the five minute mark, the urge to go to him was too much for me to ignore. Hoping I wasn't about to make a huge mistake, one which I might regret for the rest of my life or, worse, not live to regret, I started for his front door.

I pushed the door open and glanced around his living room, noting that nothing seemed out of place. I didn't call out to him, afraid I might alert any possible interlopers. Instead, I pulled the Op 6 from my shoulder holster and held the gun pointed down in front of me, in low ready stance. I glanced around the room, assessing any threats. The couch could hide someone as well as the dark corner leading into the kitchen. I took a step into the living room from the doorway until I was barely a foot or so inside, my back against the wall.

I walked the perimeter of the room, inspecting both sides of each couch to ensure no one was hiding behind them. When I reached the wall, beyond which was the kitchen, I kept my back to it, and with my gun in low ready, pivoted on my toes until I was facing the kitchen. Nothing. Nothing out of place, nothing disturbed, nothing.

I didn't stop. I continued forward, into the hallway which led to the master bedroom and the guest room. Good thing I'd been in his condo before because I knew exactly how many rooms and bathrooms I'd have to secure.

After seven minutes, I found myself at the entry of the living room again after checking the rest of the house and with no leads at all. Nothing was disrupted, no doors busted, no windows broken, no furniture overturned. No one had broken in. His bed hadn't even looked slept in. It was as if he'd never even been here …

I heard the sound of footsteps in the front entry, announcing the backup I'd summoned and I started for the living room.

"It's Dulcie O'Neil," I shouted. "Don't shoot me!"

When I emerged from around the corner of the hallway, facing the living room, I found Trey standing before me, frowning with the worst rash I'd ever seen covering half his face. It looked like he'd fallen into a tub of poison oak.

"Why the hell are you in here by yourself?" he demanded, his hands on his hips. "You should have waited for us."

Behind him was someone I didn't recognize. Probably my replacement since I'd quit the ANC several months earlier.

"I couldn't wait," I said, giving him an expression that said he better not try and argue with me.

"And?" he commanded, puffing out his lower lip until he looked like a blowfish with rosacea.

"Knight's not here and from what I can see, it looks like he hasn't been here in days."

Trey nodded and glanced around the room, as if half expecting Knight to jump out from behind the curtains. Luckily for both of us, and the ANC in general, Trey had the ability to psychically see glimpses of the past. His gift was about to come in very handy.

"Hold on a sec," I said as I started for Knight's bedroom. Walking inside, I opened his closet and pulled one of his long-sleeve shirts from the hanger. I brought it to my nose, smelling his aftershave. Good, he hadn't washed it. The washing machine had a way of dimming any trace of personal essence from clothing—essence that was imperative in assisting Trey with his ability to recreate the past.

Smelling Knight's spicy, masculine scent was almost overwhelming and I suddenly felt like I was going to be sick. Worry gnawed at my stomach and the idea that he was in trouble, that maybe he'd been in an accident and was lying in a ditch somewhere or maybe someone was holding him for ransom against the ANC. Or, worse yet, maybe he was … dead?

No! I wouldn't allow myself to even consider the possibility. Knight was a soldier for the Netherworld, trained in combat—he wasn't someone who went down easily. He'd been created by the god, Hades, to defend the Netherworld. He had to be alive. I didn't know how I knew it but it was a gut feeling. Yes, he had to be alive.

I started for the hallway and into the living room, handing Knight's shirt to Trey. He took it with a silent nod and closed his eyes, his mouth twitching as he attempted to channel the side of him that could see into another plane.

"You can do it, Trey," I said in a soft voice.

He didn't respond but clenched his eyes even tighter, his fist grasping the fabric of Knight's shirt. And then, it was as if an earthquake struck him. His eyes flew open at the same time that a tremor seized his body and he began to shake. He glanced at me, his eyes wide, but he wasn't seeing me. He was looking right through me. Remembering a time when Knight had witnessed one of Trey's visions, I grabbed Trey's wrist, hoping I'd see into his head the same way Knight had been able to when he touched the hobgoblin. But, nothing happened. It was just another Loki trait that wasn't shared by fairies. Oh, well.

I didn't drop my grip on Trey's wrist, mainly to let him know I was there for moral support. Sometimes his visions frightened him and I could only hope this one wouldn't qualify. Because if it did … no, I wouldn't allow my thoughts to go there.

Think positive.

76

Knight is going to be fine. Knight is going to be fine. Knight is going to be fine.

Trey blinked a few times and then dropped his head. He took a deep breath and glanced at me and his eyes were still wide with what appeared to be fear.

"What was it, Trey?" I asked, grabbing his shoulders and shaking him slightly. "What did you see?"

"He was here. Knight was here," he started and then seemed at a loss for words.

"What happened?" I said, not intending for my voice to sound so panicked. I also didn't realize I was squeezing his arms until he attempted to wriggle out of my hold.

"He was in his living room and someone was calling him. He reached for the phone but before he could answer it, they just sort of ... showed up." He shrugged and looked at me as if to ask if any of his garbled explanation made any sense. It didn't.

"Who showed up, Trey?"

"I don't know. They were dressed in uniforms and looked like military, maybe, or maybe like cops. But not like human cops or ANC."

"What color were their uniforms?"

Trey chewed on his lip. "Um ... they were grey."

"You sure?"

"Yeah."

I nodded, we were getting somewhere. No, the ANC didn't have grey uniforms. Not here on earth anyway ...

"Where did they come from, Trey?"

He shook his head. "It makes no sense. They just showed up in his living room, like out of thin air. Like they just dropped in from the sky or something."

It was a portal. They'd come from a portal and they were wearing grey law enforcement uniforms. I knew this because Quill had told me a long time ago that the only entrances to the Netherworld were via portals. Obviously, that information had been hush-hush because even Trey wasn't aware of it. "Then what happened?"

"They said they were here to take him into custody and he didn't even fight them, Dulce." Trey shook his head like it didn't make any sense. "He put his hands out and let them cuff him and he even said he thought they 'wouldn't have taken their sweet ass time about it.'" He paused for a few seconds and then shrugged. "And that's all I got."

I nodded and felt a shard of panic piercing me. I knew exactly what this meant, exactly who these assholes were.

"What was that about, Dulce?" Trey asked.

I glanced up at him and answered, barely recognizing my own voice. "They were from the High Court of the Netherworld, Trey," I started and then swallowed hard. "They've arrested him for something I did."

SIX

As soon as I discovered that the ANC of the Netherworld had Knight in custody, I wasn't sure what to do. I had no experience with the Netherworld—I'd never even been there. From what I understood, the Netherworld existed in the same spatial plane as Earth. Knight had described it as a cake with multiple layers—the Earth existed in one layer and the Netherworld on the next layer. As I mentioned earlier, the only way to travel from one layer to the other was through a portal. However, where those portals existed and how one accessed them was anyone's guess.

Although I didn't know much about the Netherworld in general, I did know that anyone who had been there once, knew enough to stay away. Most creatures dreamt of coming to Earth, but the immigration policy between Earth and the Netherworld was strict. Why? In order to maintain the balance; otherwise, Netherworld creatures might outnumber humans.

So now I was pretty much stuck. Other than sitting back and allowing the ANC to take care of the situation through their avenues of justice, I really had no course of action. And I'm not the type of person to sit back and let things happen, especially when I was the cause of Knight getting caught up in this whole mess. Yes, something else was entirely my fault …

Back when I first met Knight, we worked a case involving a Kragengen shape-shifter who was eating some

79

of the less than civilized members of the Netherworld community in Splendor. I discovered my boss and friend at the time, Quillan, had defected to the other side. Knight and I had busted Quill and his cohorts at an abandoned house outside the city limits and I managed to detain Quill. I fully intended to take him into custody but he slipped away from me. Well, to be honest, I had my Op 6 pointed at him but he probably knew I wouldn't pull the trigger, so he simply walked away.

That moment has plagued me since it happened. I knew then as well as now that I could never have pulled the trigger. Not when I was fully cognizant that the dragon blood bullets would have killed him. Netherworld creatures just can't handle the toxins of dragon's blood and Quill, being an elf, was no match. What it came down to was that I just couldn't do it—I couldn't shoot him and I hadn't come up with any other ideas at the spur of the moment to detain him, so I reluctantly let him go. I wasn't angry with myself that I hadn't been able to shoot him, especially because he was unarmed—I was angrier with the situation. I couldn't stop thinking about what I could have done to arrest him, to ensure that he wouldn't get away.

I shook my head, trying to clear the thoughts from my already frazzled mind. What was done was done so there was no use in crying over it now. The real bummer of the whole situation was the fact that the ANC was well aware that Quillan had escaped. Knight, being the hero that he was, had insisted it was his fault when we both knew it was entirely mine. And now Knight would suffer for my mistake.

It was a fact I couldn't stomach as I tried to imagine the crap he was in now. I didn't know much about Netherworld law, other than hearing their punishments were brutal. They still practiced more along the lines of medieval torture than innocent until proven guilty. But who knew? Maybe those stories were merely that—embellished stories. The worst part was that I had no idea what was happening—whether Knight was being tortured or merely being held in a prison cell, awaiting trial. The suspense of not knowing was driving me crazy.

I took a deep breath and picked up my phone as I collapsed into my sofa and propped my feet on the coffee table. I pretty much had already made up my mind as to what my next steps would be. Actually, I'd reached this conclusion as soon as I realized the ANC had Knight.

I glanced at the phone pad and dialed Dia's number. As head of the ANC division in Moon, I hoped she could give me some information as to Knight's whereabouts and how I could reach him.

"Diva here," Dia trilled in her sing-song voice and then giggled. She was one of those people who had no problem laughing at herself, which was one of the reasons I liked her so much.

"Hi D, it's Dulcie." I couldn't help the dejected tone of my voice. There was so much on my mind, so much to explain and I didn't know where to begin.

"Girl! How ya been?"

I sighed. "Not good."

"What's going on?" she asked in a level but concerned tone. I didn't have many girlfriends outside of Sam, but I definitely considered Dia among that small circle.

I took a deep breath and thought about the best way to relay the information, finally deciding on the most direct route. I had no time to explain the whys and hows of it. "Dia, the ANC Netherworld has Knight."

"Oh no," she said as she exhaled. She was quiet for a few seconds.

"I need to do something about it."

"Oh hell no, Dulcie girl! Doncha even think about it, you hear me?" I had to give it to her; she was quick.

"I have no other choice. I can't let Knight face punishment for something I did, Dia. It's my fault he's there." I paused as the weight of what I was saying began to sink into me. "I have to go to the Netherworld, Dia, and get him out. I have to tell them the truth."

"I get that, girl, and I see where you're coming from but you need to promise me you will push any thoughts of going to the Netherworld right out of that stubborn head of yours."

I swallowed hard. "I can't promise that, Dia, and, what's more, I … I need your help."

"Oh hell no," she said and I could tell she was shaking her head in her Diva like manner even though she was on the phone and I obviously couldn't see her. "Bad idea, Dulcie, bad idea."

"There's no other way," I insisted. I was resolute. "I've made up my mind."

"Have you ever been to the Netherworld?" she asked in a voice a parent would use on an unruly child.

"No."

"It's not like here, girl. It's dangerous with a capital D."

"Have you been there, Dia?" I asked, wanting to cut directly to the chase because I needed to talk with someone who had first-hand experience. I could only hope Dia could tell me something I didn't know.

"No I haven't and I sure as hell am not interested in any vacations to the Netherworld either, you hear me? If you were going to Mexico or Hawaii, I'd be on board, girl. But the Netherworld? Hells to the no, thank you."

I started chewing my lip as I realized it wouldn't do me any good to pursue this conversation. I needed someone who had some knowledge of the Netherworld. "Dia, I've made up my mind."

"Girl, I know you made up your stubborn fairy head up about this but you need to know the risks before you go. You are not cut out for that place. It would chew you up and spit you out."

"I have no choice, D."

"You always have a choice." Her voice was sharp, serious.

I took a deep breath. "Dia, if Knight is found guilty, what will happen to him?"

She didn't respond right away. "I dunno."

"If there's even the ghost of a chance he could end up rotting away in a cell somewhere, or something even worse, I would never forgive myself."

"So you would sacrifice yourself instead?" she demanded.

"It's not sacrificing myself," I corrected her. "It's me confessing something that is solely my responsibility and my fault."

"I get that, girl, but there was a reason Knight stood up for you. There was a reason he took this on his own shoulders. That fine man is not dumb and you know that."

"Okay …"

"So imagine for a second what could happen to you." She paused as if she were also trying to imagine the worst-case scenario. "Girl, I can't even imagine it because I haven't got a clue what could happen. But whatever does happen, it sure won't be the end of it, Dulcie. Knight lied to the High Court and that is a serious offense, punishable in and of itself."

I nodded. I had already considered that. "I can't imagine that that punishment would be any more severe than what he would face if he's found guilty of allowing a criminal to escape."

"Be that as it may, Dulcie, the Netherworld is a combat zone. It's not safe." Then she sighed. "I don't know what I'm worried about—there's no way you could find the portal and more so, no way immigration would let you in. You need proper ANC identification and a passport."

Hmm, I hadn't considered that. Technically, I was no longer employed by the ANC but I had a pretty good hunch I could just drum up one of my old badges somewhere. That wouldn't be a problem. The passport could be tough though … But I wasn't about to cave in just yet. "I can get all that."

"Knowing you, I imagine you could but that is just the half of it. You would not last one day there without a guide, Dulcie. It's all warfare, creatures eating one another. It's not civilized like it is here."

"How do you know all this if you've never been?"

"Because I once ran border control on this side, girl, and I've seen and heard first count stories of the stuff going on there."

I smiled. "If you ran border control, that means you know where I could get a passport and ID?"

She exhaled. "Damn girl, are you not listening to a word I'm saying?"

"D, I'm going, whether you help me or not. I'm not asking you to be my escort because I need someone who knows the Netherworld and you've never been. But what I will ask you for, as a friend, is your help with the legal stuff."

She was silent and then she sighed which meant I'd won. "Sometimes I bemoan the day I first set eyes on you, Dulcie O'Neil."

I laughed. "Thank you, Dia."

"Honey, you be careful and you find someone who knows what the hell they're doing, you got it?"

"Yeah, I will," I finished, although I had no clue who that person might be. "Thanks, Dia." She didn't respond but didn't hang up either so I had to imagine there was more. "Yes?"

"I have a list of all the creatures who live in California but are natives of the Netherworld." She said it like she was giving away a secret. Course, this was confidential information and she could have gotten in trouble just for letting me know she had such a list.

I smiled wide. "Dia, have I told you lately that I love you?"

"Yeah, yeah, don't give me any of that Rod Stewart bullcrap," she said but there was a laugh hiding somewhere in her voice. "Just a minute while I pull this up on my computer."

"Okay."

She started singing. "… fill my heart with gladness … Oh, hell no, girl, you got that damn song stuck in my head."

I just laughed. It seemed like my day was looking up. Dia could handle the documents I needed and she could find me someone to serve as Netherworld tour guide. I had to admit, it was incredibly funny hearing the diva sing some shitty Rod Stewart song.

"Mmm hmmm," she said as I imagined she started recognizing names on her list of native Netherworld creatures. "Bingo," she finished.

"Who is it?" I asked as I lowered my feet from the coffee table and leaned forward.

"Looks like a certain fang face who's gotta thing for you, Dulcie girl."

I smiled broadly. This couldn't have worked out any better. "Bram."

No Regrets hadn't fared badly after the introduction of its rival nightclub, Bliss. Tonight, there was a huge crowd on the dance floor, undulating to Kesha's song "Blow" and every booth was occupied. I pushed my way through the crowd, looking for Bram's tall and handsome person but not seeing him, I strode up to the bar.

As usual, Angela was bartender. Although I'd never had an issue with Angela in the past, she'd always been withdrawn. But I saw her as a strong woman whom I actually admired. Well, that was before she showed up at one of Bram's events with Knight in tow. I later learned that she had the hots for him.

"Hi, Angela," I said, offering her a quick smile.

"Dulcie," she said in response, sans a smile. *So playing it catty, are you?*

"I'm here to see Bram. Is he around?"

She nodded towards Bram's office which was at the rear of the building. A black light bathed the club in a weird, sporadic freeze frame and highlighted Angela's banana-yellow, butch-short hair. Not a good look.

I didn't say anything more as I tapped the bar top in a strange rendition of "thanks and I'll see you later" before starting for Bram's office. I was somewhat surprised that Angela hadn't tried to hightail it ahead of me, if only to ensure he wasn't necking on some chick.

I knocked on the door.

"What?" Bram called out in a tone of fatigued irritation.

"It's Dulcie," I yelled back.

There was no response but within seconds, the door opened to reveal Bram, smiling graciously at me. Bram, as always, looked extremely handsome. His pitch-black hair and light blue eyes, along with a sharply defined but perfect nose and jawline. His height gives him an air of dignity and aloofness that says he doesn't bother with trivialities. And the icing on the cake? His English accent is to die for.

He held the door open for me as I entered, the sound of classical music pouring from his speakers in a jumble of loud and less than relaxing notes. He closed the door behind him and I felt swallowed up by the darkness.

"Where are the lights?"

Bram's laugh was deep. "I can see in the dark, sweet. No reason for harsh glares."

"Well, I can't," I protested, finding myself almost screaming to compete with the music. "And what the hell are you listening to?"

"Darling sweet, this is a Norwegian composer, Edvard Grieg—In the Hall of the Mountain King. Quite famous."

86

He flipped a switch and the lighting went from non-existent to dimly lit, bathing us in a yellowish hue. I'm sure it looked like I had jaundice.

I shook my head. "You're an enigma, Bram."

"And you, my delectable little package, are an aphrodisiac to my very senses."

The last thing I wanted was a long evening of rebutting Bram's less than smooth advances. I needed to cut to the chase. It wasn't like I had a lot of time. "I need your help, Bram."

He smiled, displaying his fangs. "I find I quite enjoy your being in need of my assistance, sweet."

I frowned. "I'm sure you do."

"And what can I assist you with this eve? Perhaps you would care to remove your jacket in favor of comfort?"

Before I could respond, he was behind me, peeling my jacket from my shoulders until he had it in his hands. He deftly draped it over the back of one of his chairs. Then he ran his long fingers down the naked skin of my shoulders and upper arms until I got goose bumps. He didn't back away but stood behind me and leaning into my neck, inhaled deeply.

"I am always hopeful, my dear."

"Of what?" I asked as I quickly withdrew from him, turning around to face him.

He opened his eyes and smiled at me. "I am always hopeful that whenever you are beside me, my desire for you will be less consuming than it has been on previous meetings; and, yet, I find such is never the case."

"Oh," I didn't know what else to say. Sometimes I wished I'd had sex with Bram so he would have gotten over this stupid crush a long time ago. And I'm pretty sure Bram would agree with me.

"How can I help you, my beautiful friend?"

I glanced around his office, eyeing the black and white motif of his furniture and carpeting. I looked down at his leather couch and back up at him. "May I?"

He nodded. "Of course."

I sat down and he seated himself beside me. I took a deep breath and swiveled to face him. "What's your history with the Netherworld, Bram?"

He seemed taken aback. "The Netherworld?" he repeated.

"When was the last time you were there?"

He was silent and seemed to be reliving the past in his mind, pulling up memories that were probably long since buried. It wasn't surprising because Bram was over three centuries old.

"It has been over one hundred years since I last stepped foot on Netherworld soil, sweet."

I swallowed and glanced down at my folded hands in my lap. Over one hundred years was a long ass time. Maybe I needed a more up-to-date guide?

"Why do you ask?"

I glanced at him. "I need a guide, Bram."

"A guide?" he repeated.

"I have to go to the Netherworld and I don't want to go alone."

Bram's expression was non-existent and seconds later he exploded into a raucous laugh, throwing his head back with the effort.

"This isn't a joke," I said with no smile.

He stopped laughing and faced me. "You must forget this foolish errand, sweet."

I stood up and glared back at him. "If you won't help me, I'll find someone who will."

He stood and grasped my hand, pulling me into the breadth of his chest. "If I were to accept your proposition, may I expect a reward?"

I didn't pull away. I knew too well that I had to play his game if I wanted to get my way. "I could pay you." Even as the words left my mouth, I wasn't sure what I would pay him with. My bank account wasn't exactly something to boast about …

"I am not interested in your money."

"Bram, you and I have a good arrangement. You know I could bust you for some of your less than legal transactions."

"You have attempted to use this argument on me before, sweet. We both know that only I can offer you information that is more than … valuable."

Damn, I should have known better. Bram was a formidable foe or ally, any way you looked at it. And that meant I was fresh out of ideas.

"I will deliver a letter of my demands, should you choose to hire me as your guardian," he said as he pushed away from me. "If you accept, you merely sign the letter and if you do not, we shall continue our awkward friendship."

I just shook my head—I didn't want to touch the awkward friendship line. But as to the letter of demands ... "Last I checked we weren't still living in the eighteen hundreds."

"I must be mindful of my own needs when dealing with you, Dulcie sweet."

I nodded and took a deep breath. "Okay, you have a deal but I need your answer quickly. I have to do this and I have to do it immediately."

Bram merely nodded. "You will have your letter of demands this very evening, before midnight. Does that suit you?"

I glanced at my watch. Midnight was three hours away. I could wait that long. I looked up at him again. "Yes, that will do."

"Very well," he said, slapping his hands together. "I must start my letter."

89

I laughed and took a few steps toward the door but his hand on my arm prevented me from leaving.

"One last item to discuss," he started.

"What?"

He eyed me suspiciously. "What business calls you to the Netherworld?"

I debated whether or not to tell him for all of three seconds. "Knight was apprehended by the ANC for something he didn't do."

Bram just continued to eye me. "Something you did?"

I just nodded.

"Perhaps you should weigh the potential outcomes of your actions. The Netherworld is not an easy place in which to be a criminal, sweet. Is it not better to allow the Loki to suffer for your transgressions?"

I felt my cheeks color. The articulate way he said it made it sound even worse. "Absolutely not. It's my responsibility."

"I do not understand your great sense of morality and justice, Dulcie sweet, though I do admire it. And as to the Loki ..." He sighed. "I will relish the day when the Loki is no longer your primary concern."

I wondered if that day would ever come.

If nothing else, Bram was true to his word. At ten minutes to midnight, there was a knock on my door. I opened it to find a youngish Lamia staring back at me. Lamias belong to the shape-shifter family, similar to weres only Lamias morph into lions. I was surprised to find that Bram would have a Lamia in his employ because they are notoriously difficult to manage and rumored to be dangerous, since it was general knowledge that they delight in causing pain. They also possess the ability to drain information from their victims by simply staring at them, which was probably why Bram kept one in his employ. Like I said, Bram couldn't always be found on the right side of the law. Luckily, this Lamia was wearing sunglasses—probably Bram's way of saying I was safe.

He said nothing to me, merely handing me Bram's letter which was folded in thirds and sealed with red wax.

"Ridiculous," I muttered while I slipped my finger under the wax and broke the seal, unfolding the letter. It read:

Dear Ms. O'Neil:

This is a demand letter. If you agree to abide by each and every one of the following conditions, please sign your name at the close of the letter and I shall happily act as your escort through the Netherworld.

Yours,

Bram

Demands: All mandatory.

Once in the Netherworld and throughout our time there:

1. For as many nights as we are travel companions, we shall share the same bedroom and bed; and

2. When you dress or undress, you shall do so under my gaze; and

3. I am allowed to touch you at my discretion and as many times as it pleases me; and

4. You will deliver me one kiss a day (the French sort with tongue); and,

5. You must discourage the lust of another man (I believe you refer to this as "flirting"); and, finally,

6. Upon our return to Splendor, you consent to dine with me five times (you must dress in something no longer than three inches above your knees and the top of which outfit should extend into a low v, whereby I can clearly delineate your cleavage)

If you accept the aforesaid conditions, please sign and date below.

I dropped my hand which was holding the letter and scoffed at the Lamia. "Is he serious?"

The creature just shrugged and acted as if he had no idea what I was talking about. Good thing he had those sunglasses on or he could have just extracted any information he wanted. Course, then he'd have to deal with Bram and suffer the consequences.

"Just a minute," I said as I stomped into my living room, grabbing the phone. I dialed No Regrets and told myself to calm down.

"Thank you for calling No Regrets," someone muttered on the other side.

"Bram please. This is Dulcie."

Silence on the other end followed by elevator music as they transferred me.

"Dulcie," Bram's voice was sickening sweet, as if he were completely unaware of how absurd his list of demands was.

"Is this some sort of joke?" I insisted.

"I know not of what you speak," he said, trying his best to sound innocent.

"Your demand letter. It's absolutely ridiculous."

He sighed. "If you do not accept my terms, sweet, do not sign it, my darling."

"But if I don't, you won't come with me to the Netherworld."

"It appears you have grasped the rules of this arrangement quite well, sweet."

It was my turn to sigh. "Why are things never easy with you?"

"I often say the same of you, my dear."

I held the letter up to my face again. "I need to rewrite a few of the terms."

"Such as?"

I glanced at demand number one, about sharing a bed. "We can share a bed but I will not be expected to have sex with you."

"Very well. Add it as an addendum, darling."

"Where is this 'darling' shit coming from?" I barked. "It's incredibly annoying, so cut it out."

"What is the next item you wish to negotiate?" he asked in a bored tone.

"When I dress and undress I have to do so in front of you? Only after I've put on my panties and bra."

"No."

"Bram, there is no way ..."

"Then we do not have a deal."

I grunted and said something unintelligible as I faced the fact that I was going to have to get naked in front of Bram. "Fine. I'll give you that one. The third one, that I allow you to touch me whenever you want to? What the hell does that mean?"

"I believe you are an intelligent woman, Dulcie. Figure it out."

"Okay, I'm adding to that one that you can only touch me above my clothing and not in inappropriate places."

He sighed. "Very well. Unless, of course, you invite me to touch your 'inappropriate places.'"

It would be a cold day in Hades before that happened. "Sure, I'll give you that one, too."

"Are you finished, Dulcie sweet?"

I glanced at the rest of it. Five dinner dates seemed like overkill but I guessed I could handle them. Especially since the book I was working on (well, technically, I hadn't started it yet) was about Bram. I could use those dinners to my advantage ... for research. And the final one about a kiss a day? Yeah, I could probably handle that too, despite my aversion to it.

Yes, it did occur to me that Knight might not approve of any of this but, at this point, I cared more about his safety than anything else. So, yes, Bram could have a few cheap thrills at my expense if it meant I could save Knight from whatever punishment was looming.

"Yes, I'm finished."

"Good. Simply sign the letter and return it and we shall leave … tomorrow evening?"

I took a deep breath. There was that little problem of a passport. "Um, I need some time to get a passport and identification."

"I will take care of it."

"I have someone from the ANC handling …"

"It will take too much time, sweet. Allow me to use my connections."

Of course, those connections weren't legal ones. But, in this case, I had to turn a blind eye because Bram was right, it would take too much time on Dia's part. She most definitely would have to field a long list of questions regarding my interest in going to the Netherworld and that was something for which I definitely didn't have the time. Furthermore, I didn't want to put Dia in that position …

"Okay, Bram, do what you have to do."

"Very well. I shall pick you up at nightfall tomorrow."

I took a deep breath. I was really going to do this—travel to the Netherworld where Hades only knew what awaited me. Although I felt good about doing my part in sparing Knight the wrongful accusations, what did that mean for me?

SEVEN

The following evening, ten minutes after the sun set, there was a knock on my door. I pulled it open and found Bram leaning against the wall of my building with his hands in his pockets and a killer smile aimed solely at me. He looked every inch the bad boy, and once again up to no good. And, okay, I'll admit it … he looked hot.

"Good evening, my dear."

"Hi, Bram. Are you ready?" I, myself, was as ready as I was going to be. I'd asked Sam to dog sit for me for the next few days, telling her I was going to visit some family members I'd basically made up. Sam wouldn't have reacted well to the news that I was headed to the Netherworld. So, besides Sam and my dog, I didn't have any other responsibilities.

"I am," he said and after giving me the once-over to which he shook his head—probably at seeing me dressed in sweats and an oversized T-shirt. He glanced behind me and saw my red suitcase. "May I?"

"I've got it," I interrupted, grabbing the handle of my bag. I started down my front walkway, toward Bram's black Porsche Carrera. Then, remembering my manners, I turned back to face him. "Thanks, for offering though."

He didn't reply but smiled in that endearing, boyish sort of way and instantly appeared in front of me, courtesy of his vampire speed. He opened my door, every inch the perfect gentleman or at least trying to play one. He grasped my bag to place it in the trunk. I just nodded in thanks and took my seat, fastening my seatbelt as he walked to the other side of the car.

"Thanks for picking me up," I said, once he was seated and buckled into his seatbelt.

"It is my pleasure, Dulcie sweet." He grinned as he turned the engine on, put it in gear, and gunned it, narrowly missing old Miss Gingerly in her 1970 puke green AMC Gremlin. She screamed something at him and held up a wrinkled, furrowed hand, flipping him off.

"I need to move," I said, sighing.

Bram glanced over at me with a raised brow, insinuating "you're just now reaching that conclusion?"

"Moving on," I muttered. "Where are we going?"

He smiled and put his hand halfway up my thigh. I removed it. I thought I was somewhat prepared for this drive and Bram's roving hands, which is why I wore my sweats and bulky sweatshirt. For the time being, sexy and I weren't acquainted. He surreptitiously placed his hand on my thigh again.

"We aren't in the Netherworld yet so we don't have to abide by your list of demands," I said with a scowl as I forced his hand back onto his lap.

He chuckled softly. "I could not help myself, sweet, your body just screams for my touch."

This was going to be a long ass trip. Ignoring his comment, I reached over and turned the volume on the radio up. More classical music poured out, however, this song was far less furious than the last.

"Jeez, is this all you listen to?" I asked, even as I found myself absorbing the melody and, dare I admit it? liking it.

"I find it soothes my ever agitated nerves," he answered with a quick smile.

"Who's on now?" It was nice to focus on something other than the butterflies which were agitating my stomach and flying headlong into one another until I felt somewhat sick. I was nervous—I couldn't deny it. I hadn't slept all night, plagued with thoughts of Knight and wondering what was happening to him, if he was alright or not ... As if those thoughts weren't enough to ruin my evening, there was always the dread of what I was up against if I were found guilty. Would I end up rotting in a Netherworld cell for the rest of my godforsaken life? Or would an even worse punishment await me?

"Beethoven," Bram answered, holding his hand up and swaying in time with the music, as if he thought he were a conductor or something. "Moonlight Sonata."

Well, good on Beethoven and his Moonlight Sonata because somehow the music soothed my frazzled mind. The haunting melody gave me something to focus on, steering me away from the frenzy that was beginning to develop in my gut.

I focused on the lines in the road as they blurred before me, realizing we were coming ever closer to the destiny I'd arranged for myself, the Netherworld. I'm not sure how long I zoned out on the dotted yellow lines, or got lost in the fury of my thoughts but, before I knew it, we had driven clean out of Splendor city limits. I didn't remember turning off the main road but soon we were traveling on a back road, heading for the nearby town of Estuary. This wasn't the main road to Estuary and it was so poorly maintained and rife with potholes and overgrown weeds, few people traveled this way.

"Portals are pretty far out of the way, huh?" I asked, casting a glance at my vampire driver.

"Yes, quite so."

I took a deep breath, trying to still the beating of my heart. "Bram, are you frightened at all?"

He glanced at me and wore his confusion. "Frightened?" He said the word as if he didn't know its meaning.

"Well, it's been over one hundred years since you've been to the Netherworld, right?"

He nodded. "Yes, it has been; but, no, I am not frightened."

Did I believe him? I wasn't sure. "Why not?"

He considered the question for a few seconds. "I imagine not much has changed in my absence. The Netherworld is not as progressive as we are, sweet."

I nodded. I guess that made sense. "Then why does everyone say the Netherworld is so dangerous?"

Bram didn't respond right away and appeared to be listening to the music, his hand swaying to the tempo as he'd done before. After another few seconds, he apparently remembered my question. "Because it is dangerous. Oh yes … Very much so."

The road veered around a gnarled oak tree and Bram turned sharply, merging onto a fire road that was completely overgrown with tall weeds that whipped the front of the Porsche as we proceeded. Knowing how much Bram loved his car, I had to imagine this was a huge bummer for him. However, I didn't want to mention it—I already felt bad that I'd roped him into escorting me, ridiculous conditions or not.

"Are we almost there?" I asked, not intending to sound all of four years old.

"Yes, nearly."

As the moon broke through the clouds overhead, its milky rays highlighted another craggy oak tree off to our right and Bram put the car in park, turning the engine off. I didn't say anything but watched him close his eyes as he listened to the music.

"Beautiful," he whispered while he ran his long fingers along the steering wheel, as if he were playing the very notes we were hearing.

I thought about telling him to pay attention to the task at hand but I suddenly realized this was Bram's way of accepting the fact that he was about to embark on a voyage that maybe did frighten him. I mean, it had been over one hundred years since he'd been to the Netherworld and who knew why he'd left. Had he been trying to escape something? Someone? The ANC? It's not as though it would have surprised me to find that Bram's past had been shady—like I've said before, his present wasn't exactly vanilla. I hadn't ever considered whether or not Bram returning to the Netherworld would upset him, not to mention be dangerous for him. Who knew if he had enemies there? I was suddenly disappointed with myself. I'd been so consumed with thoughts of Knight and myself, I hadn't considered Bram's situation. Course, I also had to imagine that if Bram perceived himself to be in danger by returning, he never would have agreed to it. Still, watching him now, I could tell he was nervous. At the very least, he wasn't his usual garrulous and confident self.

The last note sounded from the stereo and Bram opened his eyes, turning to face me. He took a deep breath. "Very well."

Then he opened his door and stood up. I didn't wait for him to come around and let me out. Instead, I opened my own door which was a bit difficult considering all the tall weeds that pressed against the car door.

"Where do we go?" I asked as I stood up and realized we were completely alone, aside from a steady buzz of the insects, the shadows of a few straggly trees and the briskness of the wind.

"Straight ahead," Bram answered as he opened the trunk and pulled our two suitcases out.

I glanced around me again, trying to decipher what a portal might look like. "If this is one of the portal locations, why is it so overgrown? It looks like no one has been out here in decades."

"This portal was a gift to me, sweet."

I felt my eyes widen. "You mean, this is your very own entrance to the Netherworld?"

"Yes, quite so."

"But …"

"Of course, once we enter the other side, I must subject myself to the same treatment as other travelers." I didn't know what to think so I said nothing but had to admit I was impressed that Bram had been presented with his very own Netherworld entrance. Judging by the dilapidated environs of the portal location, it didn't surprise me that it had been over one hundred years since he'd last used it.

I watched Bram shut the trunk and lock the Porsche with his key remote. Then he picked up our luggage and started forward, looking like he'd completely lost his mind given the fact that he was out in the middle of BFE but dressed to the nines in a black suit.

He stopped walking once he was parallel with the nearest craggy oak tree and set both of our bags down. He walked to the right until he was completely in line with the tree, then glanced down at his feet and stepped to the side for a count of four. Pivoting on his toes, he turned ninety degrees and took a step forward. It seemed like he was doing the box step or something.

He held his hand out before him and seemed to run it through the air, as if he were practicing synchronized swimming. He repeated the bizarre gesture three more times before I realized he was looking for some difference in the air, probably in temperature, I guessed.

"What are you doing?" I asked, coming up behind him.

He turned to face me and held his hand out to stop my approach. "Do not stand too close, sweet. You could accidentally be pulled in."

Even though I didn't know what that meant, it didn't sound good so I stepped to the side where I didn't imagine I'd be pulled into any invisible portals.

"I am checking for the portal entrance, sweet."

I nodded. I'd gotten that much. "How will you know it?"

"The air feels heavier, denser, less airy. Similar to a gel."

Interesting. He continued to move his hand around, looking like a mime trying to get out of a box. Then a great smile spread over his mouth and he pushed his hand forward, being careful to keep his feet firmly rooted.

"Voila," he said, glancing over at me with a triumphant smile. I took a step nearer him but he held his hand out to stop me again. "There are three items to consider before we step over, sweet."

I stopped in my tracks. "Okay."

He held up his long index finger. "First, do not forget the sky."

I was about to insist he explain that one but before I could, he was onto point two, middle finger already having joined index finger. "Second, creatures in the Netherworld will not appear the same as they do on Earth. And third, fairies are a special breed in the Netherworld. Creatures will respond to you differently."

I started to insist he explain that to me but he shook his head. "I've located the portal entrance, sweet, and activated it. Therefore, we do not have much time remaining. I will walk through and once I vanish entirely, you must follow within three seconds. You simply step through, allowing your legs to enter before the rest of your body. Once you feel the gel of the portal, close your eyes and hold your breath. Oh and remove your sweatshirt."

"What?" I started but before I could finish, Bram had our luggage in each hand and with one step, he disappeared right in front of me. Remembering his three second rule, I tore off my sweatshirt and leapt forward and threw one leg into the air where he'd just gone. He was right, it did feel like gel. It wasn't cold, nor was it hot, it was just a bizarre texture. Suddenly, afraid I might lose my leg if the portal inadvertently closed, I lifted my other leg and, inhaling deeply with my eyes shut, propelled myself forward.

It was like being in a wind tunnel for all of one second. I kept my eyes clamped shut as I felt myself dropping even though I wanted nothing more than to scream. Then I remembered Bram telling me to hold my breath.

My feet landed on what felt like pavement and I could feel strong arms around me, holding me upright. Feeling like I might pass out, I inhaled and opened my eyes.

When I focused on the scenery around me, I didn't know what to think. I blinked a few times almost to make sure I really was seeing what I thought I was and not just some figment of my seriously confused imagination.

But, any way I looked at it, I was outside, on what appeared to be a tarmac, in a line, with a host of people standing single file in front of me. Beyond me were rolling green hills that looked like they were completely untouched by civilization. The green of the hills met the azure of the sky and, feeling like I just walked into the Teletubbies set, a horrible thought suddenly struck me. The sun was out, glaringly obvious in its yellow haven up in the sky, so where was Bram?

That was when I remembered the feeling of arms around me. I glanced up and felt the breath catch in my throat …

Bram was not only standing in the garish sunlight without exploding into dust but he was also stunningly … beautiful. His dark hair was blacker than I could remember it, almost blue in its glossiness and his usual blue eyes had taken on a lavender hue. But it was his skin that had me completely arrested—the color of bronze. He looked like a Greek or Roman God and he was so much … taller than I remembered.

"Bram?" I started. "The sun won't destroy you?"

"I am free to walk in the daylight in the Netherworld, sweet." He smiled down at me, completely aware that I was mesmerized by him.

"Why do you look so different?"

He shrugged. "Remember? Creatures in the Netherworld plane are not what you expect them to be."

I swallowed hard and just nodded dumbly, still unable to stop ogling him. This was beginning to get embarrassing. "Is this your natural state?"

He chuckled, apparently amused by my awe. "Yes, this is a true representation of the vampire."

"Why can't I stop staring at you?" I asked, finally okay with admitting the obvious because the truth of it was, I was getting worried.

Bram chuckled again and ran his finger down my cheek. His touch was warm … strangely so, considering he was a vampire. "My powers of persuasion are stronger here, sweet. I shall reduce them for you." He glanced away from me and when he returned his gaze, his eyes were no longer purple, but back to their usual blue.

Wanting to test my ability to break away from his hypnotic eyes, I glanced down and sighed in relief. "Thank you."

He chuckled again and before I could respond, I felt something … strange and curious. It sounded like a sheet flapping and I could feel the slightest tickling in my upper, no middle back … It was like an itch I couldn't scratch. Before I knew it, I felt lighter, as if I were floating on air. Bram's grip on my shoulder tightened and when I looked at him in complete confusion, he motioned for me to look down. I glanced at my feet and realized I was hovering a foot or two off the ground.

"What the hell?" I started as the shuffling sound began to accelerate and thrum incessantly, sounding like the beating of … wings?

With a great sense of foreboding, I turned my head to peer behind me and what I saw almost made me gag. Green gossamer wings that reflected the light in an array of glittery patterns met my delirious eyes as they fluttered madly, attempting to keep me airborne …

"You've gotta be fucking kidding me," I started as I realized fairies did have wings. Well, at least they did in the Netherworld, anyway.

Bram started chuckling again and I turned my narrowed eyes on him. "Shut it," I growled. "I don't want to hear one word about this from you."

"You must learn how to control them, sweet. If not, you will find yourself flying Hades only knows where."

He released me and, as if to prove his point, my wings began to beat with even more determination as my body drifted upward. Bram caught my arm and pulled me back down again, laughing all the while.

I wanted to cry.

"Did you know I'd sprout wings here?" I demanded. He smiled but said nothing. "A warning would have been nice, Bram."

"I seem to remember my informing you that creatures would not be as you expect them."

I frowned. "That is a damn far cry from: 'Dulcie, don't freak out but you're about to have more in common with Tinkerbell than you ever imagined.'"

"I apologize, sweet," he mumbled.

"Never mind that now," I said and shook my head, glancing around me at the people in line, only to find they were all staring at me.

"You must stay close to me at all times," Bram whispered as if, he too, had just sensed I was suddenly the center of attention.

That was when I took note of the "people" surrounding me and found an array of creatures, some in semi-human form such as elves, goblins, fellow golden vampires; while others completely defied explanation. Something that looked like a big blob of reddish fur was standing next to what appeared to be a lizard. But this lizard was standing on two feet and wore some sort of uniform. Both he and the blob of fur were intently staring at me, with expressions I couldn't read. I glanced behind myself and found another vampire, this one also tall, golden and incredibly handsome. Except he was fair-skinned, where Bram was dark. He, too, was staring at me with the expression of ... was it hunger in his eyes? I glanced at the creature behind him, something blue and lumpy, and realized they all had the same starved look but I didn't think a hamburger would appease them. Theirs was that other sort of hunger.

Son of a fucking bitch.

"Why are they looking at me like that?" I demanded, feeling myself unconsciously leaning toward the strength and protection Bram supplied.

He took a step forward, the line apparently now moving. Grabbing my waist, he carried me with him, being careful to propel our luggage forward with his leg. I watched a were, dressed in a blue and grey uniform, complete with an ill-fitting hat, start at the front of the line, apparently checking for documentation. He wasn't in his wolf form or anything but I knew he was a were all the same. Guess my ability to detect creatures also worked here. At least some things were the same in the Netherworld as they were Splendor.

"The fairy is a creature of sexual delight in the Netherworld," Bram answered and offered me a grin that said he was enjoying every second of this—every second of the fact that I had wings that wouldn't stop beating, that he looked like every woman's wet dream come to life and the fact that I was now considered a Scooby snack of the Netherworld.

"What?" I demanded, completely aware that I hadn't comprehended one word of whatever he'd just said.

"The fairy is a creature of sexual ..."

"I got that," I interrupted, exasperated. "Explain what the hell that means."

Bram sighed, like I was slow. "It means all creatures will find themselves irrevocably drawn to you, Dulcie sweet.

105

It is your smell, your taste; they find you intoxicating. You are comparable to a drug on the earthly plane." I couldn't help but notice he was holding my wrist up to his nose like he could smell the blood in my veins.

"Bram, does that include you??"

"I always have been inextricably attracted." He nodded with a devilish smile. "Though I can manage it better than … most."

"Great, just frickin' great." I shook my head at the injustice of it all. "Could this get any worse?"

"I will protect you, sweet," Bram said, offering me a cheery smile. "As long as you are with me, you will be safe."

I glanced at him with narrowed eyes. "Why, what would they do to me?"

He shrugged, still wearing a smile that said he knew more than he was letting on. "I know not for certain."

"Um, I think that's a load of crap, Bram. What is the deal with fairies here?"

"You are … how should I verbalize this? Quite like an erotic delicacy. There are only a few fairies in the Netherworld and perhaps your rarity combined with your beauty is enough to drive even the strongest of creatures to obsession."

"Oh my God," I muttered. If I'd wanted to cry before, it was now amplified tenfold. As if to remind me of the fact that my life was sucking huge balls at the moment, my idiotic wings began to beat frantically.

We moved up another notch in line and luckily, Bram maintained his grasp on my arm or I'm sure I would have fluttered away. I glanced ahead of me to see where people were going once they escaped from the line but it twisted and turned so much, I couldn't make out what was happening. From what I could see, it seemed as if we barely moved at all. And the were in the uniform at the front of the line was arguing with someone, which meant it was going to take just that much longer for us to get the hell out of here.

"Bram, where are we going once we get out of this damn line?" I asked, glancing up at him to find he was staring at me. "Hey, you said you could control your lustful tendencies!"

He chuckled. "They can be quite difficult to control, sweet." He glanced away before looking at me again. "I made arrangements for a hotel, my dear. From there, I will leave the particulars to you, as I am not mindful of your intentions."

I figured he meant my plan was moving forward. I actually wasn't "mindful" of my plan either—I didn't really have one. Not wanting to focus on my disorganization, I glanced behind me, to see where it was that we'd come from when we dropped out of the portal. I noticed a large building that looked as if it had been constructed in the seventies. Dark windows dominated the square structure and, with the white of the walls, it looked like some government-type building. In black bold letters it read: Association of Netherworld Creatures. So this was the mother ship, the headquarters of the ANC. Somehow, I wasn't too excited to see it although I'd heard so much about it throughout my career as a Regulator. If I'd always felt a part of the ANC, I didn't feel that way now. Not since they arrested Knight …

"Has it changed much?" I whispered to Bram, not wanting to attract even more attention to myself, considering everyone around me was still staring at me like I was a Big Mac.

Bram glanced around himself with what appeared to be ennui. "Yes and no."

I figured we were going to be stuck in this line for a long ass time, seeing as how we'd moved up maybe two feet in two hours. And Bram's response was just begging to be dissected. "What do you mean?"

He shrugged. "The building has been updated, the creatures and the scenery have not. It is the same and yet it is not the same."

Before I had the chance to respond, what appeared to a black-winged bat suddenly appeared in the air. It was the size of an SUV and had fiery red eyes. Its long talons curved into sharp claws, the points of which were just as sharp as its fangs. So, yeah, not exactly a bat, but close enough. It screeched as it flew over us, diving down and swooping over whoever was unfortunate enough to be in its way.

"Bram," I started as I felt him tighten his hold on me, pulling me closer.

I didn't get another word out before what appeared to be cannons suddenly rose out from the asphalt. They spun around, seemingly targeting the bat creature as it squawked and darted down again. I lost sight of it but moments later, with the cannons pointed at it, it flew straight up in the air. Something was clutched in its talons and that something was moving. I couldn't make out exactly what it was but judging by all the creatures in line screaming and running this way and that, I had to imagine the bat creature had just picked off a poor, unfortunate tourist.

"Bram!" I screamed hysterically.

"Shhh, do not attract attention to yourself," he whispered and began slinking back toward the wall of the building, leaning into it, with me right beside him.

I watched as the cannons spiraled around, trying to stay targeted on the bat creature. But the thing flew incredibly quickly. It pulled whatever was in its talons up to its mouth and began eating it, midair, its victim still trying to tear itself away.

I couldn't watch anymore and dropped my face into the warmth of Bram's neck. God! What was this place? What had I gotten myself and Bram into? And where was Knight? Was Knight even alive?

At the sound of firing, I glanced up and watched the cannons shoot a volley of bullets at the creature. But they weren't bullets that I've ever seen—they were fluorescent green, red and yellow laser-like lights. The creature dodged them and flew straight for everyone in line again, dropping whatever it had been munching on as the cannons' fire merely sizzled in the air and died away.

"Oh my God," I started and felt like I wanted nothing more than to escape, rather than standing still with Bram as we attempted to hide against the wall. My wings were beating madly.

"Do not move," Bram insisted. "It can detect movement."

I had no control over my moronic wings so Bram grabbed them none-too-gently and held them until they were motionless. I could see what looked like glitter all over his hands and on the ground below me.

"Am I hurting you?" he whispered.

Well, his hold wasn't exactly comfortable but compared to becoming dessert for the bat creature, this was like getting a massage. "No, I'm fine."

Meanwhile, the demonic beast in the sky continued to circle, watching the various creatures as some slunk against the wall in Bram-style and others continued running around the tarmac fully panicked. It soon became obvious that the creature was selecting its next victim. The cannons continued to spiral, trying to get a clean read on the creature but it always flew one step ahead, as if it were accustomed to this game of cat and mouse.

The creature suddenly leapt upward and then dove down, looking as if it were in a tailspin. Just as it was about to make contact with another creature, the cannons exploded in a coordinated rain of fluorescent bullets, hitting the monster square in the chest. There was definitely a look of shock in its red eyes as it began to plummet out of control. It dropped from the sky, its body covered in what looked like blue ink—its blood, I imagined.

It fell to the ground and the earth shook.

"Welcome to the Netherworld," Bram said with a smile.

EIGHT

After the attack of the flying rodent, all I could think about was the fact that my parents had lived in this hellish place. I was an American citizen because my mother had come to Earth when she was pregnant with me and I'd been born on American soil and thus granted amnesty but this horrible place was my lineage, my ancestry. The thought made me ill. But what bothered me more was the idea that somewhere in this godforsaken land was my father, that is, if he hadn't already died.

I'd never met my father and although my mother had died when I was young, I didn't recall her ever talking about him. And even though I hadn't thought much about him over the course of my life, I couldn't help but think about him now, wondering where he lived in the Netherworld, what work did he do, was he still alive? They were futile thoughts, really, because I had absolutely no intention of trying to find him. He'd given up on mom and me, that's all mom had ever said about him. That she'd severed ways with him and made her own start and that was that.

Yes, that was that.

With weighty thoughts of my father in my head, it felt like at least four hours had passed by the time we finally wound our way to the front of the line. The were in the ill-fitted uniform demanded our documents with an open hand and a frown. Bram handed them over with a self-assured smile and the were glanced at both passports, intermittently looking at both Bram and me with a suspicious glower on his face. After a few minutes, I realized it wasn't so much suspicion regarding us, per se, but more the natural state of his face.

"What are you doing in the Netherworld and when do you intend to return to ..." He glanced at Bram's passport again. "Splendor?"

Bram smiled, long and slow. "I am here to introduce my intended to my family and friends and we propose to return in one week's time."

His intended? I wanted to gape at him with the expression of WTF plastered on my face but kept my cool. Sometimes it was better to keep one's mouth closed—especially in a land where enormous bat-like creatures ruled the skies. Eyeing my determined vampire guardian, I'd never been more grateful to have him by my side.

The were took a final inspection of our documents and scrutinized us again. Then he closed the passports, handing them to us with a nod that said he bought Bram's story. Thank Hades for that.

"Have a good stay."

"Many thanks," Bram replied as he grabbed my hand, probably so I wouldn't float away, and we started forward.

"He didn't even act like it was a big deal that that ... thing just picked off one of the creatures in line," I said, still in shock. After the cannon guns blew the predator out of the sky, it crashed onto the tarmac and died. Everyone just proceeded with their day, as if they had never been under attack by a gigantic flying death rat. Even now, the thing's lifeless corpse lay in the same spot, its sightless eyes still wide open while other creatures in uniforms walked around it, apparently discussing what to do with it.

And the unfortunate tourist that got devoured? I had no clue what became of him or her and no one else seemed the least bit concerned …

Bram shrugged. "It is not a big deal, as you say." Then he glanced at me and smiled knowingly. "Remember this place and these creatures are not at all what you are accustomed to in Splendor."

"Yeah, I'm more than aware of that," I grumbled.

We followed the line of people who had just been admitted to passport check through two sliding glass doors. They led down a long hallway and through another pair of sliding glass doors, emptying outside. There, lined up, were what looked like cabs picking up fares and taking them Hades only knew where. As we walked through the first set of glass doors, I noticed we were inside a lobby of sorts. A long desk stood in front of me, behind which sat a bored woman, obviously on duty, who was playing with her nails. She was a shape-shifter of some sort. What sort, however, was a mystery. I couldn't make out which kind she was and that meant I probably had never come across her type in Splendor. She was attractive with long brown hair and big brown eyes, a smallish round face and a perky, turned-up, Irish nose.

Beside her stood a scaly looking creature that towered more than seven feet tall. It had the face of a Labrador retriever—long, narrow snout with large eyes and a wide mouth, but other than that, I couldn't compare it to any other creature I've ever seen before. It wore the uniform of what I imagined was a security guard, complete with what appeared to be an Uzi strapped to its chest. But what really caught my attention was the bold lettering of "ANC" above the woman's desk.

So this was the entry to the ANC headquarters ... This was the place, at least I imagined, where I needed to go and spill the beans regarding the truth of what had happened the night I let Quillan go.

113

I stopped walking and stood there for a second or two before I approached the woman behind the desk, my hand still in Bram's. I glanced back at him and shrugged. "We're here so I might as well tell them the truth." No reason to put off the inevitable, right?

Before I could think another thought, Bram yanked me backward, bouncing me against his chest. "Hey!" I started, realizing he clearly didn't want me to go anywhere near the woman, the guard or the ANC in general.

"It is never a good idea to drive blindly," he said.

"What?" I asked, not in the mood to try to figure out his sphinx-like riddles.

"You do not have a plan, sweet, and until you do, it is not a smart idea to go into situations blindly."

Okay, he had a point. I guess I didn't have a plan but really, did I need one? My goal was to let the ANC know the truth about what happened with Quillan so Knight could be free and justice could prevail. And the longer I waited …

"Bram, I should just go in there and get it done. That's what I came here for. There's no point in taking my time and prolonging it." I mean, I'd be innocent until proven guilty, right? Appointed a lawyer, that whole bit? That is, if it ever went that far. Really, I was expecting a decently brief investigation and even if I was found guilty, how harsh could my punishment possibly be? I mean, my crime was not being able to shoot and kill someone who was not only my friend, but my boss. Surely someone would understand that?

Bram shook his head and tightened his hold on me, steering me through the second pair of sliding glass doors. When we emerged on the other side, it was night, the sun having literally dropped out of the sky in, oh, possibly two minutes or three at the most. In its place was a dark velvet canopy with no stars, nothing to interrupt the inky black except for an oval shaped moon that appeared so close, I could hit it by throwing a rock.

"As your guardian, I will not allow you to act impulsively," Bram said and his tone challenged me to argue with him.

Figuring he was right and I should have some sort of plan, I just dropped my head in obedience and mumbled something unintelligible while he glanced around himself, apparently trying to figure out his next move. Ahead of us, vehicles in bright colors continuously pulled up to the curb, picking up creatures and departing again. Bram watched them, as if he were trying to understand how best to attract the attention of the next driver because as soon as one pulled up, it seemed like a horde of creatures descended on it, resulting in pushing, shoving and ugly words.

Bram turned around and faced me, wearing an expression of determination as his gaze settled on my wings. He walked me over to a bench and released my arm. "Grip this, sweet, so you do not fly away. I shall return momentarily."

I'd almost forgotten about my idiotic wings which, as soon as I remembered them, started beating frantically again. I grabbed hold of one of the wooden slats in the seat bench and begrudgingly gave Bram a nod to say I was fastened down and wasn't about to go sailing off somewhere. I did notice a few glances my way, mostly starting out as curious, probably because I was clinging to the seat like it was a life rope. Soon the expressions of curiosity dovetailed into that haunted, hungry look I'd witnessed earlier.

This was freaking unbelievable …

The faster I could get out of Dodge, the better. Course, depending on how the situation unraveled, I might be spending a lot more time in the Netherworld than I'd ever hoped or planned for. And that thought caused me an undue level of depression. I had to remind myself that, really, my punishment shouldn't be much more than a smack on the hand.

Bram waved down a cab, this one a bright yellow and shaped like a mushroom. Actually, it sort of looked like an English taxi. As soon as the crowd began to descend on the cab, Bram hissed at them with his fangs displayed and they backed away. Apparently, vampires were among the higher orders in the Netherworld.

"Come, Dulcie," he called out, his tone implying the fact that I'd better hurry the hell up about it.

I took a deep breath, images of myself floating away while a big bat-like creature crunched me in its jaws, played through my head. But I managed to let go and beelined for the cab, my feet lifting in the air as I did so.

"Bram!" I screamed as I searched, in vain, for something to anchor myself to.

He glanced around him, at the crowd who was coming ever closer to stealing the cab but apparently realizing I was about to have a lot in common with a runaway balloon, lurched for me, grabbing me by the waist and, in a vampire split second, dragged us both into the cab, slamming the door behind us. Then we were off. I could only hope our luggage had also made the transition.

"Our bags?" I started.

"In the back," Bram finished and began smoothing down his shirt, as if it had gotten wrinkled in the process of him securing me and then the cab.

"Where to?" the cab driver asked, glancing over at us. He was an elf but had nothing in common with Quillan. Where Quill had golden curls and hazel eyes, a killer smile and an athletic, lean body, this guy looked more like Jabba The Hut.

"The Grosvenor Hotel," Bram ordered and then leaned back into the seat beside me, exhaling. It was all put on, of course, because Bram couldn't breathe. As a vampire, he had no respiratory system so it was all for show—merely to illustrate the point that the last ten minutes had been anything but relaxing.

116

"Sounds nice," I said with a nervous smile. I hadn't exactly detailed who would be paying for this little trip but due to the fact that Bram was here to protect me, I had to imagine the financing would be solely mine.

"Quite so, my dear," Bram said as he began inspecting his nails. "When forced to travel, it is important to do so in luxury, with the utmost comfort in mind. Spare no detail, spare no expense."

Great. This was going to cost a freaking fortune. I didn't say anything though; Bram had taken care of the arrangements. It's not like I'd volunteered. "What currency?" I started, suddenly panicking that I hadn't taken the time to convert dollars into … whatever the hell they used here. Come to think of it, I'd been in such a rush to leave, I hadn't put any thought into any part of the traveling logistics.

"The same currency we use, sweet," Bram answered with a smile that said he was very pleased with himself since he was on top of things and I wasn't.

I also breathed a sigh of relief and leaned back into my seat, hoping this cab ride wasn't going to cost me a fortune. More importantly, I was hopeful Mr. Jabba the Elf would accept Visa because I rarely ever carried cash. Actually, the last time I checked the misery known as my wallet, I had two dollars.

Great.

"Relax and enjoy the ride, folks," our driver said. I didn't miss his lustful glance through the rearview mirror. Good thing I was wearing jeans because he was staring right at my lap. Thinking I'd rather focus on the scenery as it passed by my window, I glanced outside, eyeing the row of five square, large buildings, maybe ten floors in each. These also looked as if they were constructed in the seventies.

"What city is this?" I asked the driver, suddenly wondering if the Netherworld was broken into cities.

His brows drew together as if I were stupid for asking and then that expression of lust was right back in his eyes. "Splendor."

Hmm, so there was a Splendor, Netherworld. just as there was a Splendor, California. Interesting. But this version of Splendor really had nothing in common with the Splendor I knew so well. Aside from the few buildings in what I assumed was the city center, we passed by, maybe, five streets with houses, which also looked like they were built in the seventies. But other than those few croppings of civilization, the rest of Splendor, Netherworld, was completely untamed wilderness—just rolling hills with only bushes and trees to punctuate the landscape. Not that I could really see any of the bushes or trees because it was dark outside; the few street lamps offered only slivers of light.

"So was that the headquarters of the ANC in the Netherworld?" I whispered to Bram, not wanting the elf to eavesdrop on our conversation. ANC business needed to remain just that, ANC business. Course, the driver was probably more than cognizant of where the ANC headquarters was. It's not like it was a big secret or anything.

"It is, sweet," Bram answered as he patted my thigh. I started to remove his hand but he made a tsking sort of noise at me. "Demand number three: I am free to touch you whenever and wherever I like and as many times as it pleases me with the post script offered by you that my touch must remain above your clothing."

I just frowned. He had me.

"Besides, sweet, you do not want to destroy the cover story I so artfully created?"

"That I'm your intended?" I threw it back at him, suddenly feeling irritable with this whole situation. Most of my irritation was reserved for the wings that were completely spastic and useless; and my not being able to control them was exasperating. If that weren't enough to

118

shove my day into a tailspin, it seemed everyone wanted to bang me and that still wasn't even the worst of it. I was at risk of getting gobbled up at any second by gigantic flying rodents. That was the worst of it.

"That would be the one," he said and squeezed my thigh as if to say there was nothing I could do about it.

I glanced outside my window again, wondering when the hell we were going to reach the hotel. It was so dark outside, I could see nothing and now there were no streetlamps at all, just silver signposts every few miles, reflected by our headlights. I couldn't make out what the signs said until we slowed down to make a right hand turn. I glanced at the signpost and read:

If you experience a breakdown, stay in your automobile at all times.

There was a silhouette of some hideous flying thing just above the warning so I had to imagine this was prime hunting ground for whatever stalked the skies.

Great.

I faced Bram and frowned. "You know, you could have prepared me a little bit more for all this."

He shrugged, his hand still on my thigh. Thank God I was wearing sweats. "Time was of the essence, sweet."

"Yes it was but you could have told me more than you did. You work according to your own rules, Bram." I hadn't meant for my tone to sound so whiney but there it was.

"I cannot argue that, my dear."

He didn't have to because the cab suddenly slowed and I glanced out my window to find what appeared to be a chateau before us—over four stories tall and complete with a stone façade, huge double wooden doors, gargoyles and turrets. It looked like something out of a horror movie.

"Let me guess, this is the Grosvenor?" I grumbled.

Bram smiled. "It appears not to have altered in the one hundred years I have been away."

"Yep, it's the same old, weird place," the elf said and then turned around to face us, obviously expecting to be paid. "That'll be five hundred."

"What?!" I barked. "Five hundred *dollars*?"

"I'm not talking pesos or rubles, honey," the elf snapped back.

Five hundred dollars for a cab ride? That was just ridiculous and furthermore, I didn't think I had five hundred dollars in my checking account.

"Do not concern yourself, sweet," Bram said as he pulled out a wad of hundred dollar bills. All of them were crisp. Why did I have the feeling he hadn't acquired them by honorable means? He peeled off five bills and handed them to the elf who just nodded and folded them, putting them in his pocket. Guess tipping wasn't practiced in the Netherworld. Course, a cab ride at five hundred dollars swallowed up any tip I was ever going to offer, Netherworld or not.

"Go quick so one of those flyin' sons of bitches don't get ya," he warned and then rolled down his window to spit out a huge loogey.

Bram glanced at him in disgust and then opened his door, scanning the skies as he did so. Apparently finding the coast clear, he looked at me. "Stay here, sweet, until I return for you."

No argument there … I stayed put and watched him walk to the rear of the cab and open the trunk, pulling out our bags. Then I glanced at the elf driver with a frown.

"Aren't you supposed to help with those?"

"No way in hell," he shrugged. "I don't get paid enough to risk my life for bags."

That was arguable but I stayed silent, watching Bram check the skies again as he hurried to the shelter of the hotel and a bellhop met him at the entrance, taking our luggage inside. Bram then darted back out to the cab with the aid of his vampire speed and opened the door, leaning in.

"Come, sweet," he said as he ushered me forward. My wings started beating like the tail of a dog excited to go on a walk. I fell into his outstretched arms and looping mine around his neck, allowed him to escort me into the hotel, while I scoured the skies, looking for anything that had claws, wings or a mouth.

Apparently, the flying monster squad wasn't out tonight because we safely made it to the hotel and Bram set me on the ground, grabbing my hand to keep me from flying away.

"Good evening, Mr. ..." the doorman's voice trailed away as he glanced at the clipboard in his hand, obviously having forgotten Bram's name.

"Bram," the dapper vampire finished for him.

"Mr. Bram and his lovely lady guest," he said, glancing at me. His expression turned to hunger in, oh, three seconds flat. He was a goblin—I could tell by the slight itch in my hand but what section of the gobelinus tree was anyone's guess. I hadn't come across his ilk before.

"Thanks," I said with a hurried smile.

"Please allow me to escort you to check-in," he continued and bowed like we were royalty or something, facing us as he walked backwards and led us to the front desk. Behind it, a mermaid was acting as desk attendant. This time, I didn't need my super powers of creature detection to realize she was a mermaid. Her fish tail was obvious enough—along with the four foot makeshift water tank she was comfortably submerged in.

"Welcome to the Grosvenor, are you here to check in?" she asked in a voice that sounded artificially high—like a dolphin's. That was the only similarity between a dolphin and this legend of the sea. The mermaid was beautiful with curly platinum blonde hair that reached her waist, huge blue eyes and tan skin. I glanced at Bram, only to find he was wholly fixated on her chest which was, so typically, covered with two clam shells. The clam shells really only covered her nipples because her breasts were easily the largest I'd ever seen—like Es bordering on Fs, if those were even legitimate sizes.

"Um, Bram, hello," I said, sounding every inch the jealous girlfriend or ... intended. Sigh.

The bimbo mermaid just giggled when she realized Bram couldn't unfasten his eyes from her boulders.

"Apologies, miss," Bram said with a practiced smile. He was smooth, I'd give him that. Bram was the type of guy, or vampire, that never wanted for a bed buddy and watching him carry on with this woman illustrated why. He didn't falter—he was just pure confidence with a handsome face in an expensive suit.

The mermaid just giggled again in that horrible high-pitched sonar-like voice and Bram smiled more deeply, this time with fangs, like he was showing off. That was when I got pissed off. I wasn't jealous but I was tired, nervous and ... damn it all ... sailing off again.

"Bram, honey, can we hurry this up?" I asked, gripping my stomach, enjoying the fact that I was about to put the kibosh on his little flirtation. "Oh, I think I felt the baby move."

The mermaid silenced her giggle immediately and turned to what appeared to be her list of available rooms. Bram chuckled and shook his head, looking embarrassed if it were even possible for a vampire to look embarrassed. Then he glanced down at me with the look of death in his eyes. I just shrugged.

Hey, I wasn't interested in watching Bram get his flirt on.

"The only available room is on our fifth floor," the mermaid said. "It is a king bed." Then she glanced at me as if to ask if we intended on sharing the same bed. According to Bram's list of demands, we did.

Bram smiled. "Wonderful." Then, before I could go through freak out episode number two, regarding the price of

the room, he propped his credit card on the counter. I
promised myself I'd pay him back later.

"Do you have any preference as to dinner?" the
mermaid asked, completely ignoring me and focusing all her
attention on Bram again, as if she hadn't given up.

"What are our choices, my sweet?" he asked, his tone
so sickening sweet, I was pretty sure I threw up a little in my
mouth.

The mermaid leaned forward against the desk,
propping her breasts up against the counter until it looked
like her head was in danger of being suffocated. "I'm sure I
can arrange for whatever … tickles your fancy."

"How about sushi?" I interrupted and then laughed
acidly. I mean, come on, that had been a good one.

Both Bram and the mermaid frowned at me but Bram
realized that I wasn't in the mood to play third wheel. He
sighed and accepted the key to our room, saying thank you
as we started towards the grand staircase that dominated the
lobby.

"I do not understand women," Bram said and he didn't
sound happy.

"Why's that?" I asked but my mind was only partially
on the conversation. Instead, the majority of my attention
was riveted by the opulence of the lobby. The ceilings must
have been thirty feet high, with ornate crown molding
delineating the walls from the ceiling. In the center of the
room was a chandelier the width of my living room and
along each of the walls was a mural of the Greek or Roman
gods. I recognized Venus and Diana, the huntress, but that
was about it. The flooring was a dark, rich cherry or maybe
mahogany, covered with expensive rugs.

"You rebuff my advances at every turn and yet when
faced with the possibility of competition, you are most eager
to destroy any opportunities I might have."

Ugh, he was miffed about Flipper. Really? "Bram,
we're here for business and that should be our focus." I

faced him and it didn't appear he was buying the whole business vs. pleasure argument. "Besides, she's a mermaid, Bram. Does she even have the right ... gear?"

"Gear?"

"Looked like all that was down there was a tail."

Bram threw his head back and chuckled heartily. "I had not considered that, sweet."

"See, I did you a favor."

"So you did, sweet, so you did," he said as we reached the fifth floor and unlocked our room door. I glanced down the hallway to find the bellhop with both of our bags. They were quick, I'd give them that. Then I took a deep breath as I faced the room that Bram and I were to share for the next Hades only knew how long.

NINE

It felt like maybe I was having a panic attack. My heart pounded in my chest and I was finding it difficult to breathe, my breaths coming in short, shallow spurts. It all began as soon as I thought about my mission to march up to the front desk of the ANC Headquarters and announce the fact that I was the perp involved in a crime.

And I'd already had my opportunity, already had my chance to get this off my chest. It would have been so easy, so quick and I would have spared myself all this anxiety, which in a word, sucked. But, no, Bram insisted I needed a plan.

I sat down on the king-sized bed I would share with Bram, draped with a horrible pink, green and blue plaid coverlet that looked vintage 1962. It matched the floor to ceiling curtains, which framed the only window in our room; and the pink of the curtains was the exact shade of the shag carpeting. I took a deep breath and tried to focus on the hideous carpeting, comparing the antiqued pink to some shade I'd seen before in an attempt to calm myself down. "I thought you said this hotel was really nice," I grumbled, feeling the beginnings of a headache.

Bram smiled down at me. "I also recall expressing the idea that the Netherworld is quite behind the times."

Yeah, so he had. Not that it mattered to me anyhow. What mattered now was trying to catch my breath and breathe normally. Holding my head in my hands, I leaned over and put it between my knees, trying to stop myself from fainting.

"What is the problem, my dear?" the golden-skinned vampire asked me. I glanced up at him and felt like laughing because he was trying his best to look concerned. It wasn't an emotion that suited him at all, mainly because it wasn't real. Bram just wasn't concerned about other people, period.

"You should have let me take care of my business at ANC Headquarters, Bram. That's what I'm here for. The longer we wait, the more time we waste, and who the hell knows what is happening to Knight." My voice sounded like I was on the verge of completely losing it, which was fitting because it was probably true.

Bram arched a brow at the mention of Knight but didn't lose his cool. "I am quite certain the Loki is unscathed, sweet." A smile pasted itself on his face as he quickly abandoned all thoughts about Knight in favor of subjects more attractive to him. "And as to your rampaging into the ANC office and declaring your guilt; as I mentioned earlier, it would not behoove you."

"If I ..." I started but was interrupted when Bram shook his head and made a tsking sort of sound.

"Chaos results from a lack of planning, my dear."

"Stop calling me 'my dear.' It bugs me." And that wasn't all that bugged me. Bram was super annoying when he was right and in this case, I had to admit, he was. I mean, planning always seemed to be a good thing to do in general. And, given the fact that I really had no idea where I was and nor any clue as to the rules of the Netherworld, planning was probably not only important, but paramount to my survival.

"Very well, my sweet."

I sighed. Yes, Bram was right about the whole planning bit but his being right didn't help my feeling like I was going to throw up. "So, what? I'm just supposed to spontaneously come up with a plan?"

He nodded but said nothing and I realized how impossible that feat was. I was having a difficult time as it was just trying to talk myself out of passing out, throwing up or erupting into a fit of tears.

"I can't even think!" I yelled and, feeling dizzy, I dropped my head into my hands again.

"Perhaps you would welcome the insight of your guardian then?"

I glanced up at him, relieved. I'd welcome anything as long as it meant I didn't have to think for myself. "Yes!"

He smiled and buffed his nails against his shirt. "If I were in your situation, Dulcie love, I would first appraise what is at stake."

"I don't even know what that means." I sounded defeated—exhausted, unhappy and completely overwhelmed, which was basically how I felt. I didn't want word games; I just wanted to be advised of what my next move should be to which I could agree or disagree. I just wanted my life to ease up a little. Really, was that too much to ask for?

Bram shrugged, his expression said he didn't understand what I was so conflicted about. "It is best to understand what your punishment would entail before you come valiantly charging in only to find yourself in hot water, which could have been avoided."

I shook my head. "I don't care what my punishment is. I just want to get this off my chest and let justice run its course."

"Justice is quite different in the Netherworld than what you are accustomed to in Splendor."

I frowned, not imagining my punishment could really be so brutal. "Bram, I'm guilty of allowing Quillan to escape. It's not like I killed someone or robbed a bank. I wasn't involved in illegal narcotics. Really, how bad could it be?"

He chuckled and shook his head at my apparent naiveté. "Famous last words."

I stood up and ran my hand through my hair, exasperated not only with the conversation but the whole situation. "What do you propose I do, then?"

He smiled languidly and took a seat on the bed, focusing on me. His gaze traversed my body, starting with my bust, then traveling southward.

"I'm not in the mood for sexual innuendo," I muttered, as I realized exactly what he was proposing. I let out a long sigh and wished I could be anywhere but here. There was so much I needed to do, so much to think about and Bram's libido wasn't on my list.

He brought his eyes to my face but that flirty smile was still in full effect. "I propose we attend the Loki's hearing, learn what his punishment is."

"What if he's already had his hearing?"

"At the time we crossed through the portal, such was not the case."

I frowned, as my head began to pound from a stress-induced headache. "And how in the hell do you know that? Furthermore, how were you able to find that out?" I mean, shit, I had no idea that Knight hadn't had his hearing yet and I was much closer to ANC business than Bram was, right?

"Friends in high places, sweet," Bram said mechanically.

I wasn't in the mood to press him for details. I was too interested in the plan that was currently taking shape in his head because so far, I actually agreed with it. "Okay, so Knight's hearing hasn't happened yet and we attend it … What then?" Suddenly, something occurred to me. "What if it's a closed trial?" That would put a huge damper on our plans if it weren't a public trial. I wasn't even sure what we'd do at that point.

"That would be a regrettable detail." Bram nodded. "I will leave it up to you to find out whether or not it is open to the public, sweet."

I frowned, thinking the answer was as easy as just showing up to the courthouse to see if we could get in. "Bram, all we have to do is find out in person …"

"No," he was quick to respond. "It is not a wise idea to risk your safety."

"How is that risking my safety?"

"Until we know what we are facing, it is not wise for the ANC to know you are in the Netherworld."

"But my passport," I started.

"Was in a fictitious name," Bram interrupted.

"Oh," I said, revealing the fact that I'd been so preoccupied with portals and winged creatures that I hadn't even glanced at my fake passport. Well, it seemed Bram really had taken care of everything.

"Your identity is completely safe and hidden and I would prefer to keep it that way." He eyed me with one raised brow. "In fact, if your magic worked here, I would suggest you magick yourself a new appearance. Unfortunately, however, your magic is useless."

Hmm, that was a surprise to say the least. What a bummer this Netherworld was—making my magic utterly useless.

So back to the subject of the trial; I guess I had some homework where Bram's plan was concerned. Not a big deal. I could call Dia and find out whether or not the trial was open. I was also pretty sure I could call the ANC here; but as Bram had pointed out, it was better to be as discreet as possible. No reason to take a hot bath, or whatever Bram said. No, Dia would offer the best solution. Somehow, I had to imagine she had contact with the ANC Netherworld and could find out details regarding Knight's trial in a second. "Okay, what then?"

Bram smiled again and it was pretty obvious he was impressed with himself. "Once we learn of the Loki's punishment, we will devise our plan."

I frowned. The momentum of Bram's plan had been building up and then, smack! Right into a wall. "What kind of plan is that? We devise a plan? That isn't even a plan at all!" I shook my head, feeling like I wanted to cry again. "Seriously? Our plan is to plan?"

The smile on Bram's face fell away replaced by straight-lipped irritation. "The point, my sweet, is that the Loki's punishment might not be at all severe and if not, you should not endanger yourself unnecessarily."

And just like that, I felt like we were back to square one. That is, with no plan at all. "Ugh, that is just dumb, Bram. I should have already gone to the ANC and been done with it."

He stood up and approached me. "Think about this a moment, Dulcie." He rarely called me by my name, so this had to mean he was serious. And Bram being serious wasn't something I witnessed all too often, if ever. "The Loki insinuated himself on your behalf for a reason. He must have believed he would fare better in Netherworld Court than you would."

That was true and Knight had said as much when I first learned that he was being brought in for interrogation. "Go on."

"Perhaps the Loki is correct. What if his punishment is miniscule compared to what you would incur?"

I gulped. Now he sounded just like Knight. Thinking the Netherworld would be more lenient on him than I, given that I was an ex-ANC junior officer and he was a high-ranking official, Knight took the blame. "Okay, you have a point," I started. "But what if his punishment isn't miniscule?"

Bram shrugged. "Then you state your case."

Any way I looked at it, aside from the "we'll deal with it when and if it comes" portion of Bram's "plan," it seemed to be sound. Actually, it was the only plan I had. Maybe Bram was right and Knight would merely get a slap on the wrist. What if his punishment weren't really anything serious? Maybe he and Bram were correct; maybe I would fare much worse? But, really, where the line was drawn between a brutal punishment and a slap on the wrist, I had no clue. I had nothing to go by.

I sighed. "I guess we have a plan." It came down to the fact that I didn't have an alternative.

Bram smiled at my consent before his cheeks flushed and he looked me up and down again, obviously seeking to change the subject. It was almost like he had ADD. He seemed only able to concentrate on weighty matters for so long before hunger for blood or sex took over. His fangs lengthened as I watched him, something that usually happened only when a vampire was sexually excited or hungry. I eyed him suspiciously. "Bram, when was the last time you fed?"

He inhaled at the mention of feeding and tore his gaze from my bust, finding my eyes again. "It has been a long while, sweet."

I swallowed hard. A hungry vampire isn't something to be taken lightly. Additionally, I've never allowed the undead to snack on me and I don't ever intend to. "Then maybe you should go find a willing donor."

He stood up and approached me, as I took a few steps back, finding myself buttressed against a veneered chest of drawers from the fifties. Before I could sidestep, he was directly on me, his hands on each of my thighs. He pushed my legs apart and nestled himself between them. I considered pushing him away and trying to escape but decided against it. Running from a vampire is very similar to running from a bear—you don't do it. Better to just play dead.

"Bram, I'm not interested in playing host."

He smiled but said nothing, softly brushing my hair behind my neck as my wings danced madly. "What are you …" I started.

"Shhh, sweet," he whispered and his breath caused goose bumps along my throat. "In the Netherworld, I do not feed in the manner to which you are accustomed."

"What does that mean?" I demanded. "You're a bloodsucker any way you look at it."

He shook his head, his smile still in full effect. "Not here. Here I feed off energy, not blood."

"Energy?" I repeated, sounding like an idiot. "How? What does that even mean?"

He didn't respond but placed his hand on my chest, just below my collarbone. He inhaled deeply, closing his eyes as he did so. A slight moan escaped his lips at the same time as another smile broke across his face. He looked like he was in the throes of an orgasm.

"Bram?" I asked, wondering what the hell was going on. He was feeding; that much was obvious. And I guess it was also pretty obvious that he was feeding off me—tapping into my energy? I didn't know what to think. Yes, I vowed never to play buffet to the undead, but did this really count? The more I thought about it, the more I concluded it didn't count.

"Do you feel anything?" he asked, not bothering to open his eyes.

I was quiet as I considered his question. There definitely wasn't any pain. Some weariness, but no particular excitement or ecstasy. I basically felt exactly the same as I had a few minutes ago. "No."

He opened his eyes and focused them on me. They were the deepest blue I'd ever seen them, almost black. "Ah, shame." I watched as the indigo of his eyes dissolved, replaced by pure black, as if his pupils had swallowed his eyes. I tried to pull my gaze from his but felt trapped. And then it hit me.

Complete ecstasy, a blissful euphoria circulated my entire body, beginning at the spot where Bram's skin touched mine and arcing out in a pulse throughout my body. It was like cresting on a wave of perpetual delight over and over again. I gasped in shock and found Bram smiling down at me.

"What did you do to me?" I demanded, my voice breathless.

"I removed my screen."

"Your screen?" I repeated, before closing my eyes and trying to restrain the giddiness that flowed through me. It wasn't a purely sexual feeling. I mean, that part was certainly there, but it was more like a feeling of unbridled joy throughout my body. It reminded me of how I felt when I was taking the illegal narcotic, Mandrake.

"I have put up a guard where you are concerned, Dulcie sweet," Bram continued, bringing his other hand to my shoulder. At his touch, my knees buckled. He grabbed hold of both my arms and pulled me into him, pressing my cheek against his upper chest. I felt my eyelids clench tightly and I could barely handle the feelings of euphoria as they flowed inside me. Had Bram released me, I would definitely have fallen down.

"Are you feeding on me?" I asked, although I already knew what the answer was.

"Yes."

Somehow the realization that he was feeding off my energy didn't bother me, or even upset me like I thought it would. Somehow it was something beautiful, something that made me weak in the knees, something I wanted more of. Something that I never wanted to end.

Bram suddenly pulled away from me and walked me to the bed. He sat me down and let go of my arms, taking a few steps back as if he were afraid I would attack him, demanding more. Who knows, maybe some of his donors did.

"Do you feel well?" he asked.

I shook my head, as the remnants of bliss began to leave me and cold, hard reality started to sink in. I glanced up at him, suddenly feeling angry and betrayed, used. "So let me get this straight," I started, taking a deep breath to regain my balance, but still feeling a little bit wobbly and unsteady. "The reason for your list of demands was to secure your meals?" I mean, it all made sense … The part about sharing a room, touching me whenever he felt like it … If the only way for Bram to feed was by absorbing energy from me, he'd set himself up for that and then some.

"Very astute of you," he answered without even the trace of an apology.

Anger continued to simmer within me as I realized just how self-centered he was. "Bram, have you ever considered just asking for something instead of sneaking around like some subhuman species?"

Bram chuckled as if he enjoyed being compared to a subhuman species. "Would you have agreed?"

Hmm, that was a good question. In general, I didn't like the idea of serving as a snack to any creature but since Bram was my only ticket to the Netherworld, I think I had my answer. "Yes, albeit unhappily."

"Very well then, I apologize."

I frowned. "It's too little, too late, but never mind; I've got information to hunt down." Namely, whether or not Knight's trial was public. I glanced at the dial face and cord of the ridiculously old-looking phone beside the bed. "Will this thing call Splendor … I mean Earth Splendor?"

Bram shrugged. "Your guess is as good as mine. A century ago, the Netherworld had no telephones."

I sighed as I reached for my purse, pulling out my cell phone which had no bars displayed. I guess Verizon didn't work everywhere after all. After I found Dia's phone number, I picked out the numbers on the dial and turned it after every one. Then I waited until I heard the tinny sound of the phone lines connecting.

"Dia Robinson, Moon ANC, how may I help?" She obviously didn't recognize the number, otherwise I would have been greeted with "This is Diva."

"Dia, it's Dulcie."

"Girl, where the hell are you calling from and please don't tell me it's the Netherworld."

I sighed. "The Netherworld."

"Unfreakingbelievable!" She laughed, sort of. "How the heck did you pull that off? I never even got back to you about the passport thing. I was hoping you'd forget about this ridiculous mission but not you." Then she laughed good and hard. "What was I thinking?"

"Well, needless to say, I took care of it."

"I can see that! So how do I help you now, Ms. Nuisance?"

It was my turn to laugh. "You know I wouldn't call you if I didn't trust you like my own sister?"

"Yeah, yeah. Stop buttering me up 'cause I don't swing that way."

I laughed harder and then took a deep breath. "D, I need you to find out if Knight's trial is open to the public."

"You could call and find out yourself."

"Yeah, I know but I'm trying to keep as low a profile here as I can."

There was silence on the other end. "Sounds like you are, at least, being smart about this. That's good." Yeah, and I guessed I owed Bram for the whole "being smart about this" bit. "How is it there, anyway?"

"Crazy and horrible and if I never come here again, it will be too soon."

"That great, huh?"

I glanced at Bram who checked his watch as if to say I'd been on the phone too long. "Yeah. Well, anyway, I gotta get going. Thanks for your help though. You can call me on this line once you find out about the trial."

"Sure thing."

"Thanks, D."

"Welcome, Dulce. You take care of yourself, girl, you hear me? I want you home in one piece."

I sighed. "Thanks, D, I will."

We said our good-byes and I hung up, suddenly feeling homesick and depressed. Yes, I promised her I would stay safe but I had to wonder if I just lied to her without even realizing it.

As it turned out, Knight's trial wasn't closed. And it was scheduled for the very next day which suited my needs perfectly. I was beginning to feel like an anxious mess the longer we waited for the inevitable to happen.

After I ended my phone call with Dia, Bram took me for a quick dinner in the hotel restaurant. I thought the scenery of the Grosvenor Hotel was something out of the Brady Bunch and the food was no different. I had cheese fondue with Caesar salad, a side of macaroni and cheese and Baked Alaska for dessert. And to drink? Dr. Pepper or Hi-C Hawaiian Punch.

After that bland and less than satisfying dinner, I felt reluctant to retire for the night because I knew, only too well, what awaited me … fighting off Bram's sexual advances.

Once he unlocked the door to our room, I took a deep breath and faced him, hoping he wouldn't get any ideas although I was sure it was too late for that. "I'm exhausted."

He smiled knowingly. "Very well, you should sleep."

Vampires don't sleep much so I had no idea what he planned to do while I got my zzz's but I couldn't say I really cared either. I threw my suitcase on the bed and began rifling through it, looking for my jammies.

"Please do not forget our contract," Bram said as he watched me pull out a white T-shirt and blue and white striped short shorts.

I glanced at him and frowned. "I haven't forgotten and yes, I am well aware of our contract."

He took a seat in one of the two club chairs, each beside the bed, stretching his long legs out before him, and linking his arms behind his head as he settled in for the show. A long, slow smile spread across his face.

"I am waiting," he prompted.

I shook my head, silently bemoaning the fact that I'd ever agreed to this as I leaned over to untie my shoelaces and pull off my sneakers. As far as I was concerned, this was going to be the shortest disrobing ever. After I pulled off my shoes and socks, I pulled my sweats down and stepped out of them. I glanced up at Bram. Why? I wasn't sure, but found his eyes riveted on me.

"Very lovely legs," he whispered.

"Thanks," I said and taking a deep breath, pulled my T-shirt over my head, exposing my bra. Of course, nothing in my life is easy so the T-shirt got caught up on my idiotic wings. I wrestled with the T-shirt and my wings for about two minutes before Bram chuckled and stood up, approaching me.

He reached behind me and helped push my wings through the neck of the T-shirt. Then he stood in front of me, smiling down at me like I was some kind of big idiot.

"Would you prefer to deliver your kiss now or later?" he asked loftily.

Dammit, I forgot about the kiss I'd agreed to give him each day … with tongue. Ugh. "Let's just get it over with," I grumbled.

His eyebrows reached for the ceiling. "Get it over with? No woman has ever said as much to me before."

137

"Yeah, well, there's a first time for everything." I shook my head and craned my neck upwards. "Pucker up, baby."

I wasn't actually prepared for Bram's kiss. I thought it would just be an innocent enough peck with a bit of tongue peeking through, but such wasn't the case. Instead, he wrapped his arms around me, pushed me against the wall and brought his lips to mine gently, kissing and biting at my lower lip. After a few seconds, I felt his tongue in my mouth and, thinking I needed to keep my end of the bargain, I met his tongue with mine. After what felt like another minute, I pulled away.

I have to confess, Bram wasn't a bad kisser. In fact, he, um, was a pretty good one.

He smiled down at me. "I quite enjoyed that, sweet."

"Yeah, well, I'm getting tired so let's get this show on the road," I said, perhaps a little too gruffly, as if trying to hide my flushed cheeks and racing heartbeat.

And Bram didn't miss a thing. I silently grabbed my night shirt, unclasped my bra and pulled it off. Then, in a split second, I had my night shirt over my head, which caught on my wings again …

"Son of a!" I yelled, realizing my breasts were completely visible.

Bram's chuckle deepened as I felt his hands smoothing the shirt over my wings. "I believe I need to cut a hole in your shirt, sweet."

"Okay, fine," I said in an exasperated sigh.

Bram merely leaned down and tore the shirt with his fangs. I heard the sounds of fabric ripping, after which he smoothed the T-shirt over my wings. Glancing down to see I was finally covered, I breathed a sigh of relief.

"Thanks," I muttered as I pulled out my pajama shorts and put them on over my thong underwear, even though I usually didn't sleep with panties. In this case, however, I figured Bram had already had an ample eyeful of my breasts and I wasn't in the mood to share anymore.

"Good night," I said and before he could argue, I drew the blankets down, crawled into bed and turned off the table lamp beside me.

TEN

"**P**lease do not do anything rash," Bram said as we stood outside the ANC courthouse. It was the same building we entered at the "airport" when we first arrived in the Netherworld.

"Rash?" I repeated, shaking my head as if "rash" weren't even a consideration, as if my MO merely consisted of "even-keeled," "thorough" and "deliberate." I started for the glass entry doors and threw Bram a backwards glance. "I'm fully aware of our plan."

Bram said nothing else but, judging by his body language, it didn't appear he was convinced. He easily caught up with me and accompanied me through the double doors. Once inside, the first thing that commanded my attention was the metal detector that blocked the only hallway in the room. The same bored woman was sitting behind the long desk at the front of the lobby; and, yes, she was still entirely fixated on her nails. The uniformed guard I'd seen last time wasn't there this time.

I glanced at the metal detector and the creature behind it, who was so small, he was seated on a stool. It was a creature I'd never seen before—small as I mentioned—maybe as tall as my knees and as thin as my legs. It was covered with snowy white fur and almost looked like a monkey—like someone had taken a monkey and stretched him out. It wore a uniform so I assumed it was an

ANC employee. And I guess that was made even more
obvious by the fact that it was working the detector.

"Please empty your pockets and place your purse on
the conveyor belt," the monkey-like creature said in a high-
pitched voice that sounded almost robotic.

Good thing I hadn't brought my Op 6. Well, that is,
good thing Bram insisted I leave my weapon in the hotel
room, saying I needed to remain under the radar. I'm sure if
I happened to pull the Op 6 out of my shoulder holster now,
I'd have lots of questions I wasn't in the mood to answer.
And a blown cover to boot.

I plopped my purse on the conveyor belt and walked
through the detector, silently relieved when it didn't go off. I
waited nervously while I watched the x-ray image of my
purse on the screen as it came out the other side of the
conveyor. I snatched it off the belt and turned to see how
Bram was faring. When the vampire walked through the
detector, it screeched at him with a litany of bells and
flashing lights and, if it were possible for a vampire to look
stunned, that was how Bram looked. A few seconds later, a
burly were materialized—like the air had just spit him out.
He was dressed in an identical uniform to the elongated
monkey man and had a dour expression on his unshaven
face. He motioned for Bram to hold his arms out "T" style
and spread his legs. Then he frisked Bram and I had to admit
it was pretty amusing, despite Bram's tight-lipped
expression, which showed little humor.

"Do you know where Room 101B is located?" I asked
the monkey man. Dia, great sleuth that she was, not only
found out that Knight's trial was public but also learned
what room it was in. It was good to have friends high up on
the ANC ladder.

The monkey creature nodded and pointed down the
hallway. His hand had only three fingers, all of which were
bright orange and knobby. "First door on your left," it said in
that robotic voice.

141

"Thanks," I responded as I started for the hallway before remembering Bram. I glanced behind me and found him wearing the same vexed expression, now complete with furrowed brow, as he slipped his Rolex back on his wrist and immediately emptied the tray full of change back into his pocket.

"Stop screwing around, Bram," I said with a smile, enjoying the fact that the overconfident vampire had to be bothered with security checks.

He joined me in the hallway and I took a deep breath as I faced Room 101B, realizing this was the moment of truth, the determinant of my next course of action—which could and most probably would change the direction of my life. I suddenly felt as if my heart had jumped into my throat and was lightheaded and dizzy again, my nerves frenzied.

"Are you feeling well?" Bram whispered as he placed his large hand on my shoulder. I glanced up at him and smiled in thanks. I paused for another few seconds and opened the door.

It wasn't a huge room—maybe fifty feet by fifty feet, very plain with its off-white walls. There were about ten rows of wooden, fold-up chairs arranged in amphitheater style for the audience and of those chairs, only about half were occupied. I glanced to my immediate right and noticed the last row empty, so I slid into the second chair down. Some sort of enormous, gelatinously blobby creature sat directly in front of me, which suited my needs perfectly. I would be completely obscured behind it and, for that matter, so would half of Bram. Bram nodded his approval and slunk into the seat beside me. I didn't pay much attention to the rest of the creatures because I was searching furiously for any sign of Knight.

He hadn't yet arrived; and, as far as I could tell, neither had the judge.

As to the courtroom itself, it reminded me of the ANC courtrooms I was accustomed to. There were tables located on either side; I presumed for the defense and the prosecution. The judge's box stood in the center of the room and there was a single row of fold-up chairs to the left of the judge for the jury, I guessed. The witness' box was beside the judge's stand and the court reporter (a troll) sat beside it.

The troll looked incredibly pissed off. That wasn't too surprising because trolls, in general, are always pissed off. What did surprise me was the fact that a troll was the court reporter because they aren't especially intelligent, as a rule, and their spelling is atrocious. This one, like most, was short and stocky with a bright red, bulbous nose, long stringy hair, beady eyes and skin that looked like someone had thrown pebbles into drying cement.

Instead of displaying the United States flag behind the judge's box, there was a flag I'd never seen before. It was completely black, save a white line that ran the perimeter and four vertical lines that decorated the right side. Hmm, must have been the flag of the Netherworld, if I had to guess.

Only the disgruntled court reporter and two women who sat at the prosecution table on the left of the judge's stand were in attendance. Both women's backs were facing me so I couldn't discern who they were or what role they played in all of this.

"Where are …" I leaned into Bram and started to ask about the whereabouts of Knight and the judge.

But I was stopped cold by the sight of a Chimera as it appeared in the doorway that opened into a hallway of holding cells. I'd never seen a Chimera before but I knew it immediately—mainly by its incredible size (it had to stoop over to fit through the doorway) and its three heads—those of a lion, a ram and a dragon. The Chimera's body looked basically like an enormous goat with the tail of a dragon. Looking ridiculous, it was dressed in a blue and white uniform and, I could only guess, was acting as bailiff. It wore a nametag but unfortunately, I couldn't read what it said.

The lion head opened its mouth and said in a deeply robust voice: "All rise for the honorable Judge Thorne."

Everyone in the audience as well as the two women in the front of the room stood up so Bram and I followed suit. The troll stayed seated and just "harrumphed" unceremoniously.

My eyes were glued to the doorway as I watched a vampire saunter in, dressed in a floor-length red robe. He was incredibly handsome (I was beginning to realize all vampires were)—very tall and broad-chested with dark, wavy, brown hair and green eyes that dazzled in his face like gems. Before he took his seat, he glanced around the room, smiled at the women at the prosecution table and then whispered something to the Chimera. Something that was probably along the lines of: Where the hell is the defendant?

The Chimera seemed suddenly embarrassed, probably by the fact that it had forgotten to present the accused. Well, at least its lion and ram heads appeared embarrassed—the dragon head must've had ADD because it glanced around the room so repetitiously, it looked like it was doing an impersonation of Stevie Wonder. With a grunt, it disappeared down the hallway. A few minutes later, it re-emerged, one of its hooves dragging a long chain across the brown carpeting. I followed the links of the chain with my eyes, my heart in my throat, as I waited for it to reveal the accused and, when it did, I felt my heart stop for at least a few seconds.

Knight.

Yes, I could recognize him and yes, he was the same Knight I knew so well. But at the same time, he appeared different. It must've been due to the fact that I was seeing his true Loki Netherworld appearance. And in a word, he was … breathtaking.

Descended from the soldier race of the Netherworld, which was bred to protect, Knight was immense. He'd always struck me as a huge guy but this was beyond huge. He had to be over seven feet tall and was almost as broad as the creature seated in front of me. His hair was glossy black and the chiseled angles of his face seemed sharper somehow. He was stunning, absolutely stunning.

Once I'd gotten over my initial shock at Knight's appearance, I was able to take in the rest of him. He was dressed in a two-piece, black prisoner uniform, his hands cuffed and chained, as well as his feet. His hair was buzzed short and I glimpsed a huge gash on his right cheek that looked fresh. The other side of his face was marred by a black eye and split lip.

Anger boiled up within me and I felt my hands fisting in my lap. How dare they treat him this way! He was a high ranking ANC official! He didn't deserve to be dressed in the garb of murderers and rapists and he most definitely didn't deserve to be beaten. My breathing was coming in short spurts and it was all I could do to remain in my seat.

Luckily, Knight didn't observe the audience because I really didn't want him to notice Bram and me. Of course, we were seated so far back and obscured by the blob-like creature in front of us, that had Knight wanted to see the onlookers, he probably would never have spotted us.

I was relieved of my worry because Knight took no notice of the audience and, instead, faced the judge and there was no trace of subservience in his demeanor. He acknowledged the judge with a nod and allowed the Chimera to lead him to the empty table. The Chimera pulled out the chair as he yanked on Knight's chains, forcing him down. Knight remained silent but glared at the ugly beast.

The judge took his place at the stand and announced to the Netherworld citizens: "Please be seated." Everyone did as requested. "Following is a case regarding the Association of Netherworld Creatures versus Knightley Vander."

145

I wondered why there didn't appear to be anyone appointed to defend Knight and the twelve or so jury chairs had remained empty. How could this be fair in any way? How could there be a prosecution with no defense? It seemed like the case was already doomed.

My thoughts were interrupted when one of the women seated at the prosecution table stood up and faced the judge. She was very pretty and rather tall for a woman, probably about five foot ten. She had extremely thick, long, red hair with black lowlights that fell below her shoulders. She was dressed in a purple and black suit that contrasted with her blue eyes. In her hands, she held a piece of paper.

"Very good, Ms. Fields-Gerrity," the judge said with a smile, encouraging her to proceed.

The woman, who seemed to be in her middle twenties, had the definite aura of a witch. She turned to face the assembly and, in a nervous voice, read out: "The Association of Netherworld Creatures charges that on or about March 5, 2011, in the earth's realm of California, in the District of Splendor, the defendant, Knightley Vander, who was representing the Association of Netherworld Creatures Splendor, did fail to take into custody Quillan Beaurigard, despite ample opportunity. This is in violation of Article 23, Netherworld Code, Section 34456."

When she finished reading the formal indictment against Knight, she smiled prettily at the audience and the judge before retaking her seat. The judge nodded and addressed the woman beside Ms. Fields-Gerrity.

"Ms. Brandenburg," he said, eyeing her hungrily. The woman stood up, frowning at the vampire judge, in a tacit announcement that she didn't approve of his lascivious glances where she was concerned.

"Your honor," she said with tight-lipped reserve.

"Have you anything to say in defense of the accused?" the judge asked as he leered at her figure from head to toe.

The woman faced Knight and offered him a kind smile that seemed mired in pity. She turned to the spectators and I realized how attractive she was. She was a shape-shifter; I could feel it in my gut. It took me a few more seconds to discern that she could shift into a cheetah. Once I knew that, I could see the proof in her face—cat's eyes and high cheekbones. She appeared to be in her mid-thirties and tall, though not as tall as Ms. Fields-Gerrity who, judging from the context, might have been her assistant or coworker. Ms. Brandenburg was probably about five foot eight with long, brown, wavy hair, diffused with blonde highlights. Her eyes were nearly the same shade of blue as Ms. Fields-Gerrity's. She wore a brown two-piece suit that hugged her lithe frame and visibly appealed to the judge.

"As my assistant mentioned," she began and I gave myself silent kudos for figuring out the nature of their acquaintance, "Mr. Vander is charged with failing to apprehend Quillan Beaurigard."

"I believe this case is fairly straightforward?" the judge asked and when she nodded, he continued. "In fact, the accused has already pled guilty and yet you still demand a hearing, Caressa?"

I was surprised when he called her by her first name. Such familiarity, but, when in the Netherworld … I guess. I saw Caressa tighten her lips, making it more apparent than ever that she didn't like the judge. With the way she was glaring at him, I daresay she couldn't stand him.

"Yes, that is so," she started. "And though the accused has confessed, I believe there is more to this case than meets the eye."

"How so?" the judge asked in a bored tone.

Caressa took a deep breath. "I have known Knightley Vander for some time, your honor," she started. I felt myself leaning forward with surprise. "He and I worked together for the ANC when we were Junior Regulators and from there, we worked our way up the proverbial ladder. In other words,

147

Knightley Vander and I were coworkers for over ten years. In that time, I believe I got to know him extremely well and I believe him to be an honorable, hardworking and just man. He never shirked responsibility and he was an absolute tiger in the face of crime."

The judge frowned as if he weren't buying an ounce of her story. "That is all very lovely, Caressa, but what does it have to do with this case?" he asked. Now, I found myself beginning to seriously dislike him. At least Knight had a friend in Caressa and, since she came to the hearing (either by subpoena or otherwise), I assumed she had to have been a decently high ranking official. Hopefully, she would prove to be useful.

"If you would allow me to finish," she snapped while shooting daggers at the judge with her eyes.

"Excuse me, but weren't you brought here as a witness for the prosecution?" the judge interrupted, obviously not interested in details about Knight's innocence.

I was surprised to hear Caressa was the prosecution's witness because she had just stood up in his defense.

"I'm not a witness for either side," Caressa retorted at the asshole judge. "As there was no defense attorney supplied for Mr. Vander, I am attempting to present an unbiased case."

It was deeply disturbing that Knight had no attorney. I could only wonder why they had a hearing to begin with? Based on Caressa's statement, she, too, was appalled by the injustice of it all. I didn't know why, but it appeared the odds had been stacked against Knight on purpose. Due to Knight's previous confession, no one cared to hear anything more. No one, that is, except for Caressa and me, of course.

"Introduce any contingencies to the case, Caressa, and move on with it," the judge said as he stifled a yawn. "I'm not interested in your personal accounts of Mr. Vander."

Caressa frowned at him and then took a deep breath, turning to face the audience again. "Mr. Vander was not the

only active ANC employee the night Quillan Beaurigard
escaped. His partner that night was a Ms. Dulcie O'Neil."

I felt my heart sink as I caught my breath when I heard
my name. After I thought about it, though, I shouldn't have
been surprised. Of course the ANC knew that I was on duty
that night. Not only that, but they would be remiss not to
think that perhaps I had been involved in Quillan's escape.

"Caressa, Dulcie had nothing to do with it," Knight
suddenly piped up and the tone of his voice warned her not
to argue with him. At the same time, there was a twinge of
desperation to it, as if he recognized that she was his only
friend in the room.

Caressa cast him a look that discouraged him from any
more outbursts. It was pretty obvious she was trying to save
his ass but even more apparent that he wanted none of it.
Guilt began to spiral through me as I realized how much
Knight had put on the line to defend me—his reputation.
And I had to wonder what that would mean for his position
as the head of the ANC in Splendor? If Knight lost his job
because of me … I couldn't even finish the thought.

"Mr. Vander seems to debate the validity of your
argument, Caressa," the judge observed as he smiled at her
with fangs.

Caressa had her hands on her hips and I could see the
tension building in her shoulders. "Do we or don't we want
to seek the truth in each and every trial?" she demanded but
the judge didn't respond right away. He appeared to be
trying to preserve his patience. "Judge Thorne?" she
repeated in an annoyed tone.

The judge shrugged. "We have already found Mr.
Vander guilty, Caressa.

"Already?" she repeated, her eyebrows raised in
suspicion.

"Yes," Judge Thorne answered, hissing the syllables as
he leaned forward. "The only reason we are sitting through
this farce of a trial is as a personal favor to you."

That silenced Caressa who immediately sat down. I could tell by the fact that her arms were crossed against her heaving chest that she was about to lambaste the lecherous judge but caught herself in time. She must have realized it wasn't the best move to make. As soon as she sat down, Ms. Fields-Gerrity tried to comfort her.

When I glanced up at the judge again, his lips were drawn in a tight line. He picked up his gavel and smacked it hard against the wooden dais. "In the case of the Association of Netherworld Creatures versus Knightley Vander, the High Court of the Netherworld finds Mr. Vander guilty of deliberately failing to apprehend Quillan Beaurigard."

I felt my heart sink as a sigh lodged in my throat. Even though I expected this would be the verdict all along, somehow I wasn't prepared to hear it in person. It sounded so final, so heavy and so wrong.

The judge took a deep breath and called the Chimera over to his side, whispering something in the ram's ear before he descended from the stand and disappeared into the adjoining hallway. The Chimera faced the audience and the lion head announced: "The honorable Judge Thorne will now determine Mr. Vander's sentence. This court will take a brief recess."

The Chimera reached for Knight's chains and yanked on them, forcing him upright. Knight narrowed his eyes and tugged the chains back, jerking the Chimera and causing it to stumble over its cloven hooves. Knight chuckled and the Chimera glared at him with all three heads before snatching up the chain and forcing him through the doorway and down the hall.

"Where is it taking him?" I asked, leaning over to whisper in Bram's ear.

"To the holding cell while the judge deliberates his sentence," Bram responded. His face was stoic, revealing no emotion, nothing at all.

"How long will that take?" I continued.

150

Bram shrugged but didn't glance down at me. "I do not know."

As it turned out, the judge didn't deliberate long although it felt like an eternity to me. According to the wall clock above the judge's box, a mere twenty minutes had passed; but for all I knew, maybe time existed in a different spectrum here in the Netherworld. Nothing would have surprised me.

When court resumed, I felt my heart rate quicken, realizing that the time of reckoning was now upon us. A grunting sound came from the hallway behind the judge as the Chimera pushed him aside and moved to the center of the courtroom, obviously tardy in announcing the judge's return.

"The honorable Judge Thorne will now announce Mr. Vander's sentence," the ram head said in a voice that bleated between words. Because it said nothing, I wondered if the dragon head was mute.

The judge frowned at the Chimera as the creature disappeared into the hallway, only to return a few minutes later with Knight, who appeared exhausted.

The Chimera led Knight to the same table as before and yanked down hard on his chains. This time Knight didn't throw the Chimera a curveball, instead he merely took his seat, his attention primed on the judge.

Judge Thorne cleared his throat and addressed the spectators and I swear my heart stopped beating as I awaited his sentence.

"This is quite an unusual case as I've received orders with regards to the sentence of the convicted," the judge began as he glanced at Caressa, with a slightly apologetic expression. His body language seemed very unusual and it only served to heighten my concern.

"In accordance, Knightley Vander is hereby sentenced to …" the judge cleared his throat as his eyes belied the fact that the verdict surprised him—he was merely the messenger of bad news.

"Death."

ELEVEN

It seemed like time stood still or I was watching a movie. Everything I witnessed appeared unreal; like it was staged. I glanced around myself, at the people in the courtroom and watched the surprise register in their cocked heads and bouncing shoulders. But even their surprise didn't seem real—no, it was as if they were all just actors, performers all around me, pretending to be the judge, the prosecutor and the defendant, not to mention those observing the farce. It was all a sham, a ridiculous play or maybe it was just a dream. Either way, it remained non-threatening, just a little blip on the radar of my completely muddled and confused mind and soon I would wake up.

Soon I would wake up.

Soon I would have to wake up.

But I didn't wake up. Pretty soon, the comprehension that I was in a real courtroom, amid otherworldly creatures who cared nothing for Knight or me dawned on me. And so did the sentence … That Knight had just been ordered to … die.

Death.

Death?

Had I really heard the judge correctly? I must not have because there was no way Knight could be put to death for failing to apprehend Quillan. It just didn't make sense. I shook my head, trying to eradicate the ludicrous thoughts

153

right out of my ears. But there wasn't anything ludicrous that needed eradicating. The cold, hard reality was that everything around me was actual, true, and appalling.

"What?" Caressa yelled at the same time Knight stood up, his chains clanking against one another, making him sound like Marley's ghost. I could barely bring myself to look at him because I was so afraid of seeing his face and his reaction to his own death sentence. But I had to look at him; there was no escaping it. When I did, I found him straight-faced, stoic, almost as if he was wearing a mask of indifference. But he was hiding behind that mask—there was no way he could've expected execution; no way he would've come here voluntarily, knowing his life was on the line. No, I anticipated some shock, anger or fear veiled behind that mask of indifference and yet, even I couldn't see beyond it. There was nothing there, visibly—no surprise, dread or anxiety. Not until I forced myself to study his eyes did I realize the fury with which he struggled. His eyes were an incredibly bright, burning blue, like frantic sapphires in his face.

Still, he never said one word.

I was so stunned, I couldn't even think. Every time my mind reached for a logical thought, anything to make sense of what had just happened, my brain couldn't follow it long enough to solve the riddle.

"This whole fucking thing was set up!" Knight suddenly erupted, angst and vitriol dripping from his voice.

At Knight's outburst, the Chimera yanked his chain, probably intending to silence him. Then, seemingly unbalanced on its hind goat legs, it aimed for the hallway, its dragon head still space-cadetting out, weaving this way and that. My attention gravitated back to Knight and I watched him as he narrowed his eyes at the Chimera. Then he tugged on the chain leading from his handcuffs. The Chimera lost its footing and tumbled over, heads, arms and legs all flailing about until you couldn't tell if it was one creature or three.

I watched as Knight held the chain in his hands, focusing intently on it. His face turned bright red as he did the unthinkable and snapped the chain with his bare hands. I felt the air constrict in my lungs while I watched his pure, brute strength. As a creature created by Hades, in Hades's own image, his strength was god-given and unsurpassable. That thought led to another one …

He'd been playing the court like a game all along; playing the part of the accused, at the mercy of the court of the Netherworld, when all along, his own immense strength could have set him free. He could have easily unleashed havoc on the courtroom; yet he restrained himself and played along simply to secure my safety. But even he had been surprised by this verdict, however, and its inappropriateness. And, really, the joke was on him in the end—and now it seemed the Netherworld would get the last laugh. That is, unless I intervened.

I swallowed hard as the imaginary flood gates burst open in my mind and thoughts of my next steps overwhelmed me. I knew what I had to do now; what I'd known all along. I was foolish to think it would ever have come to anything but this. At the moment, however, I remained wholly focused on Knight, waiting for my cue.

After freeing himself from the chains, he held his hands upright and pulled against the handcuffs. I watched as they strained under the intense pressure, eventually twisting with a snap and falling to the ground below, a pile of warped metal.

Knight took a deep breath and approached the judge who stared at him with a strange expression—not one of concern, but merely interest. He had the kind of curiosity of one detachedly watching an experiment.

"That fucking bastard has been looking for an excuse to polish me off all along," Knight railed, his eyes spewing venom at the judge.

And then, as far as I was concerned, the halcyon before the storm had suddenly been given the boot. Something welled up inside me—something volatile and passionate that could no longer be denied. I couldn't comprehend what Knight had just said; it was like I went into a purely emotional state and words and logic no longer held any relevance to me.

I was acting on pure instinct now.

"No!" I screamed out at the instant I stood up. I felt Bram's hand on my T-shirt as he tried to tug me back down but I swatted him away. I was on autopilot now, almost a spectator to my inner Dulcie taking over—that primitive person inside every one of us who only comes out in times of panic.

I started to move past Bram but he stood up and grasped my arms, his eyes begging me not to do what I'd begun, step two in his plan. A step that he never expected to come to fruition. But, now that I was aware of what was happening, I wasn't about to be silenced.

"Let go of me," I said in a steely voice.

"Dulcie," he started. "Please."

I swallowed hard and tried to free myself from his hands but he wouldn't release me. "Let go."

"You will not sacrifice yourself on my watch."

"That isn't your decision to make," I said, pulling my arms from his grasp. I didn't wait for him to change his mind; I merely leapt past him and tripped over his leg when he attempted to circumvent me. For once, my idiotic wings actually proved their worth because they began to beat outrageously fast, probably spurred on by my "fight or flight" adrenaline rush against a vampire. I easily hovered just out of his range and felt like I might float all the way to the top of the ceiling which would prove to be a big problem, in and of itself. I grabbed the first anchor I could, which happened to be the arm of a creature I'd never seen before.

It faced me in surprise, its huge mouth frowning to reveal three rows of shark-like teeth that were, in a word, sharp. Its massive under bite as well as its wide, flared nostrils, and red, glowing eyes, were enough for me to shrink back but I didn't release my hold on its leathery, upper arm.

"Sorry," I offered with a sheepish smile while I gestured to my wings. "I'm not used to these things."

It seemed to understand because it merely shrugged or maybe it was the fact that I was a fairy and, as such, a sexual delicacy because it allowed me to keep hold of its arm until my wings calmed down. Then I took a deep breath, thanked it with a heartfelt smile and faced the courtroom again.

"Knight didn't do this!" I yelled out as I moved forward, making sure my wings weren't going to start up again. I glanced back at them and found them sitting peacefully. From the looks of it, I was in the clear. Thank Hades.

The judge slammed his gavel down and scowled to let me know he wasn't impressed. "Order!"

"He is innocent!" I insisted as I made my way down the aisle, pausing only at the partition which separated the audience from the participants in the court proceedings.

"Dulcie?" It was Knight's voice. He sounded shocked and even betrayed. But I saw no betrayal in his eyes. No, the expression I found there was more like dread—probably at seeing me here.

One glance was all I could spare him. I wasn't strong enough for anything more. Not when I could see that he was furious I'd come—that he'd just realized his sentence would now most likely be transferred to me. Or, maybe I was completely wrong. Maybe he was actually relieved.

Either way, tears threatened to fall from my eyes and if there was one thing these sons of bitches wouldn't get from me, it was my tears. They could have my blood and sweat but tears were where I drew the line.

"Restrain that woman," the judge ordered to someone behind me. I looked back and saw a guard at the entrance of the courtroom. He was a shape-shifter who could become a lion. He had the intimidating appearance of someone you didn't want to mess with, very large and beefy. I wondered if he'd been standing there the whole time. I also happened to notice that Bram was nowhere to be seen. Great. So much for acting as my escort and guardian. He must've decided that I'd made my bed and now I had to sleep in it and probably saw no need to further ingratiate himself on my behalf.

The guard grabbed hold of both my arms but I had too many self-defense training sessions not to know how to get away from him. With a well-placed kick, I nailed him between the legs and watched him crumble to the ground, grabbing his crotch. With no time to waste, I catapulted myself over the barrier separating the court spectators from the rest of the courtroom.

"I'm Dulcie O'Neil, former ANC Regulator of Splendor, California," I said in a loud, breathless voice as I faced the judge. "It was my responsibility to apprehend …"

"Don't listen to her!" Knight interrupted loudly as he turned his panic-stricken eyes on me. "Don't listen to a word she says. She's … she's not telling you the truth."

When I looked at him, his eyes begged me not to continue, not to endanger myself but I was already involved, as in up to my thighs. I was also determined. And if there was one thing I knew about myself it was the fact that if Dulcie O'Neil decided to do something, there was nothing that would get in the way of her accomplishing her mission.

"It was my responsibility to take Quillan into custody and I allowed him to escape," I finished, alternating my attention from Knight to the judge.

"I'm not interested in the testament of some," the judge began, glancing at my wings with distaste, "fairy." When I saw him sigh wearily, it was pretty obvious this guy simply wanted to get the case wrapped up so he could get back to doing whatever it was that vampire judges did in their leisure time.

I narrowed my eyes and fished inside my pocket for my ANC ID which, against Bram's advice, I'd decided to bring with me anyway. Hey, you never knew when you might have to prove your identity to save your favorite Loki from an unjust sentence.

I held up my ID. "What about the testament of a former ANC Regulator, asshole?" I seethed.

I heard a slight laugh that sounded like approval from either Caressa or Ms. Fields-Gerrity.

"Bring it here," Judge Thorne said with little humor and even less patience.

"Dulcie, don't do this," Knight said but I refused to give him eye contact. I wasn't going to let him pay for my mistake.

I strode up to the podium and handed my ID to the judge. He inspected it for a few seconds, frowning all the while, and then faced Caressa. "It appears to be genuine."

"Take her into custody," Caressa said with tight lips. I turned to face her and nodded, holding my arms out for her to cuff me, letting her know I was ready and willing to go.

"Please, Caressa," Knight said with a rough voice, his eyes pleading. "Please leave her out of this."

Caressa swallowed hard and when she faced Knight, I saw compassion in her eyes. "I can't let you pay the ultimate price for something you didn't do, Knight."

"Caressa, damn it …" he started but I interrupted him.

"Knight, this is how it has to be," I said as I forced my eyes up to his at the same time that Caressa snapped one handcuff onto my wrist.

"You have no idea what you're doing, Dulcie," he said, shaking his head and clenching his hands into fists at his side. Then he faced Caressa again. "They want me, Caressa. You know that as well as I do. There's no reason to sacrifice Dulcie."

Caressa inhaled deeply and paused in her task of cuffing me. She swallowed and then brought the second handcuff to my un-cuffed wrist and secured it. She avoided even looking at Knight. "I'm sorry," she muttered but I wasn't sure who she said it to, Knight or me.

"Who are they?" I demanded but neither of them would so much as even acknowledge me.

Instead, Caressa pushed me forward, toward the hallway of the holding cells.

"Caressa, please," Knight repeated.

"It's too late, Mr. Vander," the judge spewed back at him as he approached Knight, grabbing his arm. "It's too late for her and it's also too late for you."

I had no time to consider the judge's words because before I knew it, Caressa was leading me down the hallway and into my holding cell. She unlocked the cell, which was empty, and escorted me into it.

"If you need anything," she started, facing me with kind eyes, "please don't hesitate to let Alexandra know." Then she turned to Ms. Fields-Gerrity who was just behind her. "I'm leaving Alex here to ensure you and Knight are treated well."

I nodded and offered her a small smile. "Thank you."

"I don't know what your relationship is with Knight," Caressa started but was interrupted when we both turned around to see the judge push Knight, none-too-gently, into the only other cell, which happened to be right across from mine. "But he must really care about you," she finished.

I nodded but said nothing, as I watched her step outside my cell and lock it. Then she walked over to Knight and stood with her back to me. "You will both be transported to High Prison within the hour, I imagine."

He nodded as he sat on the cot, sighing. "Don't let the same thing that happened to me happen to her."

"I will push for a quick hearing for her," she started and then added. "And I'm going to do my best to ensure your release."

Knight chuckled but it was a sound drenched in acid and sarcasm. "Caressa, you know I'm not getting out of this. He has me right where he wants me."

"Knight …"

"I just don't want her to suffer for … her connection to me."

Caressa's shoulders sagged. "I will do my best."

Then she turned around, offering me an apologetic and hurried smile and motioned to Alexandra, before they both stepped outside. That was when I understood she'd done so on purpose—to allow Knight and me a cherished moment of privacy, perhaps the last one we would ever get.

"Knight, what were you talking about earlier? Who has you right where he wants you and why do you think this was planned all along? Who are they?" I demanded, my voice rising with alarm.

Knight shook his head. "It's too long and complicated to explain and I don't know how much time we have before they cart us back." He stood up and took the few steps separating him from the cell bars. Grabbing them, he wrapped his hands around the bars and sighed. "Why did you do this? Why couldn't you have left damn well alone?"

I shook my head. "I could never let you die for me, Knight."

He smiled and I felt something break inside me as the tears that threatened to fall for the last hour suddenly filled up my eyes and began pouring down my cheeks.

161

"Don't cry, Dulce, please. I … I'll get you out of this somehow."

I shook my head. "I'm not crying for myself," I muttered, wiping my eyes on the cuff of my shirt. "I'm just so sorry I involved you in this mess."

"Dulcie, it was my decision and I don't regret it for a minute. I only wish you could've left things alone. But, shit, that's who you are, isn't it?" He chuckled and I felt a smile bursting through the cloud of my tears.

"They aren't going to release you, are they?" I asked, the small smile fading right off my mouth again.

He shook his head. "No. They'll find something to find me guilty of and that will be that."

"I'm so sorry, Knight."

"None of that matters at the moment, Dulce. What does matter is that you stay alert at all times while you're in High Prison. I hope to Hades they put us in the same cell but if not, remember that you are a fairy and, in this world, you're in high demand."

"I know," I grumbled. "Bram warned me as much."

"Bram?" Knight repeated, shocked. "Is he here?"

"He came with me but who knows where he is now? If he's smart, he's on his way back home."

He nodded and then took a deep breath. "Then you know what to expect?"

"Yeah, I've been schooled in that lesson."

"And you know your magic won't work here?"

I nodded. "Yes."

"You have to rely on your ANC training, Dulce, purely self-defense." He glanced away for a second or two and then brought his gaze back to mine. "And whatever happens, I want you to know that I …"

But he never had the chance to finish his sentence because Alexandra appeared in the hallway with Caressa just behind her. "We are moving you now," Alexandra said in a small voice as she offered Knight an apologetic frown.

The High Prison was nothing like what I'd imagined, given my experience with prisons in Splendor. This was more along the lines of something from a horror movie.

As Caressa led me through the double-bolted high security door, a prison guard who happened to be a goblin, the genus of which I wasn't certain, met us on the other side. He nodded to Caressa and then eyed me, his gaze raking me from head to toe before he smiled, revealing discolored, broken teeth. I swallowed hard and, assuming this bastard was going to give me trouble, narrowed my eyes and shot him the look of death. He averted his eyes and set to securing the door behind us. The sounds of the bolts locking reverberated through my head and I don't imagine I will ever forget it. Then the goblin turned his warthog-like face in my direction, where he sniffed around me a few times and grinned broadly.

"She is off limits," Caressa said sternly. Her distaste was evident as she glared at the hideous creature that towered over us both. Even though it was well over six feet, it was hunched over and bore a huge growth on its back. It narrowed its eyes at the reprimand but remained quiet. "Did you hear what I said?" she demanded.

The guard nodded dumbly but still said nothing.

"She is to be in a cell with no other creatures. Do you understand?"

"Aye," the creature said finally with a strange sort of accent. Its breath filled my nostrils with the putrid odor of rotting flesh and I thought I might lose the contents of my stomach right there.

Caressa faced me and smiled awkwardly. "I will try to rush your hearing," she said, as if preparing me for a very unpleasant stay.

"Thanks," I answered, although I wasn't really sure why I was thanking her. The guard grabbed my arm none-too-gently and jostled me forward, toward the dark hallway. I took one last glance at Caressa, who was just watching us, the worry visible in her pretty features. "Please do what you can for Knight," I called out.

"I will," she replied.

I took a deep breath and pulled my arm from the guard's vice-like grip. "You don't need to drag me," I muttered.

The goblin remained silent as he continued limping beside me. We walked down a long, dank hallway that smelled of urine. There were a few uncovered lightbulbs that buzzed and flashed as he escorted me through what felt like a maze of winding hallways. On either side of us were walls that appeared to be made of plywood, painted grey. There were splotches of mildew and what looked like dried blood all over the cement floor.

We hit another door and the guard pulled out an O-ring, containing about four skeleton keys. He selected the third from the right and unlocked the door before giving me a healthy shove through it.

"Where is Knightley Vander?" I demanded as soon as I stepped across the threshold and saw the cells on either side of me packed with creatures. Some were crying, others were laughing maniacally, while some screamed out in anger, and others begged for food. I refused to look at any of them, keeping my gaze fixed directly in front me, on the wall at the far end of the room.

"Don't know 'em," the goblin responded, giving me a push, the cue to start walking. I did.

So that meant that Knight either wasn't here yet or else this wasn't the only High Prison? I was somewhat surprised to find the male inmates hadn't been separated from females. Instead, all the inmates were lumped together in this hell-hole.

164

"Is this the only prison here?" I demanded, turning to face the goblin who lurked behind me as he grinned at my ass.

"Aye," he answered and I felt relief. Knight probably just hadn't arrived yet. Maybe it was only a matter of minutes before I'd join my Loki again. The one thing I hoped for was that he and I would share a cell. I never felt as if I needed Knight's company more than I needed it now. Badly.

"A fairy!" someone shouted.

All the creatures suddenly piled against the prison bars and began screaming profanities at me. I felt my skin crawl.

Just focus on that wall in front of you, Dulcie, I coached myself.

"This is you," the goblin said as he paused in front of a cell that was next to last, on the right. He pulled out his key ring and fumbled for the correct key. I peered at the cell and noticed the toilet came complete with a yellowish looking ring inside the basin and a small, mildewy sink. The cot appeared to have once been white, but now was a cross between dingy grey and crap brown. Either way, it might as well have been broadcasting: "Lie here and you'll die here."

The goblin opened the cell door and gave me another hearty shove. "Make yerself comfy," he said with a smile that looked more like a grimace. "Yer gonna be here a while so ya might wanna werk the kinks outta dat bed, if ya know what I mean. I can help ya wif it." Then he laughed like he considered himself a regular comedian.

I shook my head and frowned but said nothing. Then I appraised my new digs, trying to figure out where to sit. The cot was out of the question but the floor looked equally disgusting. After observing a cockroach scuttling across the ground just in front of my shoes, I decided to remain standing.

TWELVE

"Don't touch me, you son of a bitch."

It was Knight's voice.

I looked up from my huddled position in the corner of my cell where I'd finally collapsed in exhaustion after standing for hours on end. My knees were drawn into my chest and my head was resting on my knees while I tried to figure out what the hell I was going to do. It had been three hours since I was first introduced to my Spartan accommodations, three hours of not knowing where the hell Knight was and three hours during which I could only imagine the worst. My ultimate nightmare had been that his punishment had already been carried out; that he was … dead.

"Knight!" I called out and gazed up at him, feeling pins and needles in my wobbly legs as I willed myself upright. My wings came to my aid again by letting me hover until the circulation returned. I rushed to the bars of my cell as I watched another guard, different from the goblin, thrust Knight into the cage opposite mine.

The creature who had occupied the cell prior to Knight's entry melted back into the wall and huddled there, as if trying to hide in the shadows. Seeing it skulk away as soon as it saw the second guard alerted me that this guard probably wasn't going to be the most merciful or lenient. The goblin guard didn't worry me. As I did a double-take on the creature again, I couldn't decide what it was. It was smallish—maybe my size, bald as a billiard and albino white. It sort of reminded me of a hairless cat. At any rate, owing to the fact that the guard obviously intimidated it, I figured it posed no threat to Knight. I hoped so anyway.

As soon as the guard released him, Knight immediately rushed the cell door but the guard, who I realized was a Cyclops as soon as I got a view of the eye in the center of his head, slammed it shut and locked it before Knight could overpower him. His snide smile oozed of pride and self-importance at the fact that he'd overpowered a Loki.

When I looked at Knight, I felt my heart swell just to know he was still alive. Sadly, it appeared that he'd been roughed up again. His inmate uniform was ripped and stained with drops of blood, his hair tousled and another shiner darkened his right eye. But he was alive and, at that moment, that was all that mattered.

"Knight," I said again, my voice softer.

He glanced over at me and smiled, his lower lip split and swollen. Those assholes …

I watched the Cyclops take out his baton and shove it through the cell bars just to get a rise out of the occupants in the chamber adjacent to Knight's. For one moment, I wanted nothing more than to wrest the baton from him and crack him over the head with it … hard … and repeatedly.

"You're here," Knight said, drawing my attention back to him. I could see relief in his face—but it only lasted a few seconds before it was replaced with angst, probably at the reality of my being here. Since "here" wasn't exactly the ideal place to be.

The Cyclops, suspiciously concerned as to whom Knight was talking to, turned his massive, hulking body around and faced me with his one eye. He scowled at me before he recognized exactly what I was. Then the scowl ran away and a filthy smile, complete with missing teeth, replaced it. It was a smile that said exactly what he wanted to do to me ... Yep, this one might cause me problems.

167

"Ah, we gotta fairy, 'ave we?"

Before I could say "F yourself," the goblin guard blocked him and shook his head in a mock apology. "Can't tetch 'er," it said as it sneered in my direction. "Orders from above."

The Cyclops stepped closer to my cell and I backed away, feeling suddenly nervous under his intense stare. It's funny how a monster with one eye is so much more disarming than one with two. And as much as I hated the goblin, I secretly wished he was the only guard on duty—at least he knew his place. This Cyclops was a lawless wild card. But then, most Cyclops usually are …

I'd only ever seen a Cyclops once before and this one was nothing like it—aside from the one eye bit. This guy was huge, probably over seven foot five and was incredibly fat. But it wasn't a pudgy, weak sort of fatness. You could see the muscle beneath his rolls—he was fat, yes, but he was built like a tank—like a Sumo wrestler. He appeared to be relatively young—maybe in his early twenties but he had already lost most of the hair on his head. Only a few strands delineated where his hairline once existed. His face was broad and ugly with a pointy nose, thin lips and missing teeth, as mentioned earlier. But, without doubt, his deeply sunken, round eye that occupied the center of his forehead seemed to demand all my attention. It was just so … weird.

"I ain't never seen a fairy befer," the Cyclops said as he licked his chops like he was about to sit down to Thanksgiving dinner.

"You stay the hell away from her," Knight said in a cold, calculating voice.

The Cyclops glanced at him sideways and laughed. "What're ya gonna do 'bout it, pretty boy?"

"Yer gonna git in serious trouble, Clyde, if ya tetch her," the goblin said. He shook his head to emphasize how steadfast he was in his decision to avoid the wrath from his higher-ups. I was beginning to like him even more. Well, I was beginning to tolerate him even more, I should say.

Clyde, the Cyclops, nodded but made no motion to retreat from my cell. Instead, he continued staring at me with that round, unblinking eye. Then he finally closed it and inhaled deeply. "She smells so good."

"Dulcie, back away from the bars," Knight said in an angry voice. "Get as far away as you can."

I didn't argue and did as he instructed, retiring to the far corner of my cell. The Cyclops, now no longer enchanted with the intoxication of my smell, I suppose, opened his eye and seemed back in control of his faculties … whatever faculties he possessed, anyway. What was boldly apparent to me was this guy didn't have a whole lot going on upstairs. He was primitive and impulsive and those two adjectives were going to make my stay here a very difficult one. I felt sure this monster had no moral compass to discourage him from whatever he had in store for me.

"We should git outta here," the goblin said as he reached for his friend. The Cyclops said nothing but backed away, still gawking at me with absolute lust pasted on his face. I was preparing for him to attack me, feeling sure it was going to happen all along. When he suddenly turned tail and followed the goblin back up the hallway, I was not only surprised, but more like shocked. They disappeared from view and I heard the sound of the heavy door opening, followed by the sound of deadbolts. I sighed in relief, grateful I was finally alone with Knight, well, as alone as we could be, considering we were surrounded by inmates.

"Where have you been?" I asked, grimacing again at his fat lip and the new shiner to match the one on the other eye.

"Detained for questioning, you could say," Knight grumbled as he shook his head. Then he looked directly at me. "Are you okay, Dulce? Did those bastards hurt you?"

I swallowed hard, still reeling from the fact that these assholes were treating him with such disrespect. I could feel my hands fisting around the prison bars of my cell as anger roiled within me.

"Dulcie?" Knight repeated, snapping me out of my own thoughts since I hadn't responded to his question.

"Yeah, I'm fine," I said, my voice belying my anger.

"Good," Knight said, heaving a sigh of relief before looking back at me and frowning. "I hate seeing you in here."

"Ditto." I took a deep breath and tried to organize my thoughts because I had so many questions for him, I didn't know where to start. "Knight, I need you to tell me what's going on," I managed. "You told Caressa and the judge that there are people above that have it out for you or was it just one person above you? What did you mean?"

Knight nodded, as if he, too, realized the need to get me up to speed and hopefully, now would be the best opportunity. I mean, it seemed like we had nothing but time. 'Course, how much time was anyone's guess. Somewhere in the back of my head, the thought that Knight was living on borrowed time suddenly emerged. His sentence had been ordered and I could only imagine it could be carried out any moment. That thought absolutely terrified me.

"I can't tell you too much, Dulcie, or I'd be putting you in danger."

"So tell me what you can," I prodded, wondering how deeply involved he was.

"Remember how I told you Lokis have always been stuck in the Netherworld?"

I nodded, remembering the conversation well. "Yeah."

"Well, there's a reason I wasn't. I was basically transferred to Splendor because I caused trouble for the Head of the Netherworld."

"The Head of the Netherworld?" I repeated, sounding completely lost. "I didn't even know there was a Head of the Netherworld."

Knight glanced around himself, as if to find a place to sit but apparently noticing the stained cot, he just shrugged and remained standing. As he returned his attention back to me, he seemed to finally notice the creature cowering in the corner of the cell. There was a look of surprise on his face. "I didn't realize I was sharing a cell."

The creature nodded a greeting and then swallowed hard, not appearing to have grown any sense of confidence over the last ten minutes or so. Knight smiled warmly and then faced me again. "The organization here is set up like a hierarchy and the government is more along the lines of a dictatorship. The Head of the Netherworld is at the top of the hierarchy and what he says goes."

I nodded, allowing this information to sink in. "So you upset the supreme chief then?"

Knight nodded. "Yes, so I was banished to Earth … the first Loki ever to make the trip. It suited me fine because I wanted out of here and the Netherworld gained what it wanted; to get rid of me."

"But why did the Netherworld, or more specifically, the Head of the Netherworld, want to get rid of you in the first place?"

He shook his head and sighed like it was too long and complicated to explain. "I can't get into the specifics, Dulce. Let's just say I upset the apple cart and rather than turning it into a big legal situation, they found it easier to relocate me. They laid me off here and got me a position in Splendor. And, of course, I complied with no questions asked."

"But now that you're back here?"

He swallowed and looked away, shaking his head. "I swore I'd never return—it was one of their stipulations for my transference."

I felt my heart sink. It was my fault that he'd come back here and broken his promise to never return. Now, because he'd breached the contract, the Head of the Netherworld had ordered his death. It was just so unfair. Then something occurred to me—Knight hadn't willingly returned here at all. "But I don't understand … Didn't the ANC come for you?" I started, remembering Trey's vision of the two ANC-uniformed employees who took Knight away. "It's not like you returned voluntarily!"

Knight nodded and then sighed. "Yes, they did. I'm convinced that this whole subject of calling me to the High Court for questioning regarding Quillan's escape was just a cover. The big man upstairs knew he could get rid of me forever without having to do it under the table so he jumped at the opportunity."

"And you played right into their hands by saying it was you who released Quillan instead of me …"

"Yep, I guess I did." He was quiet for a second or two and focused his attention on his hands which were wrapped around the cell bars. Then he glanced up at me again. "Don't think I regret it, Dulcie. I have no remorse for my decision, none."

I shook my head. "I don't understand you." Then I felt the sting of tears in my eyes again. "You risked your life for me."

He nodded. "I know," he smiled. "And you did exactly the same for me."

I smiled as I thought about it. "Guess we're just two love-sick idiots." I felt my eyes widen as I heard the words leave my lips. I hadn't even considered the fact that maybe I was in love with Knight. As soon as the thought crossed my mind, though, it became pretty perfectly clear. I mean, I wouldn't just risk my life for anyone.

"It's okay, Dulce," Knight said with a laugh but he still sounded depressed, probably due to the situation.

"Why … why does the Head of the Netherworld want you … out of the way?" I asked quickly, suddenly aware that I had basically just admitted my love for Knight in a prison cell complete with goblins, shape-shifters, Cyclops and cockroaches to share my joyful moment.

Knight nodded as if he understood and agreed with me—now was not the time to discuss our feelings. "I knew too much."

"And you can't tell me what that 'too much' was, can you?"

"Nope," he finished, sighing deeply. "It amounts to the fact that someone up there is threatened by my being alive." He glanced at his shoes and shook his head. "So now they've trumped up some ridiculous case and they're having the last laugh."

"Regardless of what happens to me? Regardless if I prove it was my fault all along?" I couldn't finish my statement because it did nothing but depress me. My self-sacrifice couldn't save Knight. I'd simply managed to damn us both.

He shook his head. "It makes no difference, Dulcie. They aren't going to let me go." He paused for a few seconds. "Now I'm worried about what that means for you."

I slammed my fist into the bars of my prison cell and stifled the mute frustration pounding through me. "There has to be someone who will understand, someone who will hear us out?"

Knight shook his head again, this time sighing. "Caressa is the only honest person in this whole system; but her hands are tied. She has to take orders from the Head of the Netherworld and he's as crooked as they come. He's also at the top of the so-called ladder. There's nothing she can do."

"Knight, please tell me …" I started, wanting, no, needing to know what this was all about. What was going on that was so bad that the Head of the Netherworld wanted Knight to pay the ultimate price?

Knight's eyes were hard and his lips were tight. "That's all I can say, Dulcie. My only hope now is to make sure you leave here safely and the less you know, the better off you are."

"But you," I interjected.

"I'm a walking dead man."

"Don't say that," I said in a hysterical voice, feeling a lump form in my throat. I shook my head, trying to force the tears to subside. "Don't ever say that again." But I knew the truth just as well as he did.

He smiled down at me. "Have I ever told you how much I admire you, Dulcie? How I've never met another woman like you?"

I returned the smile and felt tears starting in my eyes again but I didn't say anything, afraid my voice would crack. I was spared the need to respond though, when the goblin guard suddenly appeared carrying a tray with a few pieces of bread, some slices of cheese and a cup of water. The Cyclops came up behind him and stepped out to unlock my cell. Before doing so, he glanced at me with the same expression of hunger I'd witnessed before.

"No funny stuff when I unlock the cell," he said in a deep and dumb-sounding voice. "I ain't in a mood ta deal wif it."

"Bread and water, seriously?" I asked, shaking my head and crossing my arms against my chest. I was suddenly incredibly angry—as if the bread and water on the tray was the last straw in this horrible mess. "Don't bother. I'm not hungry."

The Cyclops faced the goblin and frowned. "Bitchy, ain't she?"

The goblin frowned. "Yeah, she got attitude."

The Cyclops faced me again and smiled a gap-toothed, ugly grin as he opened my cell door. Before the goblin could step in, the Cyclops circumvented him. "I think she needs ta be shown ah lesson."

"You keep the hell away from me," I said, my voice harsh as acid. I started to back up, toward the rear of my cell.

"Don't touch her," Knight yelled from across the way.

"You shut up," the Cyclops said, turning to face him. "Unless ya want me ta cum in there an' rough ya up again."

"Come in here anytime, asshole," Knight seethed. "But touch her and I will kill you."

The Cyclops laughed an ugly sound and glanced back at Knight again. "How ya gonna kill me when yer in there, stupid?"

"It ain't ah good idea, Clyde," the goblin said and, realizing his friend wasn't convinced, bent down to put the tray of food on the ground. Once he stood up again, he acted like he was going to come into my cell with the Cyclops but hesitated, revealing his fear of the other guard.

"Who's gonna find out?" the Cyclops asked, turning to face the goblin. "Yer so afraid o' that idiot woman Brandenburg an' she ain't gonna do shit."

"Don't do it, Clyde," the goblin warned again. "I need this job an' you do too."

Clyde waved him away like a fly and faced me again, his ugly smile back, wide and appalling. "When do we ever git a fairy in here ta play wif? Huh?"

"Never," the goblin answered as he held onto my cell bars and watched me, sniffing the air like he was trying to catch my smell.

"Stay the hell away from me," I warned again, aware of exactly how weighty my warning was, considering I had no magic to back me up. Clyde was so big, he could basically break me in half.

"C'mere little fairy; big daddy gonna teach ya how ta play," he said. He kept approaching as I continued to retreat. Pretty soon I felt the rough texture of the wall against my back. I was pinned. Great.

"I ain't gonna be rough unless ya fight me, girly," he said as he reached for my face. He ran a dirty index finger across my cheek, trailing it down my neck and ending at my breast. He paused and then palmed my breast and squeezed.

I could feel my heartbeat pounding through my body as I tried to calm myself, in order to figure out the best way out of this. "It's not worth it."

"You are going against orders from Headquarters," Knight yelled, his tone frenzied.

The Cyclops turned to Knight and that's when I pushed myself forward, easily squeezing past him and running hell-bent for the cell door, where the goblin faced Knight. All I had to do was push the goblin off balance and make my escape. 'Course, how far I could get was a good question, considering both guards still held the keys to the main door.

It turned out that I never even needed to plan that far ahead because I forgot about the little things on my back called wings. That is, until the Cyclops grabbed hold of one and yanked. I'm sure the feeling of intense agony was due to the fact that he'd just ripped my wing either right off me or in half. I shrieked as the pain hit me and then, before I could comprehend it, I felt myself being thrown against the cell wall, where the cold, lead bars met me straight in the forehead.

"Dulcie!" I heard Knight scream but everything went black for a second or two as I felt myself falling. Something cold smacked my cheek but I couldn't bring myself to open my eyes. It was like they were glued shut.

"Bitch!" When I opened my eyes, the Cyclops was on top of me, his fist right in my face. I closed my eyes, savoring the darkness as I felt my lip split and the warmth of my blood dripping down my cheek and pooling in my ear. I couldn't say I felt pain, though. Instead it was like I was in a dream state, seeing the black of night, complete with stars and then opening my eyes again to find the prison cell around me.

"You like it rough, huh?" I glanced up at the ugly face above me and felt like I wanted to cry or throw up as cold, hard reality began to set in. The stars of delirium started to fade away, and I with them. Then it dawned on me that I had to have hit my head hard against the prison bars.

I pushed against the Cyclops, deciding right then and there that I was going to defend myself. I wasn't going to make this easy for him. But it felt like trying to push a wall. He laughed in my face, the sour smell of his breath lodging in my nostrils until I thought I'd be sick for sure.

"Get the fuck off her!" Knight screamed. The Cyclops glanced up at him and with a dirty smile, grabbed hold of my T-shirt and pulled, ripping it in half. He tore it off me, until I was clad in only my bra and jeans.

I pulled my arm back and landed a good punch right across his cheek, momentarily stunning him. I flipped myself to my hands and knees and started to get up when I felt his immense weight throwing me to the ground again. I hit the cement hard and felt the air forcibly expelled from my lungs.

As I was trying to catch my breath, the bastard was on me again, this time tearing at my jeans, trying to pull them off and down my hips. I attempted to pull myself out of his grasp but since I couldn't breathe, the situation was basically hopeless.

"Leave me alone!" I screamed again, ready to claw my way from him when the vision of black dress shoes before me suddenly took me by surprise. Before I knew what to think, I felt the Cyclops's body torn from me and the sound of crashing—of something big hitting the wall.

"You do not force yourself on a lady!"

I would have known that upper class English accent anywhere.

Bram.

"Bram?" I repeated in shock, wondering if I was dreaming all this or if Bram really had pulled a total

177

Spiderman move. I took a deep breath and crawled to the far side of my cell, forcing my head up so I could watch Bram pin the Cyclops against the wall, his hand wrapped around the much beefier man's neck. What looked like glitter covered the floor but it wasn't glitter. I knew better—it was fairy dust. I glanced over my shoulder to see my wing lying limply against my shoulder, torn and ragged.

"Where is that bastard goblin?" Bram asked, turning to face me with fangs.

I figured he meant the goblin guard and I looked around, finding him slouched in the corner of my cell, as if trying to remain unnoticed.

"Assist her, you fool," Bram seethed to the guard. The guard immediately stood up and approached me, pulling me into his arms as I fought to keep myself from throwing up. I had to have a concussion from the lead bars to the head injury.

Bram stepped away from the Cyclops, allowing the bigger man to fall against the floor with a thud. Then he smoothed his shirt, brushed off his pants and turned to me with a big grin.

"Dulcie, sweet, I would say I was just … in the nick of time?"

THIRTEEN

"**I**'d say you came in the nick of time," I repeated to Bram, suddenly feeling light-headed again as I tried to break away from the goblin. I couldn't wait to get away from him; he smelled like BO and Swiss cheese. Bram immediately appeared beside me and I collapsed into his outstretched arms, wanting nothing more than to inhale his clean, spicy scent, hoping to banish the memory of the goblin's odor.

"What did that bastard do to her?" I heard Knight's voice, which was still frantic. "Dulcie, are you okay? Talk to me."

"I think so," I said in a small voice, just as a headache started behind my eyes and I momentarily saw stars again.

Bram held me close to his chest but I could tell his attention wasn't on me. I opened one eye and saw him staring at the Cyclops with stiff composure.

"You will never touch her again," Bram said in a tone that promised retribution just by its iciness. "I will conduct a strict surveillance over her and if I learn that you so much as touched a strand of her hair, you will suffer the consequences."

I wasn't sure how Bram intended to "conduct a strict surveillance" over me but my head hurt too much to think about it any further. The Cyclops said nothing but gritted his teeth and grunted, heaving himself up from the floor before fleeing my cell and elbowing past the goblin guard. I had to admit I was impressed with Bram. Even though he was a vampire and thus, one of the highest orders of creatures, and among the strongest, the way the Cyclops and the goblin responded to him … it was as if they thought he was some high-ranking official. And, for all I knew, maybe he was (I mean, he did have a private portal from Splendor to the Netherworld … Now, more than ever before, I was wondering why.)

"You," Bram said to the goblin. "Wait just one moment."

The goblin stopped walking and slowly turned around, his eyes filled with dread, as if he were wondering why he had to be detained when he hadn't even attacked me. I was wondering the same thing.

"Yes … sir?" he asked, wincing.

I glanced up at Bram in surprise. "Sir?" Why did Bram always seem to have a wild card up his sleeve?

Bram ignored me and focused instead on the goblin. "I want you to be my eyes where Dulcie is concerned, do you understand?" Bram asked, his pupils narrowed, warning the stupid idiot not to even think of arguing with him. "You will report back to me by phone every hour."

The goblin took a deep breath as he apparently weighed the subject in his pea-sized brain. It took him a few seconds before he reached the conclusion that it wasn't a good idea to irritate an already aggravated vampire. "Yessir, Mr. …"

"My name is unimportant," Bram interjected. It seemed he'd interrupted the goblin on purpose, as if he hadn't wanted the goblin to utter his last name … It was strange, to say the least.

"Yessir, I'll be yer eyes." It was at that moment that I realized the goblin knew Bram. He'd known Bram as soon as he'd walked into the prison. I wasn't sure if the Cyclops also recognized him but I was sure the goblin definitely had. And now, I found myself wondering, why? How would the goblin know him? And, for that matter, did Bram know the goblin? What was Bram holding back from me? What wasn't he telling me?

"I want her in my cell," Knight piped up from behind us, apparently close enough that he could hear our conversation. "She won't be safe unless she's with me."

"Yes," I said immediately, thinking that was the best idea I'd heard all day. Not to mention the fact that I wanted to lose myself in Knight's arms, to try and ignore the horrible reality around us. I just wanted to touch him, be close to him, tell him how sorry I was for causing him to be in this mess to begin with. I glanced up at Bram and noticed he was scrutinizing Knight and it was pretty obvious he didn't like the idea one bit.

"We ain't supposed ta house her with any other creatures," the goblin said, now playing stickler for the rules.

"Knight isn't going to attack me, you idiot," I said gruffly, the pain inside my head throbbing. I closed my eyes and inhaled deeply, wondering if I was going to pass out again.

"Yeah, but he ain't got much more time here," the goblin pointed out in a heated tone.

I felt my stomach drop as my eyes flashed open. "What did you say?" I demanded, feeling the pounding of my headache increasing with the news.

"His execution is set fer two days from now," the goblin answered like he was talking about the weather, not Knight's life. "So what ya gonna do once he's gone, huh?"

I felt bile rising up into my throat and thought I was going to vomit right there. I held my face up to the ceiling, hoping gravity might keep the contents of my stomach in my stomach.

Two days from now?! Two days ...

"I am very sorry to hear this news," Bram said and the tone of his voice also sounded dejected. I glanced up at him to ascertain if he really was sorry and, amazingly enough, he appeared sincere.

181

"Not as sorry as I am," Knight said with an attempt at levity but resulting as exhaustion.

"We're going to find a way out of this, Knight," I said as I looked up at him, hating the expression of futility in his eyes. "We will find a way." I choked on the words, feeling tears beginning to flood my eyes.

Calm down, Dulcie, and just think. I told myself. *There has got to be a way to delay Knight's sentence, a way to get him out of this.*

"When is my hearing scheduled?" I demanded, thinking I needed to get the facts of my involvement out in the open immediately. That way, maybe I could at least stave off Knight's execution. I just needed time!

"I ain't heard nothin' 'bout no hearing fer you," the goblin said with indifference.

"I will inquire with the powers that be," Bram said and smiled down at me kindly as I wondered what role he played in the Netherworld. There was no use in asking that he admit it now, though, not with the goblin and Knight in attendance. I mean, it was unlikely that he'd confess anything to me.

"Either way, I want her with me for the time being," Knight interrupted, facing the goblin again, his hands wrapped around the cell bars.

"You ain't the only one in yer cell," the goblin said as he shrugged. "Ms. Brandenburg gave me directions ta not put the fairy wif any other creatures an' I sho as hell ain't gonna git that woman on ma case."

"Move him to her cell," Bram said, in an exasperated tone. He had apparently come to terms with the fact that Knight was right—I would be safest with him. Especially since Bram couldn't guard me here twenty-four/seven, or could he?

The goblin nodded and pulled at the O-ring on his belt, finding the key to Knight's cell before opening the door. He grabbed Knight's hand and threatened him with an expression that said: *no funny stuff.* Knight frowned and

shook off the goblin's hold, leading himself into my cell.
The goblin came up behind him and locked the cell door
behind all three of us.

He glanced at Bram and cleared his throat. "Just lemme
know when ya want out."

Bram nodded and faced me again while Knight
motioned for Bram to release me. "I can take her from here,"
he said.

But Bram didn't release me. Instead, he glanced down
and seemed to study me. "She is injured."

"Dulcie?" Knight asked softly, looking at me with
worried concern in his beautiful blue eyes. "Your forehead
…"

Yep, I must have had a pretty bad bruise or maybe the
skin was broken where the Cyclops had forced me to get up
close and personal with the prison bars. "I think it's a
concussion," I said, seeing the stars start to spin around me
again.

"That fucking bastard," Knight spat out but before he
could complete his sentence, Bram interrupted.

"She must drink from me."

"What?" I demanded, the idea of drinking Bram's
blood right up there with cutting off my own leg.

I didn't hear anything from Knight and looked up at
him with inquiring eyes. He merely nodded at the idea,
studying me in a detached sort of way, as if analyzing how
badly I was hurt.

"You need your strength, Dulce," he said finally. "He's
right."

"Can't you heal me?" I asked him, remembering the
time when I'd nearly died after fighting the Kragengen
shifter and Knight healed me. And the best part about Knight
healing me was it didn't involve swallowing any blood.

"Not here," he said resolutely. And by "here," I had to
imagine he meant in the Netherworld. So, in the same way
that my magic wouldn't work in this godforsaken place,

apparently neither did his Loki abilities, or, at least, that particular one.

"Trust me, Dulcie," Bram whispered. "You will not need to swallow much."

Before I could respond, he simply bent down, opened his mouth to reveal his now extended fangs, pushed his wrist into his mouth and bit. When he pulled away, there was blood trailing down his wrist and mouth, the color and consistency of Welch's grape juice.

For the second or third time this evening, I felt like I wanted to be sick. I chanced a quick glance at Knight and noticed his jaw was tight and his eyes were piercing. He didn't like this one bit.

Bram forced his wrist into my face and I closed my eyes, realizing I'd have to do this quickly because his wound was going to heal within a matter of seconds. I opened my mouth and felt Bram lift his wrist and push it to my lips. I started to suck, feeling the warm, metallic taste of blood filling my mouth. My throat seemed to clench tightly shut and before I knew it, I was gagging.

"Swallow," Bram commanded in a voice that warned me not to disappoint him. I'm sure he wasn't exactly thrilled to be sharing his blood and even less thrilled by the fact that I was so grossed out by it. My body was basically staging a mutiny.

But I finally managed to go to my happy place and forced my throat to relax. I swallowed a good two mouthfuls of Bram's blood. He pulled his wrist away and I opened my eyes, watching the redness of his torn skin begin to knit back to tan again as his body healed itself. I brushed my arm against my mouth, wiping away any residual reminders of what I'd just done.

"I don't feel any different," I said, suddenly wondering if that episode had just been a huge waste of time. What if Bram's blood didn't act like it did on Earth? Maybe it was just as impotent as Knight's abilities and my magic? If that

184

were the case, then I was nothing but pissed off. My head was still aching, I was stuck in the most miserable prison I'd ever seen and the one man who had stolen my heart had been sentenced to die …

"Give it a moment," Bram said, smiling down at me. "Your bruise is already fading, sweet."

I felt surprise fluttering about inside of me and was about to comment on as much when I suddenly felt like my stomach was turning in on itself. I lurched over, grabbing my middle as pangs of agony doubled me over. It was like being stabbed in the gut with a pitchfork repeatedly. My insides were suddenly caught in a whirlwind, smashing against one another.

"Dulcie?" It was Knight but I couldn't look at him or even respond. "Bram, what the hell did you do to her?"

I keeled over and felt myself fall forward. Knight caught me and I bumped against his broad chest, wishing I could feel comforted by his embrace. Instead, the fire inside me continued to burn.

"She will heal," Bram said matter-of-factly. "Her body is trying to reject my blood but it will last only moments."

Even as he spoke, I could feel the pain subsiding and something akin to numbness began to set in. I found I could breathe again, shallow at first and then deeper, little by little. When I tried to stand up straight, there was a slight twinge of the previous agony that had been tearing through me but it was mild enough to where I could suffer through it.

"You could have warned me, for fuck's sake," I muttered, glaring up at Bram as I took a deep breath and forced myself to stand up straight.

"It is always better not to warn someone of impending suffering," Bram responded and there was a lilt to his voice, like he thought this whole thing was slightly amusing.

"Are you alright, Dulce?" Knight asked as he rubbed my back and gazed down at me with concerned eyes.

I thought about the question—was I alright? The pain was now entirely absent, replaced by … intense strength, strangely enough. I felt reenergized. The dizziness and stars were like a distant memory. Now I felt as if I could run a twelve kilometer marathon. And that had to mean one thing—Bram was right. "Yeah, it worked."

"Good, because we have more important matters to speak of," Bram said as he faced me with a smile. He smacked his hands together in a gesture of impatience, like he had places to go and creatures to see.

"Important matters?" I repeated, surprise evident in my voice. It always seemed that Bram was at least one step ahead of me, owing to the fact, no doubt, that he was very good at keeping important details to himself.

Bram nodded. "While I was away," he started and I figured he'd meant from the time he disappeared in the courtroom until now, "I was able to reach your Mr. Beaurigard."

"You did what?" I asked, shocked. "You got in touch with Quill?" It really shouldn't have been too much of a surprise because Quill and Bram sort of hung out in the same circles. That is to say, Quill was an outlaw and Bram dealt with a lot of outlaws, so I was sure at some point, their paths had to have crossed.

"Yes, quite so, sweet," Bram said. He became quiet again, apparently enjoying the surprise on both of our faces. He definitely liked laboring under the belief that he was as spontaneous as they came. Although I didn't know what Bram's real last name was, I was about to dub him Bram Unpredictable.

"Are you going to tell us what happened?" Knight prodded. "Or are we just going to have to stand here and deal with your smug riddles all day?"

Bram frowned at Knight but said nothing. He merely cleared his throat and faced me again. "I felt Mr. Beaurigard needed to be made aware that you and the Loki were in the prison of the High Court and being detained for his transgressions."

I swallowed hard, amazed that Bram would go to such lengths for me. I figured he'd merely booked passage back to Splendor once it looked like my fate had been sealed. But I was completely wrong. And for that I was thankful.

"And what happened?" Knight prodded.

Bram shrugged. "He told me he would turn himself in, do the honorable thing."

"What?!" I asked in shock, trying to make sense of what Bram had just said. Quill was coming to the Netherworld? To turn himself in? "You mean Quill is coming here, to the High Court?"

Bram nodded and then cocked his head like maybe it wasn't quite as simple as that. "Well, that is what he told me, in any case. Whether he sticks to his word, we shall find out." He was quiet for a few seconds. "I imagine it will be quite a decision for him to make."

Suddenly, I felt incredibly worried for Quill which really made no sense because on the flipside, Quill's arrival could mean the release of Knight and me. But what would it mean for Quill? If he came here and turned himself in, he would absolutely be sentenced to die. But would his death sentence release Knight? Would it release me? I wasn't sure and it wasn't something I even wanted to think about. Quillan's life in return for Knight's and mine wasn't a trade that I wanted any part of.

"At any rate, that is my news, as of now." Bram started for the cell door and then turned back to face me. "I will learn what is to be done regarding your hearing, Dulcie sweet."

I nodded. "Thank you, Bram, for … everything."

"Yes," Knight added. "I believe I misjudged you." Bram's eyebrows reached for the ceiling as Knight continued. "Thank you for acting as guardian for Dulcie. I don't know how I can ever repay you."

187

Bram frowned and seemed at odds with the words coming from Knight's lips. It was at that moment that I realized Bram was jealous of Knight, deeply. The vampire said nothing but took a few steps toward the cell door and then paused. He turned around to face me and smiled without humor.

"Dulcie, I believe you owe me a kiss."

I swallowed hard. "A kiss?" I repeated, suddenly realizing he was referring to our contractual kiss-a-day.

"What the hell?" Knight started.

So Bram wasn't quite the chivalrous gentleman I made him out to be. He was still looking out for himself. I took a deep breath and thought about the fact that this would not go well, not with Knight acting as sentry. I could see the impending storm already on the horizon.

I faced Knight and shook my head. "It was the only way I could get him here."

"What was the only way?" Knight demanded, anger coloring his eyes until they flamed a brilliant blue.

"We have a contract," Bram answered, his smile still in full effect. "In return for my guardianship, Dulcie promised me one kiss per day and she has yet to deliver today's kiss."

"Over my fucking dead body," Knight stormed and started forward. "I knew you were a rat bastard."

"Rat bastard or not," Bram started as he began buffing his nails against his lapel. "Your fairy owes me."

I stepped away from Knight and turned back, putting the flat of my hand on his chest. "It's a kiss, Knight, it's not the end of the world."

But judging by the expression on Knight's face, a kiss was second in line to the end of the world. I said nothing more but approached Bram and frowned. "Make it quick," I said.

"I'm watching you," Knight said to Bram, his eyes still burning.

I stood on my tiptoes, intending to give Bram a chaste peck on his lips but he wrapped his arms around me and forced his mouth on mine. Holding me captive as he kissed me, he sucked on my lower lip before biting it playfully. I tried to pull away and he opened his eyes.

"Our agreement was inclusive of tongue, my dear."

"That's enough," Knight started and before it turned into vampire vs. Loki, I grabbed Bram's neck and pushed my mouth on his, forcing my tongue deep inside his mouth so I could hold up my end of the bargain.

"Okay, that's all you get," I said angrily as I pulled away from him, wiping my mouth against my forearm.

Bram smiled and winked at Knight before he nodded to the goblin, who opened the cell door, and allowed him to leave.

Hours passed and darkness descended on the prison. With only the few overhead flickering yellow lights, it was basically a dungeon. But dungeon or not, I was happily nestled in Knight's arms as we lay on the floor and I listened to his heartbeat. I'd actually managed to fall asleep, for how long, I wasn't sure. It was the first time I'd slept in what felt like days and I sorely needed it.

"Are you awake?" I whispered, pulling away from him to find his eyes on mine. It appeared he'd been awake for a while.

"Yes," he answered and held me against his chest. "I haven't been able to sleep."

I nodded, thinking about his words, about how frightened he must have been that his death sentence was looming so closely. But I had promised myself that I wouldn't think about the future for the next few hours. Instead, I would just live in the present and enjoy every second we had together.

And suddenly I was reminded of that horrible argument Knight and I had gotten into at my apartment regarding Jack.

"Knight?"

"Yes?"

I swallowed hard. "I'm sorry about that argument we had. You were right. I was afraid of giving into my feelings for you and I acted like a child."

He chuckled but it was a sad sound. "Dulcie, it's okay. None of that matters now anyway."

I turned to face him and felt something break within me. It was the feeling that I might never hold him in my arms again, never feel him breathing down on me, never witness his beautiful smile again. "How did this happen?" I asked as I ran my fingers down his face. His cheeks were stubbly with shadow.

He shook his head and sighed. "Maybe it was fate."

"No, it isn't fate." I said and exhaled all my pent-up frustration, suddenly feeling angry again. It seemed like over the last couple of days I'd gone back and forth between anger and sadness. "If I could just have my hearing, I could prove it wasn't you, Knight."

"No," he said quickly, shaking his head. "I would never put you in this place. This is how it has to be."

I felt tears building behind my eyes. "Knight …"

"I don't want to think about it anymore." He caught my hand and brought it to his mouth. "I just want to have this, you and I, right now, together and alone."

I felt the tears continue to build and once I blinked, they began rolling down my cheeks. I didn't even try to stop them. "Whatever happens …" I lost my voice and forced myself to find it again. "I want you to know … I want you to know ..."

"I love you too, Dulcie," Knight said and much more eloquently than my attempt.

I felt my throat tighten and I could barely breathe. The tears were coming full stream now and sliding down my cheeks, only to splash against his shirt. "I do love you," I whispered, the realization hitting me like an anvil over the head. Why hadn't I given into my feelings for him a long time ago? Because the truth of the matter was that I'd been in love with Knight for a very long time.

Knight glanced down at me with the beginnings of a smile on his lips. He tilted my chin up and brought his lips to mine, kissing me. It was a kiss more passionate and deeper than any we'd ever shared. It told of the emotion within each of us, of the pain and the anger that wouldn't abate. And of the tie between us, the fact that for the next couple of days, our worlds could fall apart around us but as long as we had each other, we would laugh in the face of adversity.

I had him for two more days ...

I pulled away and shifted my body around until I was facing him. I stood up, smiling down at him as I realized what I intended to do. Not worried who could see me (probably no one given how dark it was), I slid my pants down my hips. I watched Knight's Adam's apple bob as he swallowed hard, watching my panties drop before I let them fall on top of my pants. Knight's eyes began to glow, his body pointing to the fact that he had claimed me, that I was his mate.

I said nothing as I leaned down onto my knees and ran my hand across the stiffness between his thighs. I found the flap in his prison pants and pulled his erection through it, palming him as I ran my hand up and down his shaft. He was so incredibly hard and I wanted nothing more than to feel united with him, feel him inside me as we damned both our destinies and found a small bit of happiness in one another.

I started untying my shoelaces, wanting to free myself from my shoes, pants and panties. Knight just watched me patiently as I fought with my sneakers, trying to pull them off as quickly as I could. I glanced up at Knight and at his expression of amusement, giggled.

191

"Need some help?" he asked but he didn't wait for me to respond. He merely pulled off my sneaker, helping me free my legs of my jeans and panties. Once I was completely naked, I hovered above him for just a moment, then straddled him. I reached for his erection as I ran it up and down against me, feeling myself sting with the need to have him inside me. Staring at him the entire time, I held him still and dropped myself down, throwing my head back as I felt him fill me.

He wrapped his arms around me and pushed up, until he was fully ensconced within me. Then he began pumping up and down as I rode him, fresh tears beginning to pool from my eyes again.

"I will always love you, Dulcie," he whispered into my neck.

FOURTEEN

I woke up to the sound of metal clanking against metal. I took a deep breath and opened my eyes to find the goblin working a key into our door lock. There were two plates of something that resembled slop—shapeless and colorless but definitely not odorless—on a tray at his feet. I suddenly worried that I was in a state of wardrobe disrepair from Knight's and my love-making the night before. I glanced down and sighed in relief when I noticed I was completely clothed. Knight must have taken care of the chore of dressing me once I'd fallen asleep.

Yep, he was definitely a keeper.

I pushed up from where I'd been lying against the hard cement, with only Knight's arm for a pillow. The entire right side of my body was numb, probably from the coldness of the floor. I glanced over at my cell mate and noticed he was lying on his side and smiling up at me; beautiful even though he was still covered with bruises and scabs from his rough treatment by the prison guards. Neither of us had showered since I couldn't remember, so I was sure we stunk to high-heaven, although I couldn't say my sense of smell was offended by us, only the goblin's slop.

I didn't have the chance to say "good morning" or even "hello," to my incredibly handsome Loki because before I knew it, the goblin was in our cell, pushing the plates of slop at us. I frowned at him and the slop, shaking my head at the very idea of putting the nasty stuff in my mouth.

"I'd rather starve," I grumbled.

Knight stood up and, after a quick yawn, inspected the nondescript lumps the goblin was calling food. He nodded, facing me with a quick smile, "I concur."

"Ya have a visitor," the goblin announced irritably as he turned to walk out of the cell, locking it behind him again. Then, as if an afterthought, he unlocked the door again and retrieved the tray, frowning at both of us as he did so.

"Is Bram here?" I asked after his retreating figure.

The goblin shook his head at the same time that a man appeared in the hallway just behind him. The man was incredibly tall, probably as tall as Knight and just as handsome with strong, chiseled and well-defined features. Well, nearly as handsome as Knight.

The goblin motioned for the man to approach our cell with a nod of his head and then, apparently thinking we might want a little privacy, retired to the far end of the corridor, taking the tray with him. Before reaching the end of the hallway, he called out, "Ya got twenty minutes," and then the very distinct sound of a goblin eating slop accosted my ears and I felt queasy.

I couldn't help but notice how much more compliant the goblin was when Bram was in attendance. A fact which still made me scratch my head as I wondered what level of involvement Bram had with the Netherworld higher ups. But, at the moment, I didn't want to focus on Bram or the goblin. Instead, I was curious as to who this amazingly handsome man was—a man who looked like he could have been Knight's brother. The man took a few steps toward our cell and then paused as he alternated his gaze from me to Knight.

"You must be a Loki," I said out loud even though I only intended to think the statement. Before the man could respond, I felt Knight's arm around me as he pulled me close and we approached our handsome visitor.

194

"Gabriel," Knight said and the tone of his voice as well as the deep smile etched on his face pointed to the fact that he was happy to see the man. "Took you long enough!"

Knight stepped away from me and walked over to Gabriel, offering his hand through the prison bars. Gabriel took it and pumped it heartily, covering their clasped hands with his other one.

When they broke away from one another, Gabriel's full lips broke into a dazzling smile, revealing white and perfectly straight teeth that contrasted against his olive skin. With his hazel eyes and dark brown hair, he was the second handsomest man I'd ever seen. The most handsome man award being reserved for my own Loki, of course.

"I was in the Dark World on a training mission, brother," Gabriel answered. "Otherwise, I would have been here a long time ago." He glanced around the prison cell and sighed, before his gaze settled on me. "You must be the fairy, Dulcie, Knight has talked so much about."

"That's me," I said with a smile, surprised by Gabriel's announcement that I had been the subject of his and Knight's conversation. Knight turned around to face me, as though remembering I was still there. He took a step closer and threw his beefy arm around me, inviting me into the cocoon of his chest.

"Yes, this is Dulcie," Knight said as he smiled down at me. "The one woman who has driven me to insanity on more than one occasion."

Even though I smiled, it felt odd to me that we were doing the small talk bit considering that Gabriel was standing here, in prison, speaking to us on the other side of our cell bars. Small talk was ridiculous at this point— because it was very obvious that Gabriel had come to say good-bye to what I had to imagine was one of his closest friends.

Gabriel smiled but it wasn't in any way a smile of contentment. Instead, it was laced with mourning and I could guess at the thoughts going through his head: "*they make such a great couple; shame they'll only be together for the next two days ...*"

"She's just as beautiful as you mentioned, brother," Gabriel said warmly, his eyes downcast as he offered another sad smile.

Knight nodded but said nothing, merely studied me as if he were seeing me for the first time. Uncomfortable with the feeling that I was like a rare oil painting on view, I cleared my throat and faced our visitor.

"Are you brothers?" I asked, wondering if that was the reason Gabriel kept referring to Knight as such. I glanced back and forth between the two of them, again noticing the similarities in their angular features, Roman noses and wide, hypnotic eyes.

Gabriel shook his head and chuckled slightly. It was a deep, rumbling sound. "No, but we might as well be for how close we are."

"Yeah, so close that the bastard took three days to get here," Knight said with an identical chuckle to Gabe's. Knight dropped the laugh after a second or two as he scrutinized his friend. Then he faced me. "Gabe and I grew up together, trained together, learned what it meant to become Loki men together."

I nodded and offered Gabe a smile. "Any friend of Knight's is a friend of mine."

"Thank you," Gabriel responded and then glanced around the cell again, noting the discolored cot and filthy sink with visible aversion, his eyebrows drawn together in a knot. "How are they treating you here?"

Knight shrugged as he dropped his gaze to the grimy floor and scuffed the front of his shoe against a particularly oily spot, frowning with disgust. "As you can imagine."

Gabriel nodded and then noticed the stained floor, where a few mounds of slop had dripped off the goblin's tray and lay there looking like the innards of some unfortunate beast. Were we seriously expected to eat that shit? Knight and I hadn't eaten anything in the last day or so; and, even though my stomach had been whining off and on, the image of the slop lying there like gooey entrails was enough for me to consider death by starvation not a bad way to go.

Gabe glanced back at us again and any traces of joy or playfulness were absent from his expression. "How am I going to get you out of here?"

Knight shook his head and sighed heavily. "My bed is made." He glanced over at me and smiled but I could see that he'd accepted the defeat. "It's Dulcie I'm worried about now."

"I'm going to be fine," I lied but was unable to convince either of the men. I wasn't going to be fine because even if I made it through my hearing alive and, best case scenario, was acquitted, I would never be fine unless Knight was released with me. My days of being "fine" were numbered. I could count them on one hand.

I felt my throat constrict again and tears filling my eyes. But I held them back, promising myself that I would see Knight out of this mess. I wasn't sure how, but there had to be a way and if I were nothing else, I was resourceful. Yes, I would MacGyver us out of this hell-hole known as the Netherworld and I sensed this Gabriel might be able to help me ...

"Are you ANC?" I asked him pointedly.

He glanced at me and seemed surprised that I was asking or that I'd changed the subject. As far as I was concerned, now was not the time for pity. It was time for action. And I'd be damned if the man I loved was going to die two days from now.

"Yes," Gabe answered after he considered it thoughtfully. "I'm a Senior Regulator."

Perfect.

I just smiled and pretended as if I weren't forming a plan, merely asking to distract my mind away from the ugliness surrounding me, the revulsion of the situation.

"I spoke with Caressa," Gabe started rather nonchalantly, focusing on Knight again. He leaned against the prison bars, bending down as if he were stretching out his back.

Knight shook his head. "She has her hands tied, Gabe, it's pointless."

Gabe stood up straight again and cocked his head to the side as if he were considering Knight's statement—then rejecting it. "It does appear her hands are tied," he agreed. "But we could appeal to a higher authority, Knight."

"It's pointless," Knight said with his lips in a straight line.

"We could demand another trial with a full jury. We could make it known that this is a crock of centaur shit and won't be tolerated," Gabe continued, heat rising in his voice. "Caressa is ready to go to bat for you and you know I will."

Knight laughed acidly. "Gabe, you know what will happen." When Gabe didn't respond right away, Knight answered for him. "Nothing." He shook his head and ran an agitated hand through his hair, his expression one of frustration. "I appreciate it, Gabe, but it's merely wishful thinking."

Gabe was quiet for a second or two as he watched his friend and I could see the pain in his eyes when he realized Knight was right. It was a foolish errand to try and appeal to the very ones who wanted Knight dead and, apparently, had for a while now.

"I know what this is about," Gabe said in a soft voice.

Knight's jaw was tight. "Stay out of it. The less you profess to know, the better." He glanced away and shook his head before facing his friend again. "Don't end up here, Gabe, don't end up where I am."

Gabe nodded and looked as if he were about to say something more when I heard the sound of a woman's voice coming down the hallway. I craned my neck to watch Alex as she walked past the first few cells, towards us, amid whistles and cat calls from the inmates.

Gabe immediately turned around and as soon as he recognized her, strode up the hallway, his hulking form nearly taking up the entire space. He greeted her with a large smile and a protective arm around her shoulder as if to remind her she had a bodyguard in this hideous place.

"Alex," he said and, based on the sweet tone of his voice, it was pretty obvious he had the hots for her.

She smiled up at him shyly. "Hello, Gabriel," she said, giving him a slightly more flirtatious smile. They walked down the hallway looking like a Cialis commercial. Once they were standing in front of us, Alex wiggled out from underneath Gabe's arm, apparently trying to preserve the image of "business professional." She glanced at each of us with a warm smile. "Knight and Dulcie."

"Hi, Alex," Knight said and I merely smiled with a quick nod.

"You shouldn't be here," Gabe said, suddenly facing her with concern in his eyes. The goblin merely watched from the top of the hallway, making no motion to inquire as to Alex's visit. 'Course she was sent from the ANC so I guess it made sense that he didn't ask any questions. I also wondered why I hadn't seen the Cyclops since the incident yesterday. Not that I was complaining ...

Alex nodded and met Knight's gaze, then instantly averted her eyes. "Caressa sent me," she said softly. She turned around and glanced up and down the hallway, as if searching for any sign of the goblin or some other guard. Once the coast was apparently clear, she faced Knight again. "She wanted me to give you this," she said as she fished inside her purse, producing a folded letter which she handed to Knight.

199

He accepted it and turned his back to us while he read the contents. When he faced her again, he handed her the letter and she immediately searched inside her purse until she found a small bag of what looked like purple powder, the color and consistency of grape-flavored Kool-Aid mix. She dropped the paper on the ground, and opening the small bag, sprinkled the purple contents on top of the paper. Then she simply said: "Ignite."

I watched the paper puff up with a huge flare, only to die down again after a few seconds, reduced to a few sheets of carbon which Alex then stomped out with her foot.

After her demonstration, she faced Knight expectantly.

"Please tell Caressa thank you, but no," he said graciously.

"Knight," Alex started but I interrupted her.

"What is it, Knight?" I demanded. "What did the letter say?"

He faced me and shook his head. "Nothing I want you to know about." Then he looked at Alex again. "Please tell Caressa I appreciate her concern."

Alex nodded, a frown marring her pretty face as she shook her head in apparent dejection that Knight would not be persuaded to save himself—not by Caressa, Gabriel or me. Especially not if it meant my damnation.

"Good luck to … you both," Alex added as she faced the prison around her. "I … I need to get going."

"I'll see you out," Gabe interjected and walked her up the hallway.

"What was it?" I demanded, facing Knight eagerly. "What was in the letter?"

"A way out," he answered softly, shaking his head. "But a way I would never agree to take. Until I can rest assured that you are safe, Dulcie, I won't agree to anything."

###

The morning greeted me with nothing but heartache because the following day would mark the end of Knight's life unless I could figure out a way to save him. I had a visit from Bram the night before and he informed me that he'd gone straight to Caressa to inquire as to when my hearing would be scheduled. She couldn't give him an exact date, as she was still waiting to hear from the powers above and it seemed they were taking their sweet ass time.

As far as Knight and I were concerned, we were out of time. Which meant that at this point, I needed a miracle …

Miracles are funny things because it's not as though they arrive tied with a big red bow and wrapping paper announcing them as miracles. Nope, sometimes they arrive in the shape of Caressa Brandenburg.

After hurrying past the goblin without so much as a "hello," she strode up to our cell, in an obvious foul mood. Her steps were hurried and the tapping of her heels against the concrete floor echoed the frenetic beating of my heart. She unlocked the cell door while the goblin looked on in surprise.

"Caressa?" Knight asked as he faced her expectantly.

"She's being released," Caressa said with an edge to her voice. It told me she was in no way happy about the fact I was being released. I, myself, couldn't comprehend what release meant exactly.

"My hearing has been scheduled?" I asked, standing up from my sitting position on the floor, my legs suddenly buckling with pins and needles. I braced myself against the bars and shook out one foot after another, forcing the blood flow back into my body.

Caressa glanced at me and frowned. "No. There will be no hearing."

"I don't understand," I started but she breathed out impatiently and propped her hands on her hips as if to say I needed to keep up with her.

"I've received orders from above to release you of all liability in this case and personally ensure that you go back through the portal to Splendor, Earth."

"What?" I started and then I realized what that meant. I backed away and shook my head, standing between her and Knight. "No, I won't leave him."

I turned to look at Knight, only to find he was smiling, as if this were the best thing that could have happened. Caressa faced him, shaking her head, her anger palpable. "You have no choice," she said and addressed me impatiently. "We need to leave soon so I'll give you a few minutes to say your good-byes."

She then walked out of the cell, locking the heavy door behind her as she strode up the hallway to discuss something with the goblin.

"Knight," I started as I felt tears in my eyes for the umpteenth time since I'd arrived in the Netherworld. "I am going to get you out of here."

He shook his head. "You're free now, Dulce." Then he smiled again and it beamed of true happiness. "That's all I ever wanted."

He grabbed hold of me and pulled me into his arms, kissing the top of my head. The tears in my eyes were now streaming down my face and I felt as if something inside of me was breaking.

"I'm not giving up," I said as my voice caught in my throat. "I'm not giving up."

"Dulcie, please do me one favor, that's all I ask." He took a deep breath. "Just never come back here. Go through that portal and live out the rest of your life. I want you to be happy."

Even though I nodded, I could never agree to leave him here. My mind was racing as I thought about the possibilities, the ways in which I could prevent tomorrow's execution from ever occurring. I would fight my damnedest and if I failed to save him, at least I would go down in a blaze of glory, knowing I did everything I could.

Knight gripped both sides of my face and there was fire in his eyes. "Promise me."

I swallowed hard. "I promise." And it was the first time I'd ever lied to him outright.

Knight pulled me close and kissed me with hard, passionate lips. "I will always love you, Dulcie O'Neil," he whispered.

Once I changed out of my Netherworld prison scrubs and was back in my jeans and T-shirt, Caressa escorted me from the prison and into her ANC company Town Car. We both were silent as we made the long trek to the parking lot—silent even as Caressa started the car and pulled out of the parking lot. She drove down a residential street, complete with a netted overhang stretching from street lamp to street lamp, probably to shield residents from the flying creatures.

As we exited the city limits and started on a rural road where there were no longer any netted canopies, we had yet to meet another car. After five minutes straight, I had to imagine we were en route to the airport. I cleared my throat and started in on my plan A.

"You don't have to take me to the airport," I started.

She glanced at me in the rearview mirror and frowned before turning back to the road in front of her. "I have orders."

"So break them."

She shook her head and glanced back at me again, her blue eyes narrowed. "Why?"

I shrugged and stared outside at the trees that blurred by and the azure sky, complete with white puffy clouds. It was a beautiful day, such a contrast to the dark, tempestuous storm that was brewing within me. I eyed the back of Caressa's head again and caught her reflection in the mirror. "Because you don't want me to be released and neither do I."

"So what?"

"It should be me in prison and you and I both know it, Caressa. Knight is innocent and he's being punished because someone higher than both of you in the ANC doesn't like him."

Caressa nodded but her lips were still tight. She must have taken her foot off the gas because the car suddenly slowed down considerably. Good thing there wasn't anyone behind us or they probably would have rear-ended us.

"So what do you propose to do about it?" she demanded.

I tapped my fingers against the faux leather interior of the Town Car. "Well, I won't be able to do a damn thing if you take me to the airport and force me to go home."

"So, what, I should just let you go?" she asked, laughing sarcastically and shaking her head. "So I can end up being interrogated for not ensuring your return to Earth? Yeah, that sounds like a great plan."

I was hungry, tired, dirty and my heart was broken. I really didn't want to deal with Caressa and her bad attitude. But, I managed to keep my cool. Point for me. "What if it were as simple letting me escape?"

"It would be hugely suspect."

I wasn't going to give up so easily. "You could talk your way out of it, Caressa. You know you could." I paused and took a deep breath. "Isn't Knight's life worth it?"

It took me by surprise when she suddenly jerked on the wheel and pulled to the side of the road. Good thing I was wearing my seatbelt or I'd have hit my head against the window for sure. She put the car in park but didn't turn off the motor. Instead, she turned around to face me and her expression was a thoughtful one, as if she were seriously weighing the idea.

"Let's say I let you go; what good will it do for Knight? How are you going to be able to do a damn thing for him?"

She'd bitten. Things were looking up. "I have the benefit of having nothing to lose. I'll figure out the rest as I go." Yes, I fully realized I was pulling a Bram plan; i.e., not actually having a plan but making one up as I went along, but at this point, I didn't care. I just needed to talk Caressa into releasing me and the rest would come to me. Inevitably, it always did.

She sighed and faced forward, completely quiet as she apparently considered the options. Then she undid her seatbelt and stepped out, shaking her head at her own apparent bewilderment that she was agreeing to any of this. She walked to the rear of the car and opened my door.

"Out," she said and watched as I undid my seatbelt and stood up. Then she shook her head at me and frowned. "I can't believe I'm doing this," she muttered.

"You know it's the right thing to do."

She crossed her arms against her chest and her lips were tight. "You need to make damn sure that whatever plan you're working on is a good one because I don't want to see that Loki die."

I nodded. "Well, we both have that in common."

"I don't want this to look too suspect," she started as she took a deep breath. "No one will believe me if it doesn't look like a struggle." She chewed on her lip for a second or two. "And if you get caught, you can't be picture-perfect either."

I nodded, getting her gist and braced myself for what I had coming. She smiled and drew her arm back, unleashing her fist into my face. I felt the blow all the way down to my feet and took a few steps back before losing my balance and toppling into the dirt. I gripped my injured cheek and pulled my hand away, as I noticed blood trailing from my busted lip. "Holy shit, Caressa," I started and threw her a frown.

She smiled and looked impressed with herself. Then she glanced down at her meticulous skirt suit and grabbing each side of her jacket, yanked until the buttons burst off and fell to the ground below her. She grasped her silk, off-white blouse and ripped that as well.

"Um, don't think you're going to get out of this without a little payback," I said, smiling.

She glanced at me and returned the smile. "I was just preparing myself, Dulcie."

Then she braced herself, feet shoulder-width apart and motioned for me to come at her. I took a deep breath, clenched my right hand shut, making a fist and unfurled it in the same spot where she'd nailed me. Once my fist made contact with her cheek, her head bounced back with the force and I could hear my knuckles cracking. She gripped her cheek and glared at me.

"You didn't have to make it so hard!" She checked her lip with her fingers for a sign of blood but there wasn't any. "Shit, that hurts!"

I laughed, still tasting the blood from my split lip. "You wanted real. That's one hundred percent Dulcie O'Neil."

"Go," she said as she continued cradling her injured cheek. "Before I change my mind."

I nodded, heaving a huge sigh of relief. "I need one more thing."

"Really?" she asked and shook her head like I was unbelievable; but I could see there was a smile buried there, just underneath the bravado. "What would that be?"

"I need Gabriel's phone number or his address. Both would be great." Then I took a deep breath. "And I need a ride to the Grosvenor Hotel."

"Anything else I can do for you? Maybe pick up your dry cleaning on the way?" Her levity told me that things were good between us. Not that we'd ever be friends, but we were both tough women who were fighting the man. And there's an unspoken code of respect and recognition between tough women.

Caressa walked back to the driver's seat and reached into her purse which was sitting on the passenger seat. She glanced back at me. "We'd better get in before one of those flying sons of bitches tries to grab us."

I was so wholly engrossed in our cat fight that I hadn't even considered the flying menaces. I wasted no time in opening the back door and throwing myself inside. Caressa took a seat in front of me and pulled the door shut as she picked up her cell phone. I have to admit the cell phone surprised me in the Netherworld, considering everything else seemed to be circa 1960.

Caressa thumbed through her phone and then faced me. "Do you have a pen?"

"No."

She shook her head and reached inside her purse, producing a piece of paper and wrote down Gabriel's information. Then she faced me again. "I can't take you to the Grosvenor; it would look too suspicious." Then she fished inside her purse again and pulled out two hundred dollar bills. "This is all I have on me but it should get you bus fare."

"Caressa, I don't have time to take the bus."

She exhaled and shook her head, turning around to glance at me. "Has anyone ever told you what an utter and complete pain in the ass you are?"

I smiled and cocked my head to the side, pretending to consider it. "Um, yes."

FIFTEEN

After Caressa begrudgingly dropped me off about a quarter mile from the Grosvenor Hotel (to ensure no one would see her or her car) and made me promise never to cross her path again, I collected all my things and searched, in vain, for Bram. Where the unpredictable vampire was, I had no idea but I also didn't have much time to wait around for him. Not after Caressa said she would have to protect her own ass and report that I'd escaped. She promised to give me the rest of the night but come the morning, she would have to announce to the ANC that I had overpowered her and escaped. How she planned to explain delaying the report about my disappearance until the morning, I had no idea; but as far as I was concerned, that was her problem, not mine. I had plenty of problems on my own plate to keep me occupied.

So not finding Bram, I left him a note, telling him to return to Splendor—that there was nothing he could do for me at this point because I'd taken matters and my fate into my own hands. Now no one could help me—not Bram, Knight, Caressa ... not even Quill's surrender to the authorities. I guess you could say I'd become a renegade.

After lugging my bag downstairs, the concierge called me a cab and a few minutes later, I found myself en route to Gabriel's, clutching the piece of paper where Caressa had scrawled his address and phone number.

"Here we are," the cab driver said and pulled to the side of Wilson Street, in front of a large grocery store. Even though I was still a good quarter mile from Gabriel's apartment, I didn't want to involve him and I figured it wouldn't be smart to be seen pulling up in front of his apartment building.

I glanced at the driver, and saw she was a harpy. She had a beautiful body—large breasts and a small waist that flared into broad hips. She was dressed in skin tight jeans and on top, sported what amounted to a bra. Her face, though, in true harpy style, was that of an old crone—deep wrinkles, spider-web fine, grey hair and deep-set, bubbly brown eyes juxtaposing a nose that was in a word, generous. She was the epitome of the saying: "Drink 'em pretty."

"That'll be two fifty," she said in a smoker's voice before she erupted into a coughing fit that sounded like she was suffering from emphysema.

"Um, I only have two hundred," I answered with a sheepish smile as I handed the two bills Caressa had given me to the harpy, hoping she might find it in her miserable soul to give me a discount. If anyone needed a break, it was me. Holy Hades, I'd been through hell and back ...

She frowned as she turned to face me, her beady eyes narrowing beneath her bushy eyebrows. "What else you got on you?" she demanded.

I sighed. I didn't have much and I was sure she was hinting at street potions or the like. "I've got clothes."

She craned her neck so she could get a better look at me and seemed to be raking me from head to toe. "You look about the same size as me."

"My bag's in the back. Take what you want," I muttered. She nodded and opened her door, retrieving my suitcase from the trunk. She plopped it on the front seat, opened it and started sorting through my clothes, throwing things that suited her fancy over her arm.

"We're good," she said after she'd wadded up two shirts and two pairs of jeans and tossed them onto the passenger seat. Damn, she got my Seven For All Mankind jeans. Son of a bitch!

"Great," I muttered and opened the door, rechecking the paper in my hand that proclaimed Gabriel lived at 3676 Fifth Street. I walked around to the front seat, closed up my bag and started forward.

"Have a good night," the harpy growled at me as she unrolled her window. Then, appearing to choke on something, opened her mouth and spat some sort of brownish liquid into the street.

"Thanks," I answered dismissively, trying to keep my gag reflexes under control while I watched her drive away.

I started walking down Wilson Street, looking for Fifth Street which was supposed to cross Wilson. A few minutes later, I hit Fifth and took a right, finally arriving at 3676 and heaved a sigh of relief.

The building was nondescript, seventies style and tan. It was three stories high, on a residential street lined with rental properties and tall pine trees. There was an overhead net covering the street like a huge, arcing fishnet stocking, reminding me of the one I saw with Caressa. How anyone could live in this battleground was beyond me. I'd definitely seen enough of the Netherworld to know I never wanted to come back … that is, if I ever got the chance to leave.

Not wanting to waste any more time, I ran up to the double doors leading into Gabe's apartment building. Once inside, I noticed an elevator and hit the button to call it. Luckily, it arrived quickly and I wasted no time in leaping inside and hitting the button that would take me to the third floor. Once there, I hightailed it down the hallway, searching for apartment number 354.

Finding it, I took a deep breath and knocked. Now was the time of reckoning.

Please be home, Gabe, please be home, I said to myself, keeping my fingers crossed all the while.

Apparently someone up there was smiling down on me or maybe the God of bad luck just wasn't paying attention to little ol' me because the door opened and revealed a confused Gabriel. But the important point to note was that, confused or not, Gabriel was home. My night was suddenly looking up.

"Thank Hades, you're home," I said and shook my head in relief, before noticing that his chest was bare and he was wearing a pair of worn jeans, looking like a dream come true. I gulped as soon as I saw his chest, realizing it was the exact copy of Knight's and that thought caused my heart to constrict.

Knight is going to be fine, I told myself in the hope that I wouldn't become a blubbering mess.

"Dulcie?" Gabe asked, obviously surprised to see me even as a smile spread across his face. "Did you … did you both get out?"

I shook my head and hated the look of disappointment in his eyes. "No, Gabe, and we need to talk. I … I need your help."

He chuckled. "Well, you're definitely adept at playing the part of damsel in distress." He shook his head in apparent amusement and turned around, walking into his apartment.

"Sorry," I said absentmindedly. "I guess I'm not much for greetings."

Gabe eyed me with an elevated brow and just smiled. Then, apparently noticing that I was still standing outside, he motioned for me to enter with a wave of his hand. "No loitering … Didn't you notice the sign on your way up?"

I laughed and suddenly felt intense relief. Why? I wasn't sure because it wasn't like I was any closer to sparing Knight. Of course, getting Gabe's help was a step closer and even though I had a hell of a lot more to accomplish tonight, it was a step in the right direction. And, hey, it felt good to have a friend in this shithole.

I took a few steps inside his house and noticed it was decorated decently well, considering it was a bachelor pad. The walls were a dark cocoa, combined with the chocolate leather couch and rich wood furnishings. It had a definite warm flavor to it. A huge entertainment system dwarfed one wall, complete with surround-sound speakers. Boys and their toys …

"I play a mean game of Mortal Combat," Gabe said with an infectious smile.

But I wasn't concerned with Mortal Combat at the moment. I had to imagine I'd be going through enough of that in the hours to come. Now I needed help. "Gabe," I started as I watched him reach for his T-shirt which was draped over one of his kitchen stools. He threw it over his head, pulling it down over his well-defined chest. "Caressa released me earlier today but I shouldn't be here—I'm supposed to be on a portal back to Earth."

"And obviously you aren't," he said as he eyed me knowingly. He released a pent-up breath of what I imagine was anxiety over my now being a criminal on the run whom he was illegally abetting. "How did you get here?" he asked.

"A cab; but don't worry, I had it drop me off a few blocks from here."

He nodded but that expression of concern hadn't left his eyes. "Why do I have the feeling you're a wanted woman?"

Well, that was basically the gist of it. "I'm not going to be wanted until tomorrow morning," I said as I offered him an apologetic smile—basically for involving him. But I had no other choice—I had nowhere else to go. "As of now, anyone who matters thinks I'm en route to Earth Splendor." I took a seat on his leather couch, feeling as if I could fall asleep right there. I was suddenly exhausted. It felt like I'd been going nonstop since I got here—either in court, fending off Cyclops or going through major emotional trauma. And to top it all off, I hadn't had much sleep and even less to eat in Hades only knew how long.

"But you made a stopover here," Gabe said with a secretive smile. "And I can't imagine it was to say good-bye to me."

I nodded as I thought about my next steps, what my plan entailed. I'd gotten this far and it almost felt like it had been too easy. The biggest hurdle so far had been my worry whether or not Caressa was going to agree to help me. Well, one hurdle down but who knew how many more to come ...

"No, I didn't come to say good-bye."

Gabe took a few steps closer, sitting on the arm of the couch as he glanced down at me with a sweet smile. "So if this isn't a social call ..."

I shook my head, wondering where I should start. "No, it's not a social call at all, Gabe." I looked at my knee which was bouncing nervously. I was apprehensive ... I had been for days. "I came here to ask you to help me free Knight."

Gabe swallowed hard and gazed at me, as if he saw right through me. "You know I'm ANC, Dulcie."

I nodded, thinking it an odd comment. "Yes, that's why I came to you."

He began tapping his fingers against his thigh in time to the bouncing of my leg. Frazzled nerves, anyone?

"I want to help however I can, Dulcie, but I need to be careful," he said finally.

"I'm not going to put you in any danger, Gabe. I'm accepting all responsibility in this. It's your behind-the-scenes assistance I'm after."

Gabe stood up and took a deep breath, walking toward the window. He glanced outside and was quiet for a few seconds as he seemed to zone out, probably getting lost in his own thoughts, weighing the options. When he turned to face me again, he smiled sadly. "Knight would never forgive me if something happened to you ... if I let something happen to you."

I shook my head. I'd come this far, I wasn't about to be talked out of it now. "Knight has one day left, Gabe. So his never forgiving you isn't something you really have to worry about."

"When you put it that way …" his words died, swallowed up by the air.

He dropped his gaze to the floor and seemed to be inspecting the carpet. But I knew better. He was still weighing the options, trying to decide if he should honor his best friend's last wishes or put his faith in me, someone he didn't know and probably doubted. "I know what you're thinking," I started as I offered him a wizened smile. "I'm not much to look at—small and a woman. But that's where people always make their mistake—they misjudge me because I can fight like a tiger when I care about someone."

Gabe smiled down at me and nodded. "Knight said you were the strongest woman he'd ever met." He paused for a second or two as if he was thinking about his friend's words and he studied me with narrowed but exacting eyes, sizing me up, trying to decide if he thought I could pull this off, if I could save Knight. "Okay, Dulcie, how can I help?"

I smiled, appreciating the fact that he was going to make this easy on me. I needed all the friends I could get. And already there was a plan taking place in my head, delineating itself into something real, something tangible, something that just might work. "Does the head of the ANC work in the ANC building at the airport?" I asked.

"Yes."

I nodded. That was good. No, I didn't know the building at all well but the airport was an island unto itself—separated from the rest of Splendor, Netherworld, which meant fewer onlookers. "Great. I need a map of that building, Gabe. I need to know entry points and exits as well as where his office is located." I took a deep breath. "I need to know where bathrooms are, janitorial closets … anything you can tell me."

"Going after the head of the ANC, huh?"

I inhaled deeply. The less he knew, the better but I had to admit to myself that I'd just been incredibly obvious. "It's the only way."

"What are you planning?"

I shook my head. "I don't want to involve you."

He nodded and took a deep breath, studying me intently with those beautiful hazel eyes. "You realize you could get yourself killed?"

"I realized that a long time ago and it didn't stop me then." I smiled. "It's not going to stop me now."

Gabe returned the smile and even added a slight chuckle to it, shaking his head like I was unbelievable. "I have a map of the ANC building in my desk at work."

"You have a map?" I asked, surprised.

"I guess it helps to be on the emergency preparedness team," he said with a chuckle. "We're given a map with exits clearly identified."

I shook my head as I laughed at my timely luck. "Good thing you're a good corporate citizen." Then I faced him again, thinking of the next item to check off my list. "Do you know the ANC head's hours? When he comes and goes?"

Gabe shook his head. "I don't know when he comes and goes; but I can tell you he's a workaholic. He isn't married and doesn't have any children so he basically spends all his time at the office."

I nodded. This was good news. Even better news that he didn't have a family—it would be easier to pull the trigger knowing he'd have few to mourn him. "Do you think he'll be there tonight? In a few hours?"

Gabe cocked his head to the side as he considered the question. "Most probably. Are you planning on acting tonight, though, Dulcie? That isn't much time to cement a plan …"

"I don't have the luxury of time, Gabe," I pointed out as I thought about the repercussions, should I fail in my scheme tonight. "Knight could be dead in the morning."

He nodded and glanced at the floor, heaving a sigh of what I imagined was anxiety for his friend. "Then I guess I'd better go get that map."

"As long as it won't seem strange that you're there at this hour?" I started, not even sure what time it was. I glanced at the clock on the wall. It was eight p.m. "The last thing I want is to have you attract undue attention."

He shook his head. "We Regulators come and go as we please, basically making up our own hours."

It was the same as when I worked as a Regulator at the ANC in Splendor. I smiled at him as my stomach suddenly started groaning, bemoaning the fact that I hadn't eaten in a long ass time.

"Raid the fridge," Gabe said, pointing to it as if to reiterate the fact that he wanted me to.

"Thanks and, um, while you're gone, do you mind if I take a quick shower?"

He smiled. "Mi casa es su casa."

After I'd eaten and showered, I felt better than I had in a long time. Even though I was still exhausted, the warm water had done a number on my frazzled nerves. I felt as if I could think again, and I came up with, what I considered, a pretty solid plan. The beauty of my plan was that I didn't have to rely on anyone. Well, in the actual carrying out of the plan I didn't have to rely on anyone. I would have to rely on Gabe for the lead-up.

While Gabe went to Headquarters to retrieve the map, I not only showered but, when raiding his kitchen, I managed to sate myself on frozen lasagna and two beers. My heart rate had been through the roof since my arrival here and I figured the beers might take the edge off.

Gabe returned to his apartment at nine o'clock on the dot. I finished the last sip of my Bud Light and dropped it in the trash, noticing he didn't seem to have a separate bin for recycling. Shame on Gabe ... or maybe they just didn't recycle here in Hellville.

"Got the map?" I asked with a smile, stretching my arms out and looping my fingers together to stretch them too.

He nodded and placed a few manila folders on the table. Opening one of them, he pulled out a legal-sized sheet of paper that was folded over on itself. He unfolded it and laid it out on the table in front of him, smoothing the edges as I took the few steps separating us. Standing next to him, I leaned over the table, taking stock of the map. And I was impressed—it was fairly detailed, inclusive of all exits, bathrooms, closets, and offices in the building.

"Good?" Gabe asked.

I nodded, suddenly finding it strange that Gabe didn't seem in the least bit concerned for the big boss even though he apparently worked with him. Although I hadn't detailed my plan to Gabe, it was pretty obvious that I was gunning for the man in charge. "You don't seem very concerned about the head ..." I started, wondering if there was a reason why.

"He's a bastard," he was quick to answer and then shrugged. "As far as I'm concerned, whatever happens ... happens."

I nodded, wondering what the man had done to make Gabe and Knight hate him so much. Or, what Knight had done to make the head want to knock him off. "Why does he want Knight dead?" I asked, wondering if Gabe knew or would tell me, if he did.

"It's not my place," Gabe answered. "Knight doesn't want you to know for a reason."

I wasn't going to push the subject because it really didn't matter now. It was sort of a moot point. The Head of the Netherworld wanted Knight dead and that was all that mattered. Now I had to get into that building without anyone seeing me and from there, I had a date with the head honcho, the big wig of the Netherworld.

"Did anyone see you?" I asked.

Gabe shook his head. "Nope, no one did. I parked down the street and was in and out in, maybe, five minutes flat."

"And if you're caught on video surveillance or if it turns out someone did see you?"

"I grabbed a case file that I'm currently working on," Gabe said, pointing at the manila folders sitting on the kitchen table with a dimpled, handsome smile. "I'm legit, Dulce."

I smiled and patted him on the back. "Nicely done."

He smiled in return and seemed to study me for a few seconds. "I know why Knight's so into you."

I felt my eyes widen with surprise by the subject change. "Is that so?"

He nodded. "You're beautiful, yes, but there's more to you than just a pretty face. You're a good woman and they can be hard to find."

"Well, I'd say you found a good woman in Alex."

Surprise filled his wide eyes. "Was I that obvious?"

I laughed. "Just a little."

He chuckled with me and, after a few seconds, our laughs faded to silence; and I recognized the weight of the situation. Tonight could very well be the last night of my life. At any rate, tonight would most certainly mark a turning point for me—something I might never come back from. But those weren't thoughts that I wanted any part of—what needed to wholly occupy my mind was the idea that I was rescuing Knight from certain, impending death.

"I need two more things from you before I can leave, Gabe," I said in a deadly serious tone.

"Anything."

"I need a weapon. I didn't bring my Op 6 with me."

He nodded. "I've got an Op 7."

The Op 7 was just slightly larger than my Op 6. It was Quillan's weapon of choice and I was more than accustomed to shooting one. "Is it registered to you?"

He shook his head. "No, to the ANC and it's the same registry we use for ANC employees on Earth."

This was all very good news—it meant the gun wasn't traceable. "So for all intents and purposes, it could have been a gun I brought over with me?"

He nodded. "Once we clean off my prints, there's nothing tying me to it."

"Good," I said with a smile. "Second thing, I need to use your phone."

"Sure," he answered, motioning to the corner of the room where I noticed a rotary phone on a small table beside a plush leather chair that matched the couch.

"I'm going to call my best friend who works for the ANC. It will just look like you called the ANC in Splendor, Earth, should anyone ever want to know."

"I'm not worried," Gabe said with a smile.

I stood up and approached the phone, knowing that Sam wouldn't be at work at this hour but I couldn't call her at home. It would look too suspicious for Gabe in case they ever pulled his phone records. I picked up the phone and dialed the number for the ANC, then her extension when it asked me for one.

"Hi, this is Samantha White with the Association of Netherworld Creatures. I can't take your call at the moment but please leave me a message after the beep and I'll get back to you as soon as I can. Thanks and have a great day," the chipper recording of her voice rang out.

I suddenly felt something cold and dark inside of me as I thought that I might never see Sam again. She was the closest person to family I had.

The beep sounded, prodding me to speak. I started to say something but my throat suddenly constricted around my larynx and cut it off. I made some sort of coughing sound and cleared my throat.

"Sam, it's me … I … I'm sorry I didn't say good-bye properly but I didn't have time. Anyway, things are looking bad for Knight and … for me. I just wanted to tell you that whatever happens, I will always love you and you are like a … sister to me." I took a deep breath. "I'm not sure when I'm going to be back or if I'm going to be back. And if I do come back, I'm not sure I can contact you without risk … for both of us." I sighed deeply. "As you can probably tell, I haven't exactly thought all of this through. I just couldn't let Knight die for my mistake and that's my only motivation." I paused for a second or two. "Anyway, I just wanted to tell you that I love you and I hope I can see you again really soon. Bye … er, bye for now."

I didn't know what else to say and when the tears refilled my eyes again, I hung up.

SIXTEEN

Twenty minutes later, I found myself at the rear entrance of the ANC Headquarters of the Netherworld. Of course, I couldn't just walk in through the front doors, not when there was, undoubtedly, video surveillance. Instead, Gabe dropped me off in the parking lot opposite the Headquarters lot and told me to find the back entrance which had an open door because the janitorial staff was on night duty and used it to come and go.

I borrowed a black-hooded sweatshirt from Gabe which fit me like a dress, ending at my shins; but at least the hood covered my head and the sweatshirt was roomy enough for my wings which seemed to be in hibernation for the last six hours or so—something that was totally fine by me.

I said a quick good-bye to Gabe and thanked him for all his help. I felt especially good because I doubted he would be considered a suspect in any way, if it ever came up. He was a genuinely great guy and there seemed to be something brewing between Alex and him so the last thing I wanted to do was get in the way of that. Now, more than ever before, I had new respect and admiration for love. Even though I sounded completely lame and corny, I was happy with the change. It actually felt good to be able to find hope inside yourself, to cultivate and encourage it.

What the hell had happened to me? It was like I'd been possessed by Tony Robbins.

Tony Robbins's possession aside, I had lots to do and not a lot of time to do it. Gabe pointed out the Head of the Netherworld's car in the parking lot, which was, incidentally, a brand new, sapphire blue Jaguar XKR. Gabe said they started at $100,000. So, I guess luxury items from Earth could be transported to the Netherworld—as long as you were the head honcho, that is. That nuisance aside, the important point to note was that the Head of the Netherworld was still in the building, exactly where I wanted him to be.

Pulling the black hood closer around my face, I patted my chest just to remind myself that the Op 7 was where it should be—nestled in its holster and strapped across my chest. I took a deep breath and started for the back door where I'd already witnessed a janitor coming and going. There was an industrial-sized vacuum standing unattended outside as well as four huge trash cans and a box of bin liners sitting just beside them.

I started forward from my position in the bushes at the far end of the parking lot. I stayed in the shadows as I neared the door, silently appreciative of the fact that the Netherworld seemed to be very densely wooded—it was easy to hide when you could take advantage of the shadows.

I reached the side of the building and tucked myself around the corner, lost in darkness. The moon was eclipsed—completely obscured by dark clouds that threatened to rain. If I hadn't known better, I'd say the gods of the Netherworld had been assisting me, shrouding me in darkness, offering me cover and masking the moonlight.

The janitor suddenly appeared in the doorway and started whistling something that sounded like "Hound Dog" by Elvis. He happened to be a Minotaur which was a creature that was a bull on the bottom and human on the top. Taurean horns sprung from the center of his head, twisting out left and right. Minotaurs were known for their savagery which is probably why this one was on duty at night and alone—the chances of anything threatening it were pretty slim.

The Minotaur janitor stood at eight feet tall or thereabouts and its fur was a dark brown, starting at its navel (it wasn't wearing a shirt) and disappearing under its pants. Its cloven hooves peeked out from beneath its rolled up pants and clanked against the asphalt as it busied itself with cleaning duties.

I needed to avoid the Minotaur at all costs. Since it was known for its violent temper, it only stood to get more violent when it came to sex. Given the fact that I was like a walking aphrodisiac, that wasn't a situation I wanted any part of. I already had to defend myself against the advances of the freaking Cyclops. I really didn't want to add bull-man to my list of conquests.

Holy Hades, the sooner I could get out of this damn place, the better.

It appeared I was going to be given the chance to enter the building in a matter of minutes because the Minotaur was in the process of tying four bags of trash closed and once he finished that little task, he lifted the bags—all of which were easily the size of me—and headed for the trash bins which were all the way across the parking lot.

Now he was actually singing the words to "Hound Dog" and when I looked closer, I noticed ear phones covering his ears, the cord of which was attached to a Walkman in the waist of his jeans. He wouldn't be able to hear me when I beelined for the open door … Perfect, wonderful, praise Hades!

Once the Minotaur was halfway to the trash bins with his back was towards me, I made my move and sprinted the thirty feet separating me from the doorway. Once through the door, I noticed a staircase leading upstairs. I happened to also notice the Minotaur's shirt hanging over the side of the railing, complete with a logo proclaiming the name of the janitorial company for which he worked. It was a bright green and screamed "uniform!" which was perfect for my needs. I grabbed it and took the stairs two at a time as I unzipped my jacket and reached inside my holster for the Op 7. I pulled the gun out and checked it, relishing the fact that I was armed and ready to take on whomever. I reached the top of the stairs and found myself in front of a door.

But I was expecting to reach a door because I'd studied Gabe's map and planned for everything that had happened so far ... well, with the exception of the janitor's shirt—that had just been pure luck. Once through the door at the top of the stairs, I'd make a right turn and at the end of the corridor, I'd be greeted by a restroom. I'd have to get into that restroom and put the janitor's shirt on before planning my next course of action.

I glanced through the two-foot-square window at the top of the door, checking both sides of the hallway for any traffic. Finding the hallway clear, I pushed the door ajar and squeezed through the small opening, being careful not to let the door slam behind me. Then, with my gun in low ready, I turned right and sidled down the wall as I approached the bathroom.

Not meeting with any resistance, I opened the door to the restroom, immediately dropping down on my knees to ascertain if anyone was in any of the four stalls. I encountered no one. I immediately ran to the furthest stall, locking it behind me and climbed up on the toilet. I threw off my sweatshirt and replaced it with the Minotaur's shirt. It covered my wings effortlessly since it was so much larger than I and even though it, too, looked like a dress, I decided it was less suspicious to be dressed like a cleaning woman than a thug in a hooded, black sweatshirt.

And as to the Minotaur discovering his shirt was gone? I just had to take my chances. Minotaurs weren't known for being especially intelligent and I figured I'd just have to play my lucky card on that one, hoping that this Minotaur was especially dumb or, at the very least, forgetful.

224

Once I was dressed, I slid the Op 7 into the waistline of my pants, with my thoughts on Knight. Whenever we'd worked together in the past, Knight always put his gun in the line of his pants. We joked that one day, if he kept up that habit, he might end up a eunuch. I felt a smile tug at my lips as the memory swallowed my concentration.

I'm going to get you out of this shithole, Knight, I promised him and myself … again.

I pulled out the folded map from my pocket and glanced at the black lines that detailed the second floor of the building. There was a staircase on my right that should take me to the third floor where I planned to take another break in the men's restroom located at the top of the stairs, in exactly the same position as this restroom.

Easy peasy.

I folded the paper again and shoved it back into my pocket, taking a deep breath as I stepped down from my perch on the toilet seat. Before opening the door, I bent down to ensure no one else had entered the restroom. Granted, I hadn't heard anything, but you can never be too sure.

Finding the coast clear, I opened the stall door and gasped when I saw my reflection in the mirror, my brain immediately reacting as if it were someone else. Calming my frantic heart down, I started for the door and opened it just a crack, glancing out to make sure the hallway was clear. There was no sign of anyone.

I opened the door and stepped out, immediately turning to my left where the green glowing "Exit" sign pointed to a staircase that was just beyond yet another door. Glancing around myself again to make sure I was alone, I started for the door, pulled it open and disappeared behind it.

Once in the stairwell, I paused to listen for voices or footsteps and then started up the cement steps, silently thankful that most people are lazy and wouldn't be caught dead taking the stairs if the elevators were available. That and it was nighttime so most employees were already at home with their families.

I took the steps, two at a time and paused just before the door once I reached the top. This one, too, had a two by two window so I glanced through it, scanning both sides of the hallway. This was the third floor, the one where I'd find the Head of the Netherworld so I had to be more careful. For all I knew, he might be wandering the hallway, on the way to the break room for coffee or maybe to the restroom.

But checking the hallway now, it looked empty so I opened the door and stepped into the corridor. I started for the men's restroom to my left and went around the corner. I hugged the wall as I did so, pulling the Op 7 from my waistline and into in a low ready stance as I reached the bathroom door. Pushing it open with my foot and drawing the gun, I pivoted on my toes until I faced the empty bathroom.

Bending down, I made sure the stalls were empty and, finding them clear, I started for the stall at the very end. Stepping inside of it and locking it behind me, I stood on the toilet again as I fished for the map in my pocket. Unfolding it, I followed the highlighter pen that Gabe used to show me exactly where the head honcho's office was, in proximity to the restroom. It was buttressed by two smaller offices on either side. And it was one of those smaller offices that I was targeting. Figuring I couldn't just walk in on him, with security cameras all over the place, I came up with another idea.

Eyeing the ceiling, I immediately noted the air vent that that led to all the vents on the third floor. Perfect! This would be the easiest way to get into one of the adjacent offices.

The ceiling vent was located above a stall in the center of the restroom which was good because it meant I could hide behind the stall door and stand on top of the toilet. But that wasn't going to be enough to allow me to reach the ceiling.

"Dammit," I whispered to myself as I put the Op 7 back into the waistline of my pants, stepping down from the toilet. I leaned over and searched the perimeter of the bathroom to make sure no one had entered. No one had. I opened the stall door and searched for something I could use as a step stool. My eyes paused on my reflection in the mirror, where it looked like I had a hunchback, owing to my wings which were trapped beneath my shirt.

My wings …

I tore the shirt over my head and dropped it on the floor so I was standing in nothing but my bra and jeans. But I could've cared less. Instead, my focus was reserved for my wings as I begged them to start working.

But nothing.

Please work, stupid wings, please work, I silently implored them.

Much to my relief and surprise, the ridiculously useless things actually started to flutter, as if responding to my request. They weren't exactly beating at this point, just fluttering futilely as if to say they thought I said something but they hadn't quite heard it.

Fly, I commanded them. *Get your asses going so I can float up to that air vent, dammit!*

They started beating madly, and I sounded like an enormous bee. For the first time since arriving to this hellish place, I could honestly say that having wings wasn't such a bad thing.

I started to float off the ground, little by little, gaining mere inches in the minutes that passed. I could tell my wings were straining to keep me airborne and I had to wonder if maybe I had more in common with a chicken than a hummingbird where flight was concerned.

Once I was about halfway to the ceiling, I felt inside my pocket, fingering the Swiss army knife Gabe had given

227

me and, pulling it out, selected the Phillips screwdriver. After I secured it in my mouth, I glanced up at the air vent which was now mere inches from me.

Keep going, I thought to myself, offering my wings a little support and positive reinforcement. *You're almost there!*

When I could reach out and touch the air vent, I felt immense relief flood me. I pulled out the screwdriver and started to work immediately, not stopping to think that the opening wasn't exactly large. Good thing for me, that neither was I ...

I got the first two screws loose and put them in my pocket as I started on the third. My little wings beat frantically to keep me airborne and I could feel the exhaustion setting in. I loosened the fourth screw and placed it in my pocket. Then using both hands, I popped the vent off and, turning it sideways, pushed it back into the vent and out of the way. Then I held onto the vent with both hands and lifted myself up which wasn't too hard, considering my wings were finally helping.

It was a tight fit but thank Hades I was little because I barely slid in. Once I could get my waist through the opening, I felt my head hitting the top and had to pull my knees into my chest as I pushed myself into the narrow space. I couldn't even sit all the way up and had to inchworm my way along. But I was in.

Things were looking up.

I continued inching my way through the vent, feeling like I was about two seconds away from an attack of claustrophobia. But I forced the thoughts right out of my head and focused, instead, on Knight. I encouraged myself by thinking that what I was doing right now could mean Knight's release, and ultimate safety.

I reached another grate and glanced through the slats, finding the break room just below me; the microwave was a giveaway. I had to be close because according to the map, the break room was just two rooms away from the Head of the Netherworld's office.

I was nearly there.

I continued creeping forward, feeling like I was getting nowhere quickly but thoughts of Knight and memories of the last time I'd seen him spurred me on. I wouldn't be beaten, I wouldn't be taken down. I was going to do this, I was going to see to it that Knight was released, whatever the consequences. And I knew in my heart of hearts that he would do the same for me. Hell, he was already doing the same for me.

I reached the second grate and glanced down, noticing I was hovering over someone's desk, complete with picture frames and a bottle of lotion, probably the head's receptionist or secretary.

I paused to take a deep breath, and reached down into my pocket for the Swiss army knife again. No, I wouldn't be able to unscrew the screws from the reverse side to let myself out but what I could do was cut through the thin metal screen using the serrated blade from Gabe's knife.

Before doing so, though, I peered down through the slats, listening for voices or typing or anything that would alert me to someone's presence. I heard nothing so I pushed the blade through the thin metal and started sawing. The blade sawed through pretty effortlessly and, before I knew it, I cut around the perimeter of the vent. I picked it up and placed it in the vent just to the side of the now gaping hole I'd left in the ceiling.

I pushed my head through the hole, looking for any sign of life but not finding any, dragged my legs out of the hole and, supporting myself by holding onto the edges of the vent, I lowered myself down until I was about four feet from the ground. I released my hands and dropped just as my wings began to beat frantically, allowing me to land on my toes like a stealthy cat.

I grabbed my Op 7 from the waistline of my pants and held it out before me in low ready as I moved to the wall and faced the door leading to the Head of the Netherworld's office. The door was closed and as soon as I reached it, I took a deep breath before I put my hand on the doorknob with the other hand gripping the Op 7. Yes, I realized I was about to pull a fast one on the Head of the Netherworld wearing only my bra and jeans but I couldn't say I cared.

I started counting to three.

On three, I pivoted, threw the door open and aimed the gun directly before me. I immediately found myself aiming at the back of someone's head who sat in a black, leather chair, bouncing back and forth as he talked on the phone. Apparently he hadn't heard me enter.

"Hang up, asshole," I said in an angry voice.

It felt like minutes ticked by as I watched him slowly swivel around until he was facing me.

"Quillan?" I asked in shock as I started to drop the gun but remembering myself, held it back up again. "What the hell …"

"I should be asking the same of you, Dulce," he smiled as he took in the fact that I wasn't exactly dressed.

"Are you … the Head of the Netherworld?" I asked, my voice small as the thought hit me.

He chuckled and stood up but I followed him with my gun, coming closer until only a step separated us. "No, no, far from it."

"Then you are working with him?" I said and suddenly felt sick to my stomach as I realized the extent of the double-dealing went all the way to the Head of the Netherworld. Apparently, the bastard had been in on it all along.

Ha ha, I guess the joke was on me.

"Bingo." I heard a voice from behind me but rather than turn my gun on whoever had just entered the room, I lurched for Quill and brought the Op 7 to his temple. Then I turned to face the other person in the room, who I had to imagine was the Head of the Netherworld, himself.

"Don't try anything or I'll shoot him," I said in a steely voice.

The other man glanced at me with a laugh and held his hands up as if to say he wasn't armed. But I knew better. He probably had a quiver of security agents at his disposal. If that were the case, I had already lost because even if I took Quillan out (something I wasn't planning on) the Head of the Netherworld would still be alive and Knight would still die in the morning.

Somehow I had to trade Quillan for the man facing me.

"So you didn't take that portal for Earth, did you?" the man asked with a smile as he took in my lack of clothing. "But it appears perhaps your blouse did?"

The man was an elf and he was handsome, though older, probably in his late fifties if I had to guess. His hair had once been a dark brown but was now speckled with grey to match his greying moustache. He wasn't very tall—maybe five foot seven or so but he had beautiful green eyes that sparkled out at me. He bent over a wooden cane and when he walked, he did so with a limp.

I hated him.

"I guess you could say I escaped," I answered in a tone that warned I wasn't in the mood for long-winded conversations. How I was going to get him at the end of the barrel of the Op 7 was anyone's guess. Even though he appeared to be unarmed, there was just something about the situation that told me not to believe it.

"Well, that actually works out quite well, doesn't it, Quillan?" the man asked as he faced Quill with a smile.

Quill swallowed hard and I wasn't sure if it was because he was at the end of my gun or he was nervous about the situation. "Dulcie, put the gun down."

"Fuck you," I seethed as I pushed it into his temple so he could know just how serious I was.

231

He took a deep breath. "All he has to do is touch a button on the end of that cane and you'll be overwhelmed by security."

"I will not press the button, young lady, if you agree to drop your gun," the Head of the Netherworld said, offering me a sincere smile. "I doubt you would want to harm your friend either."

"He is no friend of mine," I spat back.

"Please, Dulcie," Quill said, his shoulders sagging.

I faced the other man. "I want Knight Vander released and then I'll agree to whatever you want."

The man chuckled deeply. "Is that what this is about? You've risked your life for that of the Loki?" I nodded and he wore his surprise. "Interesting," he finished.

"I want you to call Caressa Brandenburg right now and insist she release Knight and take him to the portal to Earth immediately," I continued. "Once that's done, I'll let Quillan go."

The man nodded but made no motion to do anything. "What do you say we make a little deal?"

"Deal?" I repeated as I narrowed my eyes.

The man nodded and took a seat on an expensive and uncomfortable looking black leather couch. "I was rather hoping Caressa would not send you back to Earth."

"I thought she was ordered to?" I demanded.

"That was her plea bargain, not mine. I ordered you to be brought here but, alas, that woman seems to have a mind of her own." He shook his head and there was an expression of fondness on his face as he thought about her. Good ol' Caressa seemed to get underneath everyone's skin.

"What do you want from me?" I insisted, not interested in hearing his smooth talk anymore.

"I want you to agree to work for me," he said plainly.

"What?" I demanded as shock and anger strove to churn up my gut.

"I have lost my ears and eyes in the ANC," he started as he glanced at Quillan with a frown. That meant Quillan had been his informant in the ANC all along and once Knight and I discovered Quill was double-dealing, the head had to find a new ANC man.

"No way," I started.

"You do value the Loki's life, do you not?"

I swallowed hard. The bastard had me.

The fucking bastard had me.

I didn't respond so he continued. "Yes, Dulcie dear, I want you to work for me, take over Quillan's position in the ANC."

I felt tears stinging my eyes. "And you will allow Knight to live?"

The Head of the Netherworld laughed. "Yes, quite so, I'll even put him back on duty and you both can work together. Of course, he could never know that you work for me; it must remain top secret. Anything else would mean the end of his life."

I couldn't respond. I felt like throwing up or collapsing into a mass of tears. I glanced at Quillan and realized I'd been beaten and dropped the gun. "How could you do this?" I demanded of him, even though I suspected he probably was pushed into a corner just as I'd been.

But Quillan never responded. Instead, he lowered his eyes and shrugged like he didn't have an answer for me. Not that it mattered because the Head of the Netherworld was suddenly on his feet and approaching me.

"I have wanted you for a long time, Dulcie girl," he said with a smile. "You are very good at your job."

I didn't want to correct him about the fact that I'd failed to apprehend Quillan … mainly because he already knew that.

"Do we have a deal then?" he asked.

I gulped as I thought about it. "You swear Knight's life will be spared?"

233

He glanced at Quillan. "Once she says the word, you will call Caressa and instruct her to release the Loki and take him immediately to the portal." Then he faced me again. "Well?"

I didn't have any other option and even though I hated the thought of working for this bastard and selling my soul to the proverbial devil, I would if it meant Knight's safety …

I didn't say anything but nodded.

The man clapped his hands together and a huge smile spread over his lips. "We will be a family again."

I faced him in surprise, wondering what the hell he was going on about but I never got the chance to speak.

"Ah, I haven't introduced myself, dear," he said as he extended his hand. "I'm Melchior O'Neil, your father."

H. P. Mallory is the author of the Jolie Wilkins series as well as the Dulcie O'Neil series.

She began her writing career as a self-published author and after reaching a tremendous amount of success, decided to become a traditionally published author and hasn't looked back since.

H. P. Mallory lives in Southern California with her husband and son, where she is at work on her next book.

If you are interested in receiving emails when she releases new books, please sign up for her email distribution list by visiting her website and clicking the "contact" tab:
www.hpmallory.com

Be sure to join HP's online Facebook community where you will find pictures of the characters from both series and lots of other fun stuff including an online book club!

Facebook: https://www.facebook.com/hpmallory

Find H.P. Mallory Online:
www.hpmallory.com
http://twitter.com/hpmallory
https://www.facebook.com/hpmallory